347 MILLION

PAUL SHADINGER

A MATT PRESTON NOVEL

Edited by: Ellen Campbell
Cover design by: Kevin G. Summers
Formatting by: Kevin G. Summers

This Book is Dedecated
to long time fan and friend Tom Walbourn,
who kept asking when this book was coming out.
Sorry, Tom it wasn't done in time for you. RIP

PLEASE NOTE:

ALSO BY PAUL SHADINGER

Fiction

Houseboat (2016)
Code Name: Crescent (2017)
The Gypsy Queen (2018)
Quick, Quick, Slow (2018)
Snooker's Legacy (2019)

A Matt Preston Novel

DEDICATION

As always, I dedicate this novel to every one of you who has read my past novels and continued to encourage me to keep writing. I don't know if it was because they enjoyed reading about Matt Preston, or they figured if I wrote enough, I just might improve. Without a doubt, none of my novels would exist without your words of inspiration, encouragement, and support. Positive words are truly food to any author, and I cannot begin to describe the number of banquets so many of you have provided. Thank you all for your wonderful comments and inspiration. I've said in the past I would love to make a list of everyone who has encouraged me, but for fear I might forget somebody which would be inexcusable, I will refrain.

Thank all of you for your kind words. They mean a great deal.

My novels are also dedicated to my wife, Sandy. The book you have in your hands is a testament to her faith in me. She saw something in my writing I never saw. Without her encouragement, I'd never have started, or continued to write. Without her, Matt Preston would have never seen the light of day.

And finally, I dedicate my books to all of my faithful Cocker Spaniels. First to Buttons who was my inspiration for BJ in *Houseboat* and to the others: Pepper who we lost way too soon, Max, Brenna and Samantha. Over the course of writing this novel we lost Samantha who at 14 + had so many things going wrong inside her little body, she was miserable, and it wasn't fair to her to keep her with us. All of them are greatly missed.

Between my last novel and this one, we have taken on two new puppies. Bijou which means jewel in French and

Boots because she is all black except for four white feet are our new additions.

I'm always surprised how much animals enrich our lives and what pain we must endure when we have to send them over the rainbow bridge. They give us so much more than they ask of us. Regardless of how our day has gone, when we come home, they act like the best thing that will ever happen to them has just happened. They are always overjoyed to see us return. How do you beat that? I know all of my dogs are waiting for me, just over the rainbow.

Thank you for reading my novel.

Regards …
Paul Shadinger
NFM 2021

LIST OF CHARACTERS

Abdulaleem al-Zaman, leader of the United Islamic Brotherhood of Allah, UIBA

Albert Bradson, President-elect of the US

Anthony Zampuchini, younger brother of Sal Zampuchini

Bob Carity, Janitor at Todd Hoss' bank, works for Mouse

Dominick, Pilot for Henry Walbourn

Dude, Poker player with Matt

Farouk al-Hashim, Second in charge of the UIBA

Glen Troutman, Mossad

Guido Sabbatini, Messaggero

Henry Walbourn, Matt's business partner

Jacob McNaulty, Matt's former commander

Jade Fox, Mouse's wife

Jeff L. Davenport, Commissioner of Seattle Police

Jesi Carson, Matt's partner in Alaska

Johnathan Apple Orchard, Matt's friend

Kaye Mann, Todd's love interest

Leslie Oldman, Veterinarian

Lightning, Puppy

Little Matt McLaughlin, son of Walter

Lois Tollifson, Matt's love interest

Marshall Wells, Mouse's head of security

Martha, Matt's housekeeper in Florida

Masood, Troutman's number one

Max, Mat's dog

Melissa Jones, The Gypsy Queen

Mouse, Steve Fox, Matt's friend

Peter De Jonker, Manager of Amsterdam Hotel

Roger, Henry's Friend

Sakol Hasaphonhse, Captain of detective, Seattle Police

Salvatore Zampuchini, Capo di tutio capi, head of the Mafia

Thien McLaughlin, Walter's wife

Thunder, puppy

Todd Hoss, accused Banker

Tom Frost, Snooker

Vladimir Schreiber, Concierge of Amsterdam Hotel

William Tate, Tubs, poker player and band leader

CHAPTER ONE

Whirr.

Click.

Click.

The dealer tapped the deck to align the cards, split the deck of cards into two parts and shuffled.

Whirr. Click. Click.

Again, he split the deck and shuffled.

Whirr. Click. Click.

Jason, the dealer, set the cards in front of the player to his right to cut the deck.

I leaned back, folded my arms across my chest and tried not to smile. It amused me. Jason had performed his trick fairly well — not perfectly, mind you, but pretty good compared to many cheaters I'd witnessed over the years. Now I faced the problem of how to call him out without tipping off the others at the table. I had no desire to alienate any of the players, especially since it was my first time playing with this group.

"Excuse me, I know this is unorthodox, but before you deal, may I see the deck? I'd like to show you something." The players looked at me strangely.

I picked up the deck and before I turned over the top card, I said, "Nine of hearts." Then I flipped the card over and showed it. It was the nine of hearts. Now I had everyone's attention.

I put the card back on top of the deck and split the deck, shuffled, split the deck again and shuffled, then split the deck into three piles and put them back together. I put the deck on the table and turned over the top card.

"Nine of hearts," I said and showed the players.

This time I buried the nine of hearts in the middle of the deck. I put the deck on the table and turned my hands over twice, showing everyone, I didn't have any cards palmed. I was wearing a short-sleeved shirt, so it was obvious I didn't have any cards up my sleeves. I split the deck into two piles and shuffled, tapped it together and shuffled again. I turned over the top card. "Nine of hearts."

I handed the deck to Jason and asked him to cut it. His hand trembled as he did it. I asked him to cut one more time. Along with his trembling hands his face was flushed, and he'd started to sweat. I could see fear in his eyes—he knew that I knew, and he was afraid I'd call him out. After he cut, I took the deck and shuffled again. I put it in front of Jason and pointed to the top card. "Turn it over."

It was the nine of hearts.

I took the cards again and spread the deck out across the table. This time I pointed at a player everyone called Dude and asked him to point to a card. I pulled the card he indicated, reassembled the deck and put Dude's card on top. I shuffled twice more, cut the deck and turned over the top card.

"Nine of hearts."

Everyone at the table grew still. Dude murmured, "What the...?"

Harris, the player directly across from me asked, "What the hell are you? Some kind of card shark?

I gave him my most disarming smile and held up my hands. "I've been playing cards for a long time, even before I was in the service. I've seen a lot of cheaters in my life. In Nam there was a guy in our outfit who was a veritable master with a card deck. He should have taken his act on the road; he was that good. He could have done two shows a night in Vegas. He taught me some tricks and showed me how to spot a person stacking the deck.

"My point was to kind of warn you, if someone you don't know is sitting in on your game, pay attention to the way he handles cards, how he shuffles and how he deals. I also wanted all of you to know I've played cards before, but I'm trustworthy." Most of the players laughed. "I didn't want any problems down the road if one of you discovered I can manipulate a deck. I promise never to do what I just did during one of our games. Of course, now I don't dare win any good pots." That broke the ice, and everyone laughed.

Harris said to Jason, "I believe it's your deal."

Jason shook his head and pushed the deck toward Harris. "Hey guys. I don't feel so good." He knew, but he had no idea if I would tell or not. I'd showed him I knew, and also how much better the trick could be done. Now it was up to him.

"Jason, do you want to leave?" Dude asked.

"Yeah, sumpin' Ruth made for dinner ain't agreeing with me. Sorry about this, I'll see you guys around." He stood and walked away. I wouldn't have exposed him to the others. This was a small community, and he had to live here. There was no reason to poison everyone against him, but I wanted him to know whenever I played, I'd be watching him.

Watching him very carefully.

~ ~ ~ ~ ~

3

It was a warm, beautiful Tuesday night and just a few days ago we celebrated Halloween. Because we were in Florida, the major topic for discussion tonight was the FIU – Miami college football brawl which had transpired, last month in October of 2006 between University of Miami and Florida International University which had led to suspensions of 31 players of both teams. The windows and doors were wide open. Everyone was in short-sleeved shirts and most of us were wearing shorts and sandals. This isn't what I'm used to. I'm used to the four Ds of fall in Seattle. You know, damp, dreary, dark and dismal. Florida in the fall is a pleasure.

I've been living in North Fort Myers for a few months and every evening at five, in honor of Snooker, who'd bequeathed me his condo, I blew on a conch shell just like he did, to celebrate five o'clock. The yacht club tradition started right after the condos had been built—most of the original residents had bought their units to be with friends. But time moves on and things change, many of the original owners have either moved back up north at their children's behest or passed away. With the passing of the old guard, the tradition ended. When Snooker purchased the unit he left to me, the ritual was still observed by what was left of the old-timers. He liked the idea and had kept the tradition. He told me about the tradition and that to him it was a remembrance of fallen comrades. I'd been doing it every night since I moved in.

About a week ago there was a knock on my door. My housekeeper Martha ushered three gentlemen back to the lanai. Shaking hands, we exchanged names and they told me they lived in the complex. I asked them to sit. When one of them introduced himself as Dude, and I made the comment, "No way, really?"

"Well, kind of. I won't tell you my real first name, but in my high school class there were nine other guys with the same first name. No shit, ten of us with the same first name.

A buddy of mine kept calling me Dude, and I liked it better than my real name. Okay?"

"I'll call you whatever you want."

"Just don't call me late for dinner," Dude replied. The fellow who had introduced himself as Denny kidded him he could afford to miss a few dinners.

"We wanted to come over and thank you for blowing the shell every evening. After Tom passed away, we thought it was the end of the conch shell. Please don't take this wrong since we all like hearing it, but why do you do it?"

I smiled. "I'm not the least bit offended. I think Snooker..." From the blank looks on their faces, I realized they had no idea who Snooker was. "I'm sorry, I guess you didn't know Tom's nickname was Snooker. It's not because he played Snooker. If you ever played pool with him, you got snookered. He won a lot of money over the years."

Dick, the third fellow said, "Most of us here called him Top. Did you know he was a top sergeant in the Army?"

"Yeah, but I didn't know him then. He got that nickname when he was in the Army. His skill with a pool cue was the stuff of legends. I have a friend who lost five hundred dollars to Snooker. The closest my friend got to taking a shot was holding his cue stick while Tom ran the table, more than once. It was an expensive lesson for my friend.

"Anyway, I think Tom would have been pleased to know you're happy about it."

Dick explained, "Well, we wanted to thank you. One of the hardest things to get used to it how fast things change around here. A few of the old residents pass every year and new people buy the units. There are only a couple of the original owners left. I'm not an original owner but I've been here long enough sometimes I walk around the complex and remember who used to have a certain unit. A lot of nostalgia down here. Anyway, we wanted to ask you, do you play poker?"

I couldn't help it. "Poker? Poker, don't recall ever playing that game." I laughed. "Well, I've been known to play a hand or two." I had no intention of telling them about my regular game in Seattle or the insane pots we played for.

Dude smiled. "Should we be calling you Snooker?"

"No. But I understand the basics of the game."

"On Tuesdays at 6:30 we have a game over at the clubhouse and we wanted to invite you to play with us. We only play for quarters. It's just a bunch of old guys who play to get a night off from our wives."

Dick added, "If the truth be known, our wives are happy to have us out of the house for an evening. We have several 'chick flick' DVD's and when I'm gone, my wife settles in with a box of Kleenex and one of those sappy chick flicks. I'm just glad I don't have to endure that pain." Everyone laughed.

"I'd love to play with you guys. Thanks for the invite," I told them.

Dick spoke up. "We knew Tom was in the Army, were you in the service?"

"Yeah, I was in the Army too."

"What did you do?"

This was the part I hated, it sounded so gay, but I told them what I was supposed to. "I was a bandsman. I played piano and drums."

Dude said, "Hey, I had a buddy who was in the Army. He used to say he was a bandsman, but that was just a cover story. He was in some top secret; black ops kind of group and he wasn't allowed to talk about it. Were you really in the band or is that a cover story?"

I laughed and shook my head. "If I told you the truth, I'd have to kill all of you." Their eyes got gigantic. "Stop. I'm just kidding. Guys, the Army was a long time ago. I was a bandsman. How about we just leave it at that? And for what it's worth, I really do play the piano...a little."

6

I changed the subject. "Have you guys ever heard of Bill Tate? Tubs? The Bill Tate quartet?" They had. "Back in Seattle he was in the poker group I played with. I got to sit in with Tubs on a few gigs. I've been pestering him to bring his quartet down and play around here some weekend."

"I'd buy a ticket to see that," Denny piped up. "Did you really play with the group?"

"Yeah, and I have to tell ya, it was the thrill of a lifetime."

Dude said, "Well, the offer stands. We'd love to see you at our games."

"I'd love to play cards with you guys on Tuesday. Thanks for asking."

And now you know why I found myself seated at a large round table with seven guys, happy to be there. "I hope none of you will be offended if I don't remember names," I laughed. "I can remember Dude, but it will take me longer to get everyone else."

Harris piped up, "I play with these clowns every Tuesday and I still can't remember half of their names, but I think my problem is age related." The way everyone at the table joked among themselves reminded me a lot of the games my buddies and I used to play back in Seattle.

Between the third and fourth hand I'd felt my cell phone vibrate in my pocket indicating I had a text, but I ignored it. A few minutes later I felt it again. Between hands, I pulled out the phone and checked the message. It was from Admiral John Orchard. The first one said, "Call me."

What? I felt that was a little rude. No reason; just call me. The next message was even more rude. "Call me now. I mean NOW!" I thought to myself, he can wait till the game is over. I don't work for him and the last couple of encounters with him had left me with some physical scars and a few mental ones. We may be friends, but I'm not at his beck and call.

The evening passed quickly and before I knew it, it was crowding 10:00 PM and because most of them had spouses waiting for them at home, it was time to wrap it up. It amused me since the games back in Seattle usually lasted until the wee hours of the next day. To be honest, I think this was my first-time playing poker with a bunch of guys who folded this early in the night. I thought about mentioning how long I was used to playing, but after my demonstration with the cards at the start of the game, I decided I'd better not.

The game finished and while we cleaned up and were putting the tables back the way we'd found them, one of the group asked me, "Were you comfortable with the size of the pots tonight?"

"Yes, they were fine. I had a grand time." I didn't mention the '57 Chevy convertible I'd lost once, or the houseboat I'd won in another game.

A guy who'd won several pots snapped his fingers and pointed at me. "Tom told us one time about a guy he kind of knew from the service. His granddaughter was dating a fellow down here who owned a dance hall or something where somebody was murdered. Tom asked this guy he knew to help the boyfriend, and this guy got the entire thing straightened out. Tom was sure impressed. Was that you?"

"Guilty!"

"Tom was sure captivated by you. Well, I guess he'd have to be if he left you his condo. Did Tom do the same things you did in the Army?"

"Yes and no. He didn't do any field missions like I did, but he was involved in ops. Tom was at the top of the food chain in the Army, a command sergeant major. He was as high as you can go in the enlisted ranks."

Someone else added, "I served in the Army too. After ROTC in college, at my first duty station another second lieutenant got his ass chewed off by a sergeant major. I was taught never to piss off a top sergeant major. After I graduated, I learned real fast when Top spoke, you listened and did exactly what he said. Sarge may have been enlisted, and I might have been an "officer," but he outranked me where it counted."

"Were you overseas?" I asked.

The fellow laughed. "No, I was in supply. After basic officers training, I got stationed at Fort Sill, Oklahoma and never left. My God, talk about the butthole of the world."

The guy who knew Tom said, "Hey, I did my basic training there and I can attest it's a miserable place to be stationed."

"I guess I was lucky," I said. "I did my basic at Fort Ord in California. It was beautiful. The weather was perfect. Gentle breezes in the morning and little humidity. I lucked out."

"Where did you do advanced training?"

"Sorry. I can't tell you that." That seemed to impress them, but that's not why I said it. "Look, I don't want you to think I was more than I was. I was just doing my job. It was what you did…it was part of the war."

Everybody seemed to understand.

CHAPTER TWO

I enjoyed the short walk back to my condo. In Seattle, I'd be all bundled up, if I even went for a walk. I missed my dogs, too. A lot! They made things fun. It had been a few months since I'd seen them, and I missed them. My buddy Walter was watching them at his place near Seattle.

Life is strange, sometimes. I'm a Seattle boy. I definitely hadn't planned on ending up in Florida. Never in my wildest dreams did I imagine I'd end up here. On the positive side of things, being on the East Coast made it a lot easier to get up and see Lois. And Florida had been good for me.

The slower pace had done wonders for me—my stress level was way down. However, having my dogs would make it even better. Not too long ago I'd been severely beaten. The physical scars were gone, but the mental ones were more permanent. I recalled my return from Nam and how I'd felt regarding what had happened. I didn't seem to have any mental hang over from that like I did from my Middle East adventure.

My phone vibrated and yes, for a third time it was a message from Orchard. "God damn it Matt, call me *now*!" I hadn't liked the tone of his previous messages and for sure I didn't care for the attitude of this one.

I decided to head him off. He answered on the first ring. "You sure took your sweet time," he snapped.

John and I have been friends for a long time, or I would have immediately hung up on him. "Why hello, John. And how are you?" I said. "I'm fine, thanks for asking. The weather here is delightful. Oh, in case you've forgotten, I don't work for you. Where do you come off busting my chops? Call me when you mellow out. Good bye."

I hung up. He called back immediately. When I answered, he said, "I need to see you as soon as you can get up here."

"Why? Why, John, do I need to get up there as soon as I can?"

"I won't discuss this on an open line. I need to see you. Now!"

"Why?"

"Damn it, Matt. There are things you don't understand. I need to see you in person."

"John, I don't like the sound of this. You need to tell me more than that."

"No! I need to see you. When you hear what I have to say, you'll understand. Shit Preston. I'm afraid to even think about this in case someone reads my thoughts. Matt, this is important."

"I don't like the sound of this. Look, Lois is coming down for the weekend and I'll fly back with her Monday morning."

"That's as soon as you can get here?" he groused.

"Look, John. If it's that important, have Henry bring you here."

"I can't get away. Are you sure you can't come up any sooner?"

"You can't give me a hint?"

"No."

I wasn't going to bust my ass without a reason. I didn't want to go, and he wasn't making it tempting. Besides, I was still a little incensed. "I'll be up Monday."

"If that's the best you can do..."

"Goodbye, John."

The line went dead. John's lack of courtesy didn't engender any guilt. His attitude deserved my lack of immediacy.

I had no intention of giving up any of my time with Lois. I need that time for a lot of reasons, not least is that time with her helps heal those scars I collected in the Middle East. Lois is my...

Wow, what do I call our relationship? I'm too old to have a girlfriend. Besides, what we share is much more than any boyfriend/girlfriend thing. Lover? It goes well beyond that. I'd even been having thoughts about a more permanent relationship with her.

You just dropped the book, right? But when we're together, I do better with life and stuff. When we're apart, I miss her, and stupid things will really piss me off. Like the phone call from John who expects me to drop everything because he said so.

For instance, a friend of mine had a problem recently. I'm not at liberty to disclose my friend's name or what the problem was. What I can tell you is when he enters a room, a special song is played, and everybody stands. He lives in a big white house back east, near Arlington, Virginia.

I was trying to get some information for him and ran into two goombahs. They were waiting for me in the basement of a Las Vegas hotel with biscuits in hand, (and I don't mean the eating kind) ready to shoot me. I got the drop on them. When I told them not to move, one of them was stupid.

So, I shot him.

That's not like me, honestly. I'm usually much calmer, but events have left me a lot more on edge than I used to be. Being with Lois helps a lot

Both physically and mentally.

CHAPTER THREE

Monday morning a plane was waiting for Lois and me at Page Field, but Henry appeared to be MIA. I stepped up to the plane and rapped my knuckle on the side of the plane. The hatch popped open and Henry leaned out, motioning for us to get in. "Are you ready to go? Did you have an enjoyable weekend?"

"Yeah." I was grinning from ear to ear, as they say. "We had a great weekend, but Lois needs to get back to work.' Sides, the admiral is insisting he needs to see me. Urgently!"

"Why?" Henry asked.

"No idea. I was wondering if you knew anything?" He shook his head.

The flight to D.C. was fast and just before we landed, I asked Lois, "Babe. Do you know anyplace I can stay while I'm in D.C.?"

"Let me think about it for a while and I'll get back to you." She smiled and put her head on my shoulder. "I'm so glad you'll be in town for a while. I enjoy having you there when I get home."

"Why do you think John wants to see me so badly?" I said, even though we had beaten the topic to death over the weekend.

"Sorry, I don't have a clue."

"I'll ride in with you to work and see him now. When I finish, I'll go to your place and wait, that is, if it's okay to stay at your place?" Lois made a vulgar suggestive comment and I told her to keep that thought in mind and I'd try to take care of it later.

~ ~ ~ ~

A limo was waiting for us when we landed. One thing for sure, it made getting through traffic a lot more enjoyable. I made a comment about how nice it was to be in a limo in the middle of a morning commute, and Lois drew me close and kissed me. When I grabbed for her, she pushed me away and told me to behave. I whined, and she laughed at me.

Walking into Lois' office, I noticed a tall stack of mail on her desk and another stack of phone messages she needed to return. She saw me look at the work piled up. "I'll be home tonight," she promised.

John came out of his office and after greeting us, said, "Matt, let's go for a walk."

Fall was well underway. The leaves had turned and were falling off the trees. The air had a cold bite, and I was glad I had on long pants and a jacket. It dawned on me it was the first time in weeks I had worn long pants and I kind of enjoyed the novelty.

We came to a Starbucks and stopped to purchase a coffee (Grande Drip), then started up Independence Avenue, walking until we found an empty park bench. John glanced around furtively.

"Okay, what's so secret we have to come out here in the cold and freeze our asses off? You keep looking around like you expect a sniper to pop up."

John didn't smile. I could tell he was working up the courage to ask me something and I had a grim feeling I wasn't going to like where the conversation was heading.

Finally, he said, "I hate to ask this of you because you've done so much, but I think when I explain, you'll understand."

I let out a deep sigh, took a big sip of my coffee, and muttered, "Damn, I don't like the way this is starting. Okay, lay it on me." For the first time in a long time, I wished I had a cigarette. Both for the cup of coffee and to help my anxiety. But it had been a pain in the ass to give up cigarettes, so I dismissed the thought.

"Do you remember that little island up in Alaska where we went fishing?"

"Of course, I do. Shit dude, that trip is one of the highlights of my life. I still remember sitting on the dock, smoking cigars and drinking that great Scotch you brought with you.

"And before I forget, I found a place up in the northwest corner of Colorado where we can go horseback riding and wade out into a lake on horses and fly fish from the saddle. Interested?"

"Seriously? On horseback?"

I smiled at him. "Yep."

"Damn straight. When do we leave?"

"It's a little cold right now, maybe next summer. I'm sure the lake is frozen solid. Anyway, why did you ask about Alaska?"

"Matt, our organization heard a rumor regarding a clandestine meeting up near Craig, Alaska, not far from that fishing camp. And not just any old meeting. A super-secret meeting between Salvatore Zampuchini and Abdulaleem al-Zaman."

That stunned me. "You've got to be kidding me." I'd wondered if I should tell John about my recent contacts with Zampuchini. More important, what were Abdulaleem and Sal cooking up? "John, are you shitting me? Isn't this al-Zaman dude the leader of one of those crazy factions in the Middle East?"

"Yes. He's the leader of the United Islamic Brotherhood of Allah. The UIBA. These guys are the worst of the worst. We had Abdulaleem in custody in Iraq in '03 and he somehow got released. Nobody really knows why he was cut loose, but I have my opinions. He's very difficult to pin down—more aliases than you can shake a stick at. He almost never shows his face. Most of his followers have never seen him and there are only two known photographs.

"We've arrested or killed a man by that name better than half a dozen times. He's like a specter — most of our agencies aren't sure where the line is between fact and fiction. His followers work very hard to promote the idea he's invincible. It's possible there are several people using that identity.

"The truth is, I'm not certain he'll be there. But I overheard something that makes me believe he will. If you go up there and it doesn't pan out, the only people who will know are you and the agent I'm sending with you. I'm sure you understand this isn't something I want getting out."

"No John, the person you overheard also knows about this. Who was it?"

John shook his head. He didn't know, or he wasn't telling me.

"You know I met Zampuchini?"

John shrugged.

"According to Mouse, Zampuchini is now the undisputed head of the Mafia. Or at least on the West Coast," I said.

John frowned. "You're correct. We know Salvatore was responsible for the Parisi Massacre. We believe he also orchestrated the deaths of Ermanno Ungaretti and Vince Santoro. Vince and Ermanno died under strange circumstances and after the smoke cleared, Ol' Sal was the only one of the old dons left."

"According to Mouse, two hit men named Grasso and Carbone did the deed. Now, am I hearing you right? You're saying the Capo di tutti Capi, the Godfather of the Mafia, might be meeting the commander of UIBA?"

"Exactly. Abdulaleem is coming from Russia on an old tramp steamer under Syrian registry. The steamer will drop anchor behind an island near Craig. Sal's yacht will be anchored behind another island nearby. They're supposed to meet on Zampuchini's yacht.

"Matt, I have people who can handle small boats, what I need is someone I can trust. I have a photographer I want to go with you. You'll stay at the same place you and I were at on our fishing trip and your cover is you're on your honeymoon. That shouldn't be too hard for you." I told him to do that physically impossible act.

"I need you to take the photographer to that fishing camp, check in and act like a couple of honeymooners who happen to be into fishing. Take out a boat and fish. Naturally, you'll be moving around, looking for hot spots. The agent with you will get whatever pictures she can without blowing your cover.

"We've made reservations at the fishing camp under your name. You get there two days before the meeting and take your bride fishing."

"When is all this supposed to happen?"

"Soon, why?"

"Because it will be damn cold up there. And storm season is getting underway. Besides, what if it's too rough to go out?"

"If it's too rough for you, for sure it will be too rough for al-Zaman and his people to be out. Remember, they're used to a lot warmer climate and they're not boat people. We'll just have to hope for semi-decent weather."

"Do you have any idea what the meeting is about?"

"There is a rumor of a large cache of arms that's gone missing. I haven't been able to find out where the alleged arms came from or where they are right now, but the rumor is Salvatore and his people know something about it.

"Whatever the reason for the meeting, only two people in the agency know about it. I kept it quiet. Until we know what's going on and why, you can't tell anybody. Even Lois. Understand?"

"What? You don't want me to talk to Lois about this?"

"No!"

"Is that an order?"

"If it has to be, yes! Don't tell her where you're going or what you're doing."

"I don't like that at all. Do I have a choice?"

"No." John smiled. "You do, but I wish you'd take care of this on your own for now. I have total confidence in you, and I feel safe knowing you'll take care of our young lady."

"Do I have to give you an answer right now?"

"Can you tell me by tomorrow morning?"

"Yes."

"I'm sorry to ask this of you. After what you just went through I wasn't even going to ask, but you're the only person outside the agency I can trust with this.

Every fiber of my being said this was terrible. This whole situation was bad juju from top to bottom. I knew I should just shake John's hand and go back to Florida. Yeah, that's what I should have done. But I needed to ponder this some more.

"John, let me think about it. I'll give you an answer tomorrow." We stood and John headed back to his office and I headed toward Lois' apartment.

I enjoyed fishing in Alaska though I didn't like the idea of fishing in late fall, but it could be interesting. I really didn't like the idea of being with another woman without Lois knowing about it. And even more, I did not like taking clandestine pictures of two high-powered individuals, either of which could wish me out of existence in a heartbeat. Ghastly things can happen when you mess with people like that.

Nope, I didn't like it.

Not one single bit!

~ ~ ~ ~ ~

The evening with Lois was going well. We had a pleasant dinner and then curled up on the couch. She kissed me a number of times and then asked, "Why did John want to see you?"

"Nothing important. Just stuff."

"What do you mean *just stuff?*"

"You wouldn't be interested."

"I'm interested. Now tell me, what did you and John talk about?"

"He wants me to do something for him."

"What?"

"Something."

"What?" I sat there wondering what to tell her.

"Didn't you talk to John about our visit?" I asked.

"No, we didn't have time. What does John want you to do?"

"I can't tell you. He asked me, no, that's wrong, he *ordered* me not to tell you."

"What? He really ordered you not to tell me? He specifically forbade you not to tell me?"

"Yeah. He asked and when I balked, he made it an order. I finally told him I wouldn't say anything. But if you want to pressure him, that's a different story. It's up to you."

"You damn well better believe I'll pressure him. For as many times as I've had to bail his scrawny ass out of a sticky situation, he can confide in me. God knows if whatever the two of you are cooking up blows up, he'll expect me to fix it. I'll be stuck dealing with his shitstorm. Again!" Lois sat for a moment with her arms crossed over her chest. "That son of a bitch! Shit, I'm so annoyed he would do that I could spit tacks." She snapped at me. "Are you going to do whatever it is he asked?"

"I think so, but I'm still thinking it over."

"And you won't tell me?" I shook my head. "That asshole. My God, am I going to make his life hell tomorrow!" Her anger was obvious.

Sheepishly I asked, "Does this mean I need to find a room somewhere else for the night?"

Lois pointed toward her bedroom and growled. "I need to find your little butt in there in ten seconds ready to do your duty!"

"Yes ma'am, on my way." As I headed off to her bedroom, I made sure she heard me singing, "Hi ho, hi ho, it's off to work I go."

"I'll show you work buster," Lois warned.

Oh damn! When am I going to learn I should keep my mouth shut?

There are a lot of pleasant parts of our relationship and one of the best is the physical part. Her body is perfect for my taste, even though she thinks she's too heavy. I told her I liked round rather than bony which got a laugh and a hard pop on the arm. But our relationship is so much more than a physical thing.

But I have to admit when she comes to me, takes me by the hand and leads me to the bedroom and I ask, "Something on your mind?" is one of my favorite things.

"Yes." She informs me in a sultry tone of voice.

And by the time the view starts getting interesting, I've figured out what she wanted.

See, I may be getting older, but not too old to enjoy that.

CHAPTER FOUR

I called John the next morning and told him I'd do what he asked, against my better judgment. I also warned him how angry Lois was.

"I know Matt, I've already had my ass chewed."

"I don't care! Don't expect any sympathy from me, you earned it."

Except for John's request, the few days I spent with Lois were wonderful. As usual, the more time I spend with this wonderful lady, the more I appreciate her. One of us would begin to stay something and the other one would exclaim, "Get out of my head. I was just going to say that." When it came time to leave, I didn't want to go. Being away from her was getting harder every time. I needed to make some decisions about where our relationship was heading.

~ ~ ~ ~ ~

The next Monday morning Henry and I had a quick flight to Seattle. I rode in the right-hand seat and we chatted about our growing business. "I'm bidding on a new plane next week," he told me. "The largest one so far—a lot bigger than we're normally interested in, but it gives us a shot at more government contracts. Larger and a lot more lucrative contracts."

"I know you have pull, and that's how we get lot of those contracts, but are we counting on too much business from just one source? Are we getting enough private customers?"

"Actually, we're getting too many from both sides. The new plane I want to get could be busy thirty hours a day. You wouldn't believe how many inquiries we're getting."

"Do I want to know what kind of contracts we're talking about?"

"No."

"Oh, like that huh? Do I need to learn to fly?"

Henry laughed. "No! I need for you to keep making money so I can keep buying planes."

"I thought the money to buy new planes was to come from the business, not me personally."

"Oh, you caught me. We're making enough to pay for the new planes. I was just giving you a hard time to see if you were paying attention, seeing as how you in live in Florida now, I figured you might think we retired you."

"Hilarious. Not much chance of that with John around," I groused.

About halfway into our trip, I called Mouse. It went straight to voicemail. "Mouse, it's Matt Preston. When you have a moment, can you please call me?" I gave him my number, hung up and slipped the phone back in my pocket. Before I secured it, it rang.

"Hello."

"Matt, it's Mouse. I didn't recognize the number, so I didn't answer. It's great to hear from you. What can I do for you?"

"Are there any suites available at the Steve Fox board-inghouse?" I used his actual name.

His laugh was infectious. "Of course, my friend. But how come you need a place? What's with your condo downstairs?"

"I never got my stuff out of storage; the place is empty. Do you have a finished unit I can use for a few days until I get my stuff brought over?"

"No problem, I have just the place for you."

"I have some things to discuss with you." I was wondering how much Mouse knew about the mysterious missing arms cache. If anybody knew anything about them it would be Mouse. Mouse's nickname is a reference to his small stature, but his knowledge of what's happening around the globe is beyond belief. His friendship is a veritable treasure.

Mouse replied, "Well, I have some interesting news. You bank at First National Bank of Puget Sound." It wasn't a question. "I believe you're aquatinted with the vice president at your local branch?"

"Yeah, Todd, Todd Hoss, what about him?"

"The rumor is, he embezzled an enormous chunk of money from the bank and there's a warrant out for his arrest. In addition, my sources tell me the Honored Society is looking for him, if you catch my drift."

"I understand what you're saying, but come on, Todd Hoss? No way."

"Why do you say that?"

"Not to be cruel, but Todd isn't swift enough to steal." After I said that, I realized that was cruel and I wasn't being fair. "No, let me rephrase that. He is way too straight an arrow to steal."

"The word is there's no doubt he did the deed. We can discuss it when you get here."

"Well, I'm on my way to Seattle. Thanks for the place to crash."

"Matt, text me before you land, and I'll have a car waiting to take you to the condos."

"Sounds good."

As we were landing, Henry pulled the boom on his mike down and said, "John said you were going to need a ride up to Craig, Alaska. I can land at Ketchikan, then you have to take a float plane over to Craig. If we had a float-plane, I could take you all the way, but we don't have enough demand to justify tying up so much money."

"Yeah, John and I flew up there a long time ago when to a fishing lodge. We had a great time."

"I've been to the lodge. The food was beyond amazing. Any idea when you want to leave?"

"I have to find out when the reservations are for and when the other half of this mission will be ready to go."

"Let me know when you have a plan."

"Will do."

~ ~ ~ ~ ~

When the plane pulled up to the gate, Mouse was waiting next to his limo. I crossed the tarmac and extended my hand. He pushed it out of the way and wrapped his arms around my waist. I told you he was short.

"Damn it's good to see you my friend."

On the drive through town, it dismayed me because the traffic was even worse than the last time I'd been here. So many of the buildings I remembered were gone— I was glad I was pulling out of Seattle. I mean, I still love the place and my memories, but it wasn't the city I grew up in.

~ ~ ~ ~ ~

Mouse's limo pulled up under a portico and Marshall Wells, the head of security for the Olympus, opened the door on Mouse's side. When he saw me, a big smile spread across his face. Marshall came around the back of the car and extended his hand and exclaimed, "Matt, how good to see you."

"Marshall, you look well."

"No choice but to be." Mouse and I grabbed an elevator. It wasn't in the regular bank and I noticed it only serviced the top two floors. The top floor required a key Mouse pointed at the only button. "This is your floor. There are only two condos. Yours is to the left. Remind me to give you a key for my floor."

When I stepped into the foyer, his wife Jade came flying across the room and leaped into my arms and started kissing my face. I gave her an enormous hug. She took my face in her hands and placed her lips on mine. What ensued was a kiss less like friends and more like lovers, at least on her side, anyway.

"If I wasn't a happily married woman, I'd be chasing you, Matt Preston. You know I'll always love you for saving me." I'd helped her out of a bad situation, but that's a story already told.

I mouthed, "Help me!" at Mouse.

He laughed and shook his head. "You're on your own."

Finally, she unwrapped her legs and I set her down. She tugged on my hand, pulling me into the front room. Even though I'd seen the view from the condo before, it still stunned me for. We were over seventy stories in the air and despite being a little cloudy, I could see all the way across the Sound to the Olympic Mountains.

Jade pushed me into a chair and disappeared. She returned with an enormous cup of coffee exactly the color I like. I thanked her.

Mouse commented, "See, she really likes you. She'll bring you a cup, but not me."

Jade turned red and disappeared again. When she returned, she bowed to Mouse and extended a cup of what I assumed was coffee. "I'm sorry, sir. I was so excited to see Matt I forgot. Please forgive?"

"I'm happy to see him too Jade, I forgive. I understand." The warmth in his voice was obvious.

They made a cute couple. His teasing her was all an act. Mouse has a deep respect for Jade's abilities and even though at times she acts like a maid or a mistress, she's far from anything like that. Jade is exceptionally intelligent, and Mouse counted on her feedback and advice in his various enterprises. She was often present during business meetings, sometimes acting like a maid. Later Mouse would ask for her opinions. Her ability to accurately analyze what she'd seen and heard was valuable to Mouse.

Mouse said, "I'm always happy to see you and you're always welcome. Is there anything you need besides a place to crash?"

"I'm not supposed to talk about what's going on, but since it's you I'll take the chance John won't have me locked up for having this chat. I'm on my way to Craig, Alaska. Orchard heard a rumor that Sal Zampuchini is meeting the head of UIBA—"

"Abdulaleem al-Zaman?" Mouse interrupted. "al-Zaman? Holy shit. First time I've heard anything about this. I wonder what it's all about?"

"Rumor is, there's a large cache of arms floating around and Zampuchini either has it or has access to it and wants sell it to the UIBA."

"I'd heard the rumor. But it was my understanding they don't exist. Supposedly, whole thing was a plan to rip somebody off. If it's the UIBA they plan on ripping off, then somebody is monumentally stupid. You don't mess with crazies. Anyway, I interrupted you. You mentioned that you need a place to stay?"

"When I sold my apartment, I put everything into storage. Now I need to get my stuff and move into the condo.

When I get back from Alaska, I'll move and then it's over to rescue my dogs. I'm just going to take Max and Bean. The dog that Nicki brought with her from the old man will stay with Walter and his family. Walter's son Little Matt loves the dog, and it's the best place for it. Then it's back to Florida. You know my friend Snooker passed away? I still have several classic cars I have to dispose of for the estate."

"How's that going?"

I told Mouse about my old buddy Digger and about the Amelia Island Auction—my friend's granddaughter ended up with two and a half million dollars. He left her a business park too, which brings in a tidy sum every month. I ended with, "Everything turned out very well for her."

"It sounds like your move to Florida is working out for you."

"Yeah, I'll really miss you two. You will come and visit me from time to time in Florida?"

"We will. Promise!"

"Great. Now, tell me again about Todd Hoss. I can't believe what you said."

"From what I understand, the police have all the proof they need. The computer he used right down to using his own passwords."

"Sorry, I still can't believe it. I know the man. If you look up the word timorous in the dictionary, there's a picture of Todd Hoss. The man is a straight arrow and I'm just not buying it."

"Why not?"

"He's as boy scout as they come. This guy was the class president in his senior year at the university. He belongs to every service club I know of in addition he's a deacon and an usher at his church. If you met him, you'd understand. I just can't get my head wrapped around that idea. Mouse, there's no way he could have done it. Anyway, you said you had a place I could crash for few days. Where?"

31

"Right here."

"I can't do that. It would be an imposition."

"No, it won't, and we want you to stay." It was Jade insisting now. I was fighting a losing battle.

CHAPTER FIVE

The first thing I needed to do the next morning was contact the woman John asked me to escort to Craig. I had her number stored in my cell phone and I called it. The answering voice was low and sexy. "Good Morning, this is Carson Photo Studios, Jesi speaking."

"Good Morning, Ms. Carson. This is Matt Preston. Admiral Orchard gave me your number and said I should call you.

"Yes, hello. Admiral Orchard told me you'd be calling. I guess we should meet and make some plans."

"Sounds good. When and where?"

"I have a studio in the north end of town. How about this morning at eleven?"

She gave me her address, and I was about to hang up. "Sir, sir…"

"Yes?"

"I'm sorry. What did you say your name was?"

"Preston. Matt Preston."

"Until then, Mr. Preston."

"Yes, ma'am."

Jesi Carson sounded sexy as hell. I was looking forward to meeting this woman.

~ ~ ~ ~ ~ ~

The building was yellow and white and even though it was located in North Seattle; it looked like a building in old Florida back in the day. It was even on cement blocks. White shutters hung above the windows to keep out the strong afternoon sun with a cupola at the top of the building to vent the sultry air. I wondered why anybody would build such a structure in Seattle.

I found her photo studio with ease. Inside a woman with brown hair tinted blond on the ends and attractive large brown eyes greeted me. She also had tattoos covering both arms and a small gold ring dangling from the bottom of her nose. I had a million questions about the nose ring, but I kept them to myself. Personally, I don't care for tattoos and jewelry dangling from the nose is a definite no-no.

Okay, stop! I hear some of you hollering, "Wait a minute, you have a tattoo on your shoulder. That's not right to feel that way."

The thing about my tattoo is it happened when I was totally shitfaced, or at least that's the excuse I always use. To be honest, I've always wished I didn't have one. Let's face it, you don't put a bumper sticker on a Ferrari! Or a Rolls Royce. So far I've never had to decide whether I would sleep with a tattooed woman, and I didn't see how it would be an issue this time either. The young lady extended her hand, and asked, "Mr. Preston?"

"Yes. And I assume you are Jesi Carson."

"Guilty." She had a killer smile.

We shook hands and I looked around her studio. Motioning with her head, she showed she wanted to step outside. I agreed, and we went out to the far end of the parking lot and stood at the edge.

"It's probably safe to chat inside the studio, but doing the things we're going to do, one can't be too cautious. Especially considering some of the players involved in this affair," she explained.

"I take it you've done things like this before?" I wanted to know exactly what kind of experience she had.

"Yes, Mr. Preston, I've done things like this before." Her tone was condescending.

I explained I preferred Matt, and she told me to call her Jesi.

"How soon do you want to leave?" she asked.

"Things are already set up for us at the fishing camp; our reservations are in three days. You know what our cover is?"

"This is our honeymoon. I'll tell you I've used this cover before, and it didn't go well. Also, if this was for real, there's no way I'd spend my honeymoon fishing. Not only that, but there's no way I'd go to Alaska this time of year. But that's the assignment and I'll do my best to make sure people believe we're newlyweds and I'm excited as hell to spend it fishing. Are you okay with all this?"

"I understand fishing isn't everybody's idea of a wonderful time."

"Why don't you contact Orchard then and tell him it's a go? Then let me know where to meet you and our plane."

"That's a deal. Do you have a burner phone?"

"You mean like an inexpensive model?"

"Yes. One you intend to throw away, so nobody can trace our calls."

"No, I don't have one! Will you get me one?"

"I'll take care of it."

I left and called John on a phone he kept in his desk. There was no way I wanted to tell Lois. John must have recognized my number as he answered, "What do you need Matt?"

"I've met the Carson woman, and she's ready to go. The dates work out for her."

"Can you handle everything?"

"Get real. Yes John. If you have doubts, then why did you ask me to do this? Are you telling me everything I need to know? By the way, who is this Carson person? She seems to know a lot about what's going on with you and the agency."

"The agency has used her a few times before. I trust her. I trust you too, but I'm worried about what might leak. I'm counting on you to make this happen."

"Like I have a choice?"

"NO! Goodbye, Matt."

He had hung up, so he missed what I said next. I'm sure you can figure it out. Right?

~ ~ ~ ~ ~

I got a hold of Henry and told him when to meet me at Boeing Field and asked him to line up a float plane for us to get from Ketchikan to Craig. I picked up Jesi and started toward Boeing Field.

"Where are we going? she asked.

"We're headed to the airport to catch a flight up to Ketchikan."

When we pulled up next to the little jet at Boeing Field, Jesi's mouth dropped open. "Is this yours?" she asked.

"Kinda sorta... well, not exactly. I own part of the company that owns the plane."

We got our stuff out of the car and stored it on board the plane. We'd hardly gotten our seatbelts fastened when the plane rolled. Jesi was enthralled by the whole experience. I leaned my seat back and promptly fell asleep. I was jaded, flying in a private plane was no longer a big deal.

After we landed in Ketchikan, we moved our stuff to a float plane. I tried not to let Jesi know I wasn't a happy camper. I don't like little planes with just one motor. But we arrived at the fishing camp in one piece and got all checked in.

CHAPTER SIX

And now you know how come we ended up in late fall off Fish Egg Island, Alaska in a drizzle while shivering and freezing our buns off and acting like we're trying to catch fish, but actually hoping to take clandestine pictures of bad guys, if they ever show up!

Jealous?

Sound like fun?

Not even kind of! I won't even tell you the things I was mentally calling Orchard, however I'll bet you can guess. He owed me big time for this favor.

I was wearing a parka and heavy pants. Jesi wore sweatpants over long johns and a sweatshirt under a heavy parka. We both wore beanies, but the clothes weren't working very well. It was a damp cold, the kind that goes straight to your bones.

Jesi spent most of her time adjusting her camera and if I didn't know what it was, I'd have sworn it was a genuine fishing pole. On the tip of the pole, the first eyelet was a set of miniature optics which provided an almost 3-dimensional effect on a screen. The next eyelet was a miniature microphone. All you had to do was point your pole at what you wanted to view, and a live feed would come up on your cell phone. The third eyelet was also a camera with a wide-angle lens. The picture quality was incredible. I wouldn't have thought such a small camera could produce such amazing clarity. "Where did this come from?" I asked.

"I'm the one who built the pole. The Admiral connected me with the firms who manufacture the camera optics and directional microphones. All of the technology is top secret. When I created it, I didn't know I'd ever use it. It was more like I wanted to see if I could do it. When Orchard found out what I'd done he sent me on an assignment. This is the second time I've used this device for him."

This was an impressive young lady. I'll admit I can be chauvinistic, but I'm working on changing it. My problem is my brain is in my pants at times. Forgive me ladies, I really am trying.

In case anybody was watching us floating around out here freezing our butts off, we trolled back and forth for two hours and picked up two nice-sized silver salmon. We had established our presence and when we came out tomorrow, it wouldn't be so strange if we ran into Zampuchini and entourage. Because of the fish, the day wasn't a total bust for me, but I'm not so sure how Jesi felt about it.

~ ~ ~ ~ ~

The next morning as we were getting ready to leave, I noticed Jesi had used every towel and wash rag we had in the room and left them lying on the bathroom floor. Finally, I had to ask why she used everything we had. She stepped up to me and whispered in my ear, "Remember darling, we're on our honeymoon. We should have lots of sex. When you finish, you want to clean up. And since the towels are dirty, why put them back?"

"Okay. Now I understand."

I'll bet you never thought I'd have to get lessons on what to do on a honeymoon. I guess it's the age thing.

~ ~ ~ ~ ~

Because we were the only guests at the resort, we received the best boat they had. It was a typical boat that most fishing resorts used. The boat was not designed for speed, but it was stable when you leaned over the side to net your fish. Assuming you were lucky enough to catch one. This boat was around 21 feet long with a 125 HP Evinrude outboard motor. The motor idled slow enough so I could troll for fish and Jesi could get nice steady pictures but still fast enough so it didn't take all day to get out to suitable fishing spots.

We tried fishing in a new spot the next morning and I was pleased to see the drizzle had stopped. The sun was sickly, but still trying its best to shine. However, it wasn't any warmer than the previous day. But being dry really helped my spirits.

After eating the lunch the fishing camp packed for us, we moved around to the other side of the island. Jesi noticed an old dock sticking out from the shore and she requested we tie up and explore. After getting out of the boat, she headed inland and motioned for me to follow. We found a trail of sorts which led toward the center of the island and we followed it. Eventually the trail wandered up a hill in the middle of the island, and at the top we found besides a magnificent view an old picnic table. Jessie sat on top of the table and smiled up at me. "How come?" I asked.

"We are playing honeymoon games. Now come and sit next to me for a while."

"You are taking this seriously."

Jesi was quiet for a moment. When she started talking again, her voice had taken on a serious tone. "Listen, I need to explain something. One mission I did for the Admiral, they teamed me with a fellow and it was his first mission after graduating from academy. Between his chauvinistic attitude and that he thought he knew everything; he didn't want to listen to a thing I had to say. Our mission was a lot like this one where we were to be newlyweds. He didn't feel we needed to act like it was our honeymoon. They captured and questioned us at length. The opposition noticed several things that didn't look like we were on our honeymoon. Actually, rather stupid things like we only used two towels, and we'd never snuck off alone and fooled around. We also found out they bugged our room, and they'd listened to our conversations. We hadn't had sex once and they figured out we were not what we claimed.

"The fellow lost some fingers while he was being grilled and John's people had to rescue us in the end. The entire thing was frightening and I have no intention of getting caught like that again. This time I want us to look like we are what we say we are. What could be more normal than for us to sneak off and have sex during the day when we are on our honeymoon?"

We sat there for a while and then we heard people coming up from the dock area on the trail. Quickly she stood and removed her jacket and unzipped her pants. When I just sat there, she glared at me and told me to hurry and get my pants and underwear down. I'm sure that my face looked totally puzzled as I wondered why she'd told me to remove my clothes. "Just do it!" she snapped at me.

Jesi had removed her pants and panties and she threw her coat on the table and then climbed up on it. She motioned for me to crawl up on top of her. I was barely settled between her thighs when two men came into the clearing. Since they didn't know what was happening, it appeared like we were having sex. The two men seemed embarrassed and quickly turned and left. We stayed locked together for a few more moments and I have to admit, things were starting to wake up. Jesi pulled my face down, gave me a big kiss and wiggled her hips. "I'm glad to feel I'm not a total bust when it comes to being desirable, but this isn't the right time... even if we were trying to convince people differently."

I stood and reached out and helped her off the table. When she was standing in front of me, I reached out and touched the small gold ring she wore in the bottom of her nose. "No offense, but for me, this is a turnoff. I've never understood piercings or face jewelry. Call it my hang up."

Looking at her, it was the first time I'd really looked at her carefully and I had to admit; she was a very sexy lady. Tattoos and all. As we dressed Jesi stepped close to me and whispered, "Did you noticed both of them were carrying pistols in holsters on their belts?"

"You feel that isn't normal?"

She looked at me with one eye closed. "Are you packing a weapon?"

"No."

"And we are fishing. So, why were those two guys packing when they were just fishing, and you and I aren't?" I thought her supposition was a little weak, but she had a point. I've never heard of a King Salmon attacking anybody. But since the guys were walking in the woods and there are bears and other wild animals around, carrying guns isn't that uncommon, nor is it a bad idea.

When we got to our boat, as I helped Jesi in, I looked carefully at our fishing poles. I know when we left, the two poles were secure along the side of the boat. Now one of them was lying down the middle of the boat. I wondered what the two men were looking for. As we cast off, I noticed my pole which had been moved. Jesi's pole wasn't touched.

Still, I wondered what they were after. Was our honeymoon ruse not believed by everyone back at the fishing camp? It was something to consider.

We went back out and did some more trolling. I caught one more small silver, but we released it. I thought about taking it to the local cannery and have the fish smoked and canned and then shipped home, but this was not the purpose of the trip and I was sure we would catch bigger ones tomorrow. I still hoped if anyone was checking up on us, my actions by releasing the fish wouldn't create any problems down the line.

Next morning, we were up early and grabbed a couple lunch sacks the fishing camp provided and headed out. Orchard had given me a little idea when and where the two men were expected to meet. When we got close, I set up my pole and Jesi's pole and we started trolling. Jesi's pole was set up to look like she was fishing with a line dragging through the water with a sinker tied to the end. It was just there was no hook on the end of her line.

We'd been out fishing just over two hours and I'd caught a nice-sized silver and released it when we noticed a good-sized cruiser in the distance coming our way. From the size of the yacht, I guessed it had to be close to one hundred feet long. The design was the one I'd like to have if I had a boat. The yacht continued into the small bay on the south end of the island where it dropped anchor.

Hanging off the side of the yacht on two davits was the yacht's tender. The tender was about the same size as the fishing boat we were in, but a lot classier. This tender had two outboard motors and even though I couldn't see the numbers on the side, I could tell they were larger than the one on my little fishing boat.

I watched two men lower the tender on the davits and then climb in along with some fishing gear. Since the boat wasn't designed for fishing, I wondered what they were trying to prove. One man started one of the outboard motors and the boat pulled slowly away from the yacht. After they were away from the little inlet, the men on board dropped their fishing gear into the water and trolled back and forth close to where we were fishing. The entire time Jesi was carefully taping them.

I'd shown Jesi a picture of Zampuchini and when we were at the end of the island getting ready to turn around for our pass back, Jesi leaned over and whispered, "Neither of them are Zampuchini and neither of them look like they're of mid-eastern descent." I agreed. She continued, "But, the men in the tiny boat are the same two who found us yesterday on the island where we acted like we were fooling around." I took a closer look, but without a camera or an aide, it was difficult to tell, but considering things, I felt she could be correct. To me, they still looked like two goombahs who might work for Zampuchini.

By mid-afternoon we worried that perhaps we were keeping anything from happening by being so close to the anchored yacht. For the next few passes I went as far to the end of the island as I could. One time we even drifted around the end of the island. When we came back around the end, we noticed there was a new small open boat tied up alongside of the yacht, but the yacht's tender was still out. Jesi and I noticed neither man in the tender had a fishing pole in his hand now.

The yacht's tender was staying close to the yacht, and I observed what looked like an AK-47 in the hands of the passenger riding in the yacht's tender. We kept our distance as we trolled past the yacht while Jesi kept her pole aimed at the large boat as much as she could. It was difficult not to be obvious while she tried to act like she was fishing.

Passing by the yacht, we noticed two men sitting in the cabin located on the fantail and one was wearing a headscarf. After my first quick observation, I made sure not to look at the yacht again. Jesi surreptitiously kept her pole aimed at the stern of the yacht.

When we reached the point where we'd normally turn around, the yacht's tender with the two men was now sitting directly in our path. If we wanted to troll past where we had been fishing all afternoon, it would have been obvious we were doing more than fish, we were checking out the yacht. Jesi whispered she had some excellent pictures of the fantail and perhaps it was best if we headed back to the camp. I reeled in my line and Jesi acted like she was winding in her line. Once we had our fishing poles stored, we turned and headed back to the camp.

We tied up our boat and carried our poles to our room. Once we were inside of the room, Jesi motioned for me to be still and I just stood quietly as she pulled something out of the bottom of her suitcase. Slowly she walked around the room and three times she made a sign. Someone had installed bugs in our room. While we'd been out fishing somebody had planted listening devices,

Jesi moved over to the bed and motioned for me to come over. She wrapped her arms around me and kissed me on the lips. I guess I was a little slow on the uptake and she leaned back and frowned, "You call that a kiss. If I guess I should have married Peter if you can't kiss me with anymore passion than that on our honeymoon."

I pulled her to me and this time I pulled out all the stops. Our lips met, and I nuzzled my tongue against her lips. The kiss got a lot more passionate, but I had to admit her nose ring was a big distraction. When we broke again, she whispered just loud enough so anybody listening would hear, "Make love to me. Please."

For the next half hour, we bounced on the bed and made many sounds like we were playing the honeymoon game. Finally, Jesi moaned, and she sounded like she was having a climax which would have put the faked climax in "When

Harry Met Sally" to shame. I got the hint I should make sounds as well when she poked me in the chest and rolled her hands. I gave a big grunt, and we brought the complete show to an end. Even with the nose ring and tattoos, I had to admit, I was getting a little turned on. We lay on the bed for a little while and Jesi put her head on my shoulder. It was sweet to lie there and quietly laugh to ourselves about what we had just done. I wondered how realistic we had sounded.

After about fifteen minutes, Jesi sat up and asked, "Can we get dressed and then go for a walk? Sitting all day in that compact boat has made me want to go for a walk."

We made noises like we were getting dressed and one time I reached out and pulled her to me. She pushed me away and exclaimed, "Knock it off. We just did that. I want to go for a walk."

"Yeah, but seeing you all naked, now I'm in the mood."

"Hold on to the thought. When we get back."

I made it sound pitiful, "Okay!"

~ ~ ~ ~ ~

We walked across the island and when we got to the other side away from the camp; we walked up the beach. I had looked around just before we stepped onto the beach and I could see nobody who could overhear our conversation, even with electronic listening gear. "Do you think our cover is blown or are there just some very cautious people around?"

"So far I think it's just some cautious people. I think we did the right thing to leave our fishing spot when we did."

"I would agree. I wanted to look at some pictures you had, but I didn't want anyone noticing me looking at my phone when I was to be fishing. When we get back to the room, can you show me some of the pictures you got?"

"Yes. I could look at several of them as I was taping, and I think we got some excellent pictures of the two men sitting on the back deck."

"How do we get them back to Orchard?"

"He was watching a live feed from the fishing pole."

"No shit?"

"Yeah, the entire thing is cool. There is an aerial built inside the pole. Inside of the butt of the pole are four powerful batteries. I was hoping to hear for sure the men on the back of the boat were the two we wanted to get pictures of."

"We can always try later."

"Matt, about that, from now on, when we are in the room, I want us to be newlyweds. I know you don't like the nose ring, but can you try to have sex with me in the room? Bite the bullet. I don't want an episode like that one job I did for Orchard. I think we did an okay job making them believe our fake, but I would like for them to hear the authentic thing." I must have been still too long because after a while Jesi asked, "What's the matter?"

"Jesi, time for truth. I've never cared for tattoos. I know this sounds weird, but they're really distracting. I also have a lady friend I've been seeing. There are no promises between us, but things look good. However, I see if we must sell this just married thing, we need to make it sound and be as real as we can. From here on out, I'll try to be the best newly married guy you've ever seen."

"And I promise to do the best I can. Oh, I like the way you kiss."

"I aim to please." We both laughed.

~ ~ ~ ~ ~

That evening I discovered if Jesi and I were married, our marriage would have only lasted one evening. Our marriage would have other major problems besides the tattoos. I'd tried hard to ignore the ink on her shoulders, arms and the weird little tattoo I found on the lower portion of her tummy, but when it came time to fondle her breasts, I wasn't prepared to find little gold rings inserted through each nipple. With that discovery, I found I'd lost all my abilities, if you catch my drift. I tried to get back in the mood and I gently slid my hand down over her tummy, trying to ignore that strange little tattoo and then between her legs; much to my surprise, I found something hard there too. I was curious, and I leaned over and when I peeked, I found a small gold ring protruding from a place I didn't think should have a golden ring. At that point, I lost all hope of saving the situation.

Houston, we have a problem.

I didn't expect to find gold in that valley, and I lost all interest in any fun and games. I didn't care for the piercings of her nipples; but finding something in her nether region? Sorry, things would not happen. I whispered in her ear she needed to fake it again and we would discuss it tomorrow.

I thought we did a splendid job of selling the idea we were playing slap and tickle and we cuddled afterwards. I had no idea how I would explain to Jesi when you get to be my age. There are certain physical things are off-putting, and they can make things cease to work during sex. Not to be chauvinistic, but I don't feel a woman should have buried treasure. Finding gold rings in areas where I don't feel pieces of gold belong is a real turnoff for me! I deflate quickly and chances of getting me interested are slim. I know, I hear you saying I've become an old man. Stuck in my ways. Well, I guess I have to agree. Perhaps the old saying about old dogs and new tricks is accurate…

At least for this old dog they are.

CHAPTER SEVEN

The next morning Jesi and I returned to the bay where the yacht had been anchored. Rounding the promontory, we discovered the bay was empty. I tried not to let Jesi see how discouraged I was at the sight. Since we didn't know where to search for the boats, I decided for now, we should continue to fish and hope for the best.

As we settled in, Jesi told me she didn't like to fish and having to act like she was fishing was even worse.

I laughed. "Hate to spoil your revelation, but I was already aware how you felt about fishing."

"Didn't do a wonderful job of disguising it, huh?"

"No dear, you suck at deception. But I am sorry you're so unhappy out here. It wasn't my idea. If you're that unhappy, you need to take it up with Orchard."

After we'd made two passes, she turned to me. "Okay, you want to explain what happened last night?

"Sorry Jesi. I'm a stone's throw away from my sixtieth birthday and I'll admit I'm set in my ways, especially about sex and stuff. Your age group views things differently than mine. Things like tattoos and piercings are more common for you than they are for me. I wasn't prepared to find rings in your nipples and especially....

I couldn't believe how difficult it was to explain.

"Caught you by surprise, huh?" I agreed. "Okay, a suggestion. When we get back to the room, I'll take off my clothes and you can examine things, you know, kind of get used to them. Would that help?"

"I don't know. I doubt it. Remember, normally I'd have no qualms about us having sex, but I'm seeing someone. If we did anything, I'd feel like I was cheating. It's not that you're not desirable, because you are. Tattoos and piercings aside, you're a very sexy young woman with a darling body. It might be kinda kinky to suck on your little chunks of metal and see what transpires...but, my lady friend keeps popping up in my head."

"You know, that makes me want to have sex with you even more. Call it forbidden fruit, or knowing you have such deep feelings. I'm jealous. I want something like that. Most of the guys I know just want a quickie."

I felt sorry for her. She seemed like a like nice gal and I hoped she'd find the right fellow.

She said, "Okay, we have to keep faking it. But if our two guys don't show up, this may all be a moot point."

As if summoned by her words, the yacht came around the end of the island and into the small bay. While she was dropping anchor, two men lowered the tender again. One I recognized from the day before and one was new. After they launched the tender, the men loaded weapons and climbed in. Before it pulled away, Sal Zampuchini stepped out on the fantail and said something to them.

From the way the men had gotten into the boat, it was obvious they were not comfortable around small boats. Today they had difficulty getting the outboard started. They finally got it running and the tender came out of the cove and started patrolling the opening of the small bay. Today there was no pretense of fishing.

Jesi and I continued our act. Twice I tied into a nice-sized Silver too large for us to throw back without causing suspicion so I tossed them on bottom of the boat. Jesi was not happy about having fish flopping around between her feet. I didn't think to bring any kind of Billy club to knock the fish out. At least I'd remembered a net. Jesi maintained a running commentary regarding the fish which I'll bet would have made a sailor blush.

Just after lunch, the small open boat we'd seen yesterday appeared. It was a long way out and I didn't want to scare them away. I turned away from the yacht, still trolling for fish. As luck would have it, I hooked into what felt like a big one. I had to play the fish until it got tired and because I was occupied, I couldn't pay much attention to the open boat's approach.

By the time I got the fish into our boat, the newly arrived open boat with Abdulaleem al-Zaman and his party had tied up to the yacht. Jesi told me three men got out, and one of them was wearing what looked like a turban. "I'm positive the man in the turban is Abdulaleem. Orchard showed me a picture they think is of him."

Jesi had kept her camera on the men as long as she could while I was fighting the fish.

I started the motor and dropped my line, starting another pass. When I came around we'd picked up a breeze and the water had developed a little chop. It wasn't bad, but Jesi wasn't happy.

We were about even with the yacht when there were two *bangs*, a few seconds apart. They sounded close to each other, probably from the yacht. But it was impossible to pinpoint where.

The tender patrolling the bay immediately turned towards the yacht, fired up the second motor and gunned it.

When they reached the yacht, they barely took the time to tie the tender to a cleat as they leapt aboard. When the two men in the tender started towards the yacht, I quickly reeled in my line. Jesi made no effort now to act like she was fishing. "Get closer," she urged.

"I'm trying." I snapped.

Without warning, one of the men from the tender staggered and fell in the water. As he fell, I heard a gunshot. This shot had come from the hills, not from the yacht. It was still impossible to tell where the shooter was. My guess was he was somewhere on the left side of the little inlet.

The other guy from the tender ducked into a cabin and came out with another man behind him. This was either one of Sal's henchmen or someone with Abdulaleem. They headed aft, searching the hillside for the shooter. One of the men crumpled to the deck. The sound of the shot that got him came at the same time the second bullet dropped the other guy.

Now I had a better idea where the gunman was and I told Jesi, asking her to get some pictures. Evidently the man on the fantail wasn't badly wounded because he scooted behind cover and started scanning the hills.

Jesi told me, "The bearded man on the deck was with Abdulaleem." And then Abdulaleem stepped out of the cabin. His companion pulled himself up from the deck and they stood side by side on the stern, searching the woods surrounding the inlet. I assumed that the man wearing the turban was Abdulaleem because he was barking orders at the other fellow. Abdulaleem was carrying a semi-automatic rifle and fired several bursts around the inlet.

Evidently, the sniper took it as a challenge. The sniper shot both men and they fell, one after the other over the rail to the water below, the sound of the shots coming eerily afterward.

I thought, *Oh shit, I just witnessed the assassination of the head of the UIBA*. I could tell they were dead before they hit the water. No doubt some heads would roll over this.

The third man in Abdulaleem's party hadn't come out of the cabin.

Jesi told me, "The shots are coming from halfway up the left side of the slope. See the old dead tree sticking out of the brush about halfway up the bank? I think the shooter is behind it."

I couldn't see any shooter, but I believed her.

An armed man appeared in the doorway—the other guy from the patrolling tender. He looked out at Jesi and me and raised his pistol. I pointed at the bank. The shot was much louder this time and I realized, the goombah was shooting at us.

I wasn't waiting for any more shots. I gunned the motor and we got out of there as fast as the boat would go.

I moved the outboard back and forth to make our little boat a tougher target. When I looked back, I saw the shooter topple into the water, but I didn't hear the shot over the sound of the motor.

The guy on the deck disappeared into the cabin and emerged with what appeared to be an AK 47. He fired several bursts into the woods. Just before we rounded the island, a man jumped into the tender.

We were already tying up to the camp's dock when the tender came into view around the end of the island. We hurried to the camp's office.

A woman behind the check in desk asked, "May I help you?"

"Can you get in touch with local law enforcement?"

"Yes, why?"

"I'm an undercover federal agent. We were watching a yacht anchored in an inlet behind Fish Egg Island and witnessed several men being killed by a sniper."

The woman seemed nonplussed but picked up the phone. "I wonder who I should call? I can call the Coast Guard, but they're so far away. I can call the sheriff, but I think his deputy is up north with the county's boat."

I was really getting upset with this woman, "Call and get him here now, and I'll take him out in my rental."

The woman said okay and dialed her phone. It seemed to take a long time for the call to go through.

"Hello Becky, this is Henrietta. There are two people here in my office who say they're government agents and they saw several people get shot on the back of some boat anchored behind Fish Egg Island. What do you want to do? Uh huh...yes...I see. Okay, thank you."

She hung up the phone and said, "The sheriff is kinda busy right now. If he gets some time later, he'll come out and decide what he wants do."

"Henrietta? Is that correct? By that time they'll be gone."

"Well, what did you expect? Your story is a little far-fetched. And if you're a federal agent, where is your identification?"

"I told you we're undercover. It's not wise to carry ID when you're undercover." There was no way this woman would be any help. On the way back to our room, I told Jesi we should go. There was a plane leaving in less than an hour and I thought we should be on it. Jesi agreed. When we opened the door, we were shocked to find our room totally trashed. The pillows were slashed, drawers pulled from the dresser and emptied onto the floor, suitcases thrown around. Jesi exclaimed, "What the hell were they looking for?"

"I would imagine they want to find any evidence we have of what we saw yesterday. I don't think they know your pole isn't a fishing pole, but right now nothing would surprise me."

We packed and lugged our stuff down to the wharf. The seaplane was on time and as it taxied a boat came from behind Fish Egg Island and started west towards Ursua Channel which would take them to the Pacific Ocean.

Once aboard, I closed my eyes and crossed my fingers and promised the powers at be I'd change my ways and be the best person I could if the Gods would just let this little plane get into the air and get me back to Ketchikan safely.

Luck was with me. Fish Egg Island was visible out my window and the yacht was still anchored in the bay. A boat was pulling out of the cove and it looked like the boat the Arabs arrived in. The boat was moving fast and when I looked down again it was out past Cone Island. Beyond Cone Island, a large tramp steamer was lying idle in the water, smoke drifting lazily from the smokestack. The plane banked, and the last thing I saw was the small open boat making a beeline toward the tramp steamer.

Curious…

There was no way of knowing if they assassinated Zampuchini in the fight. From the way Abdulaleem fell into the water, I was positive he was dead. Only one of the three Arabs on Sal's yacht, was still alive when I left. Also, who was the shooter on the hill? Who was the target? Abdulaleem or Salvatore?

I was not looking forward to my next conversation with Orchard. The screw up wasn't my fault, there was nothing I could have done to prevent any of the things which just transpired, but I was sure I would catch an earful about the catastrophe.

I called Henry and asked when a plane might pick us up in Ketchikan. When he told me there was a plane still at the airport waiting for our call, I was relieved. As soon as we could get on board, we could get out of here.

Silently, I thanked Henry for his foresight.

CHAPTER EIGHT

After we landed in Seattle and got all our gear separated, I took Jesi home. When we arrived, she invited me in. "I've got something I need to show you."

We went into her office, and while the computer was firing up, Jesi said, "I should have said something sooner, but we were so busy I kind of forgot."

Jesi removed the reel from her fishing pole, opened one side and pulled out a USB cord. She plugged it into her computer and clicked through the menu, and a picture appeared. A direct shot of the yacht's stern.

"Watch," she instructed and zoomed in close. It was like I was on board the yacht looking in at two men sitting at a table. The picture was a little hazy, but it looked like Zampuchini and Abdulaleem al-Zaman.

The turbaned man picked something up off the table, then put it down. He chose something else, looking it over carefully. Before he put it down, he showed it to the man directly behind him. al-Zaman put it back down and began to argue with Zampuchini. Without any warning, Abdulaleem drew a pistol from inside his robe and shot Zampuchini in the chest. The mobster clutched his chest and fell to the floor.

A few minutes later the two men from the tender appeared and I saw the whole thing again from a different angle, up until our boat took off.

"I need to call Orchard," I told Jesi, "which is something I'm not looking forward to. When I hear from him, I'll get back to you. I think you need to hide that recording."

Deep in thought, I headed for Mouse's condo. Mouse and Jade were so happy to see me it picked up my spirts. Jade wanted to know if I'd stay for dinner and since I had no other plans, I agreed.

At dinner, I told them, "I'm going over to see Walter and Thien in the morning; it's been a long time since I've seen my dogs. I want to take them back to Florida with me. Do you mind if I have them here for a few days?"

Mouse grinned at me, "Of course not. Marshall have one of his people come up three or four times a day to take them out."

My dogs would have their own valet.

He continued, "When you get back, I'll have a surprise for you."

"What?"

"You'll just have to wait."

What a pill!

CHAPTER NINE

Standing on the top deck, I watched the ferry pull away from the dock. I knew I was going to miss this part of Puget Sound. I'd grown up in Seattle and I love the clear water and the lush green hills. My parents used to have a summer home on one of the islands and I'd grown up boating on Puget Sound. I watched the churning white water from the ship's propeller and the green waves rolling away from the ferry, there was no doubt I was going to miss this part of home.

Once on the peninsula, I drove to the familiar clearing and parked the truck, ready for the hike to Walter and Thein's. I'd hiked the trail in so many times I could probably do it in the dark. The last time I'd shown up I'd surprised them making love on the deck, so I called a hello. I rounded the cabin and found Bean dancing with happiness and Walter and Thein smiling. Thein was tiny again; she'd had her baby.

She wrapped me in a hug and Walter grabbed my hand and pumped it. Bean pawed at me to pick her up. Walter and I sat down on chairs he built himself from fallen wood he found in the forest and I marveled again at how comfortable they were. I always meant to ask him to build me a couple of chairs I could take back to Seattle with me. I had barely settled in my chair when Bean came over and started pawing me to pick her up.

"How long are you going to be with us?" Thein asked.

"At least overnight. I came over to pick up my dogs." At that point Max bounded out of the cabin and jumped into my lap. I sat on the deck and played with the dogs for a while. I'd missed them. I was glad to be taking them back with me.

Little Matt came wandering out after waking up from his nap. When he saw me he screamed, "Uncle Matt," and ran to me. I picked him up, and he threw his little arms around my neck and hugged me for a long time. Eventually he released me and said, "Thank you Uncle Matt, for Rascal. I love him to pieces. Are you going to take Max and Bean?"

"Yes. I miss them. You have a dog now and I need my dogs back. Is that okay with you?"

He nodded. "I'll miss them. But you're right, I have Rascal and I just love him."

I heard crying, and Thein fetched the baby. Those of you who know me know I'm not a big baby person, but Walter and Thein's baby girl was a doll. "What did you name her?" I asked.

"Tuyet. It means snow. Actually, it's a verb — it means snowing. Many of my people believe snow brings good luck. The day she was born it snowed, and I promised if I had a healthy child, I'd name if after the snow," Thein told me.

"That's cool. Your little girl is adorable. Congratulations!"

Tuyet fussed and Thien pulled up her top and placed the baby to her nipple. The baby girl latched on as if she hadn't eaten in weeks and Thien winced and gently pulled the baby away, telling her, "Hey, slow down. Nothing is going away. You don't want to hurt mommy." As if Tuyet understood, she seemed to suck softer with less intensity. When Thein looked at me with a grin, I had to laugh.

The three of us sat on the deck while Thein fed her daughter. Little Matt played on the deck with the dogs. He said, "Daddy says that you live a long way from us now. Will you come back and visit?"

When Little Matt spoke to me, I realized he was talking more like an adult than a child. "I'll come back often. I hope you and your mom and dad and Tuyet will come and visit me."

"Dad says to visit you we need to fly in an airplane. I've never seen one up close, but I see them fly overhead a lot. I think I'd enjoy a plane ride."

"Well, it's possible to drive, but it would take about a week. Flying is much faster, but even then, I'm about six or seven hours away."

"Dad showed me where you live on a map. He said that you live on a river that goes into an ocean."

"That's true. If you come and visit, I'll take you to see it. It's called the Gulf of Mexico."

"I know, I saw it on the map."

His remark stunned me. "You can read?"

"Of course." He sounded like I was mentally deficient for not realizing he could read.

"Umm, how old are you, Matt?"

With pride, he held up four fingers, "I'll be five on my next birthday." Walter could see my surprise.

"We don't have a TV or anything like that," Walter explained. "We never talked baby talk to him and as soon as he understood the concept of letters and words, we started teaching him to read. Right now he reads at a sixth grade level."

"Are you serious?" Walter nodded. "Holy shit!" I exclaimed.

Little Matt spoke up. "You know Uncle Matt, that's not a word you can use in front of everybody. Daddy says it sometimes, but when I go to school, I'm not supposed to say things like that."

He embarrassed me. "Your daddy's correct, and I shouldn't have said that word in front of you. I'm sorry."

"Why? I know what shit means. And I know when not to say it."

This conversation was getting way too deep for me. Little Matt sounded like someone twice his age, or more. I didn't say anything, but I wondered how he would do in school. If he went to public school, they wouldn't know what to do with Little Matt. Calling Little Matt gifted was like calling Shaquille O'Neal big.

Tuyet finished, and Thein changed her. Thein put her to bed and when she came out, she expressed how pleased she was I was staying. Dinner was fantastic as always, and I ate too much. I asked Thein where she got her spices; I was positive they had nothing like them on the peninsula.

"Amazon."

"What?" I blurted out.

"We have a cell phone with a solar charger. You wouldn't believe the reception we get up here. I order what I want, and they deliver to the little store down the road." The island had a small general store with a post office substation.

"I thought a lot of the delivery services won't deliver to a post office box."

"They know us at the store. We have their permission to use their physical address. Actually, there is nothing we can't get up here." Walter explained.

After dinner Walter and I were curled up in his comfortable chairs and he asked me if I wanted some smoke.

"It's been a long time. The last time I had any smoke was up here with you. I guess I'm growing up, it just ain't the pleasant pastime it once was."

"To be honest, I don't do it often myself," he confided.

"What is this, now that it's legal in several states with more states moving towards legalizing, it isn't fun? Was the fun in smoking because we were breaking the law? Is this another way we're getting old? Take a puff, don't let me stop you."

Walter put the pipe down and leaned back in his chair. "Funny how things keep changing."

"How so?"

"Take smoking weed, for instance. The last couple of times it wasn't as enjoyable as it used to be. I thought it was just me. Now I find out you don't care for it anymore. Like our youth has moved on and we didn't even realize it."

I told Walter about Snooker's passing and how he'd left me with the duty of getting his car collection sold. I mentioned the changes I was seeing happening in the buyers. "The millennial generation don't have as much interest in old cars like we did. If a person was into '57 Chevy, they probably have to be in their 60s to appreciate the car. As our generation ages, the pool of people who are interested in our cars is growing smaller by the day. Soon Walter, cars that weren't allowed into the parking lots of some of those up-scale auction houses will start going over the block as collector items."

At one point in the evening, Walter sat up. "What?" I asked him.

"I just remembered something I wanted to share with you."

"And?"

"Do you remember Squirrel?"

"Yeah, kinda. How come we called him Squirrel?"

"Because he kept everything. He kept the strangest things squirreled away. I saw him at the VA hospital in Seattle. That cat was taking some major drugs."

"I remember back in country he'd do anything to get high."

"Anyway, he gave me his address. I've written him twice just to stay in touch. He lives up in Bellingham now.

No idea what he's doing. Well, I got a note from him after your last visit. Do you remember Don Wykoff?"

"Yeah, he was on that one mission where everyone in his squad got killed. He'd gone ahead to the next village and when he got back to his unit, everyone was dead. Why?"

"Squirrel stayed in contact with him. Don had a ton of stuff wrong with him. He was a two pack a day smoker — unfiltered Lucky Strikes of course, so there was cancer along with heart problems and lung problems. He was in a lot of pain when he went. Squirrel heard from Don's sister when Don passed."

"They're leaving us fast, my friend."

"No shit! Makes me wonder what's happening inside me. We were out there breathing all the crap that was being dumped on the VCs. At the end Squirrel said Don told his sister he would be joining his buddies. They were waiting for him back in Nam. He always thought he should have died that day with the rest of his mates. He felt guilty he came back when they didn't." Walter got that thousand-yard stare and whispered, "Over thirty years he's been back. Thirty fucking years, Matt, and the last thing he talked about was what happened back in country. Shit Matt. Talk about still being in Saigon."

Walter's comment jogged my memory, and I remembered some words from the old Charlie Daniels Band song about still being in Saigon in the mind.

Don came back from Nam, physically but not mentally. I wondered how many of us were still back in Saigon in some way. I recalled the last night I was with Snooker before he passed away, and how we'd killed several Scotches as we remembered those who never came back. Walter reached over and put his hand on my knee.

"Matt, are you okay?"

"Yeah, sorry about that. I guess for a second I was back in Saigon myself. Most of the time I'm good at keeping it all locked up, but there are moments."

That was as good a time as any, so I told Walter about what happened in Alaska.

He was as shocked. "Any idea who was behind it?"

"Maybe. I think McNaulty is involved. But that's just a feeling. Mouse doesn't have any ideas, either. He had heard about the arms cache, but he thought it was just a fairy tale. Some kind of scam somebody was running. But with Sal and Abdulaleem involved, he wonders it there might be a grain of truth. There's nothing out there regarding any missing weapons of any kind that Mouse is aware of. Face it, the amount of stuff involved sounded like somebody had to have ripped off a weapons depot or something, but nobody knows a thing! My question is, who was the shooter trying to kill, Sal or the Arab dude? Or Arab dudes? There's a lot of people who'd like to see either one of them dead—or both of them."

"Are you safe? Is there anyone that could have identified you?" Walter asked, concern in his voice.

"I don't know. I don't think so, but who knows? When people like those guys are murdered, the fallout spreads a long way."

"Take care, my friend. I couldn't replace you." For the longest time we sat in the twilight lost in our thoughts. Eventually Thein came out asked if we were becoming bumps on a log.

That night after I went to bed, I heard Walter and Thein making love. In that moment, I realized how much I missed Lois. I missed her so much it actually hurt. I needed someone in my life. I had someone for a while, and I thought she was the one. Things changed, and she moved on.

That's not exactly true, we both moved on.

I'm probably not the easiest person to live with and I wondered if it was possible for me to change. I wanted

Lois in my life, hell, I needed her. Without her, I was a real curmudgeon.

What nagged me was I'd had these thoughts before. I'd felt this way about other women, but as time passed, my feelings would change. Being on my own, answering to no one, was what made me happiest. Had that changed? As I fell asleep, I promised myself the next time I was with Lois, I'd sit down with her and start working on ways to spend more time together.

Tomorrow.

Something to work on tomorrow.

~ ~ ~ ~

The next morning was overcast — fog filled the valley beyond the cabin. It wasn't raining but the air was damp with the threat of heavy rain. The weather matched everybody's mood. Walter was quiet and Thein hardly said a word. I had a cup of coffee and it was time to head out.

Thein hugged me for a long time. "Be kind to yourself, Matt Preston. I want to see you again," she told me and then kissed me. "I love you," she mouthed.

I kissed her forehead and turned to leave. Walter said he would walk me out to my truck.

The dogs seemed to know what was up and they took off down the trail. When we got to the parking lot, I had two damp dogs to place into the truck.

Facing Walter, I could tell he had something to say. To help things along, I said, "What is it Walter? What's wrong?"

"Well, I'll admit I'm unhappy to see you move so far away."

"Walter, I'm only a few hours away by plane. You have the number for my air service. Call my people in Seattle and they'll send a car to take you to the Port Angeles airport.

Henry or one of the other pilots will pick you up there. You don't even have to go over to Seattle, It's really that easy. There's no reason to feel bad. Is that all?"

"No. Matt, I want to say something, but…"

"My friend, considering all that we've been through together, I can't believe you'd keep quiet. Speak!"

"It's you." He blurted out.

"Me? What do you mean?"

"You. I don't like the person you're turning into. You're better than you were on your last visit, but you still have an anger, a rage inside of you. Matt, you've gotten kind of cold. It's like you've lost your sense of humor or something."

"What is this? I don't get high with you and now I'm cold and unfeeling."

"Matt don't be an ass. You know that's not it. You're alone. I know what Thein has done for me and I think you need a woman in your life."

"Well, it's not the first time we've had this discussion."

"Okay, I'm just worried about you. You've done so much for me. I'd be dead by now had it not been for you. Giving me this land and all, I owe you so much."

"No, you don't. Chill. What I really want from you is to figure out a time to come and visit me in Florida. Okay?"

"Deal. Be safe."

As we hugged, I had a problem with my eyes. They seemed to be leaking. It touched me that Walter cared that much about me.

"I promise you I'll come back and visit you here. I love this place."

Walter stood in the middle of the road, watching me go. I was sad to leave. I wasn't so sad I wanted to stick around the Puget Sound, but I was sad to leave my friend.

For the rest of the trip back to Seattle, I was in a funk. I stayed in the truck on the ferry. When I got to the Olympus, I pulled under the portico and Marshall opened the door.

The dogs bounded out of the cab and Marshall jumped back laughing. "And who are these two?"

"Marshall, meet Max and Bean. Long story, but they're mine. They're staying with me."

"If you ever need them walked, let me know. It's part of the service we provide for residents of the Olympus."

"Thanks. I'll keep that in mind."

Later, when Mouse and Jade came to check on me, they found the three of us in a big chair, the dogs sleeping and me gazing out across the sound. I needed to get back to DC. I really missed Lois. And the Admiral wanted to talk to me.

It wasn't my fault what happened in Alaska.

Was he going to listen to reason?

Don't hold your breath.

CHAPTER TEN

My surprise from Mouse was great. All my belongings in storage had been delivered. The problem was, now I had to go through all that crap. Excuse me, my stored stuff.

After a few hours I was tired of rummaging through boxes while deciding which items to pitch or to keep. Some stuff just needed to be put away, but a lot of the stuff needed tossing. Why is it we keep stuff we have no use for? We carry stuff from place to place when we really should have thrown it away a long time ago. I'm sure some researcher has a theory about this, I just don't know what it is. Finally, I needed a break, in addition the dogs were pestering me to take them out.

"Okay, let's go for a walk." I didn't have to say it twice. They knew exactly what 'go for a walk' meant.

I headed for the basement to get a vehicle to take the dogs over to a trail to let them run. The trail was perfect for them and worth the effort to get them there. I'll admit it, I've become lazy in my old age. The few times I need a vehicle, I call down to Marshall and have his valet bring the vehicle I wanted up to the building's portico. Today, however, I decided I'd fetch my own. I knew where our chief of security and sometimes valet, kept the keys and this way I wouldn't have to disturb anybody to fetch my car. Besides, the car I wanted to use was an old van I didn't use much, and I didn't know if it would even start.

Each condo has two assigned parking spaces, and Mouse was kind enough to give me three more, plus another crappy space wedged in amid the HVAC units that nobody wants for the van. Five spaces, six counting the crummy one was unheard of for any person to have in our condo building. Obviously, I kept that tidbit to myself.

I got the keys and took the elevator to the garage. As I crossed the parking level I caught a flicker of movement in the corner of my eye. I passed my van, then ducked behind it, using it as a screen. I peered around the front of the van and saw the shadow crouch, ducking behind another car. It took just a few quick steps to get past the two cars between us and cone up behind him.

I growled, "Freeze! Don't turn around. I'll shoot you if you turn." I wasn't armed, and I was praying this person wouldn't call my bluff.

He didn't. He raised his arms. One over his head, the other only partially raised. "Please don't shoot me, Matt. I'm unarmed."

The voice was familiar. "Turn around slowly." I told him.

It took me a minute. The pants from his expensive suit were ripped, exposing bloody knees, his shirt in shreds and bloodstained. He was missing his jacket and his usually handsome face showed traces of a recent beating. The hand he hadn't raised was dripping blood, he could barely lift it to shoulder height. I'd never seen him in anything but a three-piece suit before but today he looked bedraggled. "Todd?" I asked. "Todd Hoss, is that you?"

He sobbed, "Matt. Oh God, help me. Please, you have to help me."

"From the looks of you I agree you need help. Put down your arms. What the hell happened to you? And how the hell did you get down here?"

"I hid in an alcove and waited until somebody came out one of the back doors. I kept my head down so they couldn't see me and I acted like I was trying to find my keys. I then slipped in before the door shut. The reason I look like this is that several men attacked me before I escaped. Later I had a fight with two cops at my house who were trying to arrest me. I hit one with an empty bottle and I pushed the other one down a flight of stairs. Somehow, I got away, and I ran."

"What? Todd, what the hell are you talking about? What were you doing fighting with the police?"

I heard what Mouse said, but I wanted to hear it straight from Todd.

"How about you come up to my place and let's talk?"

Todd didn't move. "Are you going to turn me in?"

I shook my head. "I hadn't planned on it. Come upstairs and let's talk. I want you to tell me exactly what happened."

"I'm sorry to bother you, but you're the only person I know that might be able to help me that I can trust."

"Come on Todd, let's go up to my place and you can tell me your version."

In the elevator's light, I could see just how he's been beaten. His left eye was swollen shut, his bottom lip split. There were two deep gashes on his forehead and his face was bloody.

We got to my place and I led him to the guest bathroom. Max and Bean came out from wherever they were hiding to investigate. Both of them sniffed at Todd and departed. I guess they could tell Todd was in no mood to pet them, so there was no point in sticking around.

In the bathroom, I put the lid down on the toilet and told him to sit. I got a washrag and ran the water until it was warm then wiped most of the blood off his off his face.

His clothes were ruined — he couldn't wear them without attracting a lot of attention. I thought I had something that would do, though he was a little shorter than I am.

"How about you take a shower and I'll get you some clean clothes."

"No, it's okay. I don't want to put you out, Matt. I'm just grateful you didn't turn me in. Let's talk."

"No Todd! Let's get you cleaned up first and then we can talk. Take off your stuff and get in the shower." I left him as he was taking off his shirt. I found a few things I thought would fit him. When I returned with the clean stuff, he was taking a hot shower. I got out a towel and told him where to find it. "I left you some clean clothes. When you're done, come out and we can talk." I cleaned out his pockets and placed the items on the countertop and took his old clothing with me.

One of the other owners in the condo building is an ER nurse. We've never dated, but we're good friends. I called Mary Ellen's cell phone and was pleased when she answered.

She must have had caller ID because she answered, "Matt Preston. Well, hello. What a pleasant surprise."

"Hello, Mary Ellen. I need a big favor."

"What do you need?"

"I've got a friend here. He's been beaten up, but he can't go to the ER. It's a long story. Would you mind coming up and looking at him?"

"I'm on my way."

Next, I called down to the front desk and asked Marshall if there was anybody who could take the dogs for a walk. I wanted to do it, but I needed to get Todd to a place where I could send him on his way.

I went out to the kitchen and started a cup of coffee for myself and mixed Todd a drink. He liked bourbon with diet cola and I made it extra stiff. When he came out, he looked a lot better.

"Let's sit down. I made you a drink. Bourbon and Diet?"

"Oh God, Matt, I didn't want you to go to all this trouble."

"Todd, stop! You look like you need a friend." Tears filled his eyes, and I was embarrassed.

I handed him his drink and motioned him toward the front room and my doorbell rang. Ted panicked.

"Stop. This is a friend of mine. She's an ER nurse, and she's here to look at your face."

"No. She'll turn me in."

"No, Todd. You need to trust me. She won't turn you in. Now go sit in the front room." Todd looked like he still might cry. I handed him his drink, and he took a seat.

I let Mary Ellen in. The dogs came running and danced for attention. Mary Ellen likes dogs, that automatically makes her one of their favorite people. They know a soft touch when they see one.

"What's going on?" she asked, scratching both dogs behind their ears.

Mary Ellen is also one of my favorite people. She's a short blond with tinted curly hair, shiny blue eyes and a fantastic warm smile. She's lovely and outgoing, and if I ended up in the ER, she'd be the nurse I'd want taking care of me.

"I don't know all the details of the story yet, but you can see he needs medical attention."

We entered the room, and I sat down across from him. Todd took a sip of his drink. He took a deep breath and took another, much bigger sip. Mary Ellen waited for him to finish then checked his face. She gently pushed and prodded and he flinched a few times.

"You've done a good job cleaning him up. Nothing seems broken but his face will look pretty bad for a few days. Can you get me a plastic bag with ice for his eye? Let me see if I can fix some of these cuts."

I heard a knock on the front door. I rounded up the dogs and took them and their leashes with me. It was Marshall. He told me he wanted to take the dogs himself. The dogs were all over him, jumping for joy.

Mary Ellen finished up and excused herself. I walked her to the front door and whispered, "I'll either call you or come down and tell you what's going on." She nodded. "Thanks kid. I owe you for this one."

She smiled. "There's a restaurant I understand it's impossible to get reservations for. Rumor has it you have something to do with Hanney's Hideaway. You can take me to dinner."

I laughed. "Mary Ellen, I have nothing to do with it, but I'm friends with the owner. And I'd love to take you to dinner." She slipped out the door.

I returned to the problem at hand. "Okay, Todd. Tell me what the hell is going on? Who are you running away from and why were you fighting with the cops?"

"Matt, I don't know where to start…"

"I don't care, Todd. Just start talking and if I have questions, I'll ask." The promise I'd made to myself about not getting involved in other people's problems anymore flashed through my mind and I almost laughed.

But just looking at Todd and how battered he was, and how forlorn, how could I refuse? I had to do something. Didn't I? Besides, I was curious how he ended up getting beaten. I know what Mouse told me, but Todd wasn't a person who gets into fights, or into trouble, or steals money, for that matter.

"Matt, to start, there's a warrant out for my arrest."

That was a surprise. I mean, I already knew that but to hear him say it made it more real.

"For embezzling?"

He nodded. "But I didn't do it," he mumbled.

"Really?" He reminded me of a kid who got caught doing something wrong. "How much money are we talking about here?"

"Three hundred and forty-seven million dollars."

Silence!

I couldn't help it. When I finally spoke my voice rose two octaves and several decibels. "What? Three hundred and forty-seven million?" He nodded. "Shit Todd, you mean like with an M, Million?" Again, he nodded. "How the fuck do you steal Three hundred and forty-seven million? How does anybody take that much money from a bank? And how come you didn't go for three hundred and fifty million?" Todd opened his mouth to speak, and I held up my hand. "Sorry, I don't mean to be flip. Okay, you have my attention. Explain please."

I've known Todd a long time, and I was positive there's no way he could, or would, steal a dime from the bank, let alone three hundred and forty-seven million. I'm sure he knows lots of ways to do it, but I believed there's no way he would steal from the bank. Something was wrong. Very wrong!

"I didn't take the money. Matt, I don't care what anybody says; I'm telling you I didn't steal a dime. There was a routine audit and the numbers didn't add up. The next thing I know there are computer security types all over the place looking at every move I made for the last couple of years.

"Then to make matters worse, they summoned me to the home office to appear before the board. I had to foot the bill for the flight and when I got there, they demanded an explanation. When I couldn't explain why the books were wrong, I was put on paid leave and sent home with an admonishment not to leave town, so to speak. Actually, it was more like don't leave the country.

"Yesterday, when I was getting in my car, two men grabbed me and took me to an abandoned warehouse where some more men tied me to a chair and beat me. They kept asking me where the money was. I told them I didn't know where the money was, I didn't even know any money was missing until the audit.

"After a while, they left me alone, tied to a chair. I got loose, and I hid. When someone came back, I hit him with a stick and took his gun. Another guy came in and I made him show me the way out. But I had to shoot two guys to get out. I might have killed one of them, I didn't stop to find out for sure.

"I took the guy's car keys and his phone and started for my place. I called a friend at work who told me that all the files were turned over to the FBI and there was a warrant out for me.

"I got home and the police were waiting to arrest me. I was positive if they arrested me I'd never prove I was innocent. Anyway, I hit one of them and pushed the other down the stairs and ran."

"Interesting story. But why did you come to me?"

"Matt, I've heard the rumors about you. I sort of know what you did in the service and I have a pretty good idea about what really happened on Ross Island." I couldn't help it, that made me wince. "You've mentioned once about your service time and I saw you just after you got back from the Middle East a short time ago. I figured if anybody could help me, it was you."

When I was in the service, I served in an ultra-secret black ops unit. I don't think what I did was amazing or wonderful, and I always wondered what it was about me that seemed to attracted trouble. Why do people come to me with their problems? I thought over what Todd had told me as I leaned back in my chair peering into steepled fingers in front of my face.

There was a knock at the door and after reassuring Todd he was safe, I went to see who was there. Marshall was returning the dogs. "Matt, they're such sweet dogs. Anytime you need them walked, I'll be more than happy to do it."

"Thanks Marshall. I appreciate it."

"Can I ask a question?"

"You just did," I laughed. "Sorry about that. Go ahead."

"Have you seen anything strange or anybody lurking in the parking area? A tenant reported seeing a vagrant a little while ago."

"I haven't seen anything. If I do. I'll let you know."

"Thanks, Matt."

I eased the door shut and returned to the living room. "Okay Todd, what do you want me to do?" As soon as the words left my mouth, I regretted them.

"Aren't you going to ask me if I did it?"

"No."

"Why?"

"I don't need to."

"Huh? Why? You think I did it?"

"Todd, I know you too well. No offense, but you make Dudley Do-Right and The Lone Ranger look like button men for the mafia. I don't know anybody who's as straight an arrow as you. This isn't a putdown, but you really are Mr. Vanilla. I'd trust you with anything. When I set up the airline business and told you to take care of it, I never gave it a second thought. With you taking care of things, I was as safe as if I was in my mother's arms. I know you're innocent. And because I know it, I'm wondering how the hell somebody framed you."

Tears flowed down Todd's face. This was getting embarrassing. "For the past few days everyone treats me like I'm the biggest crook since Dillinger. Carol doesn't believe me — she wouldn't even let me explain. One of her buddies whose husband is manager of a different branch called her and told her the FBI was after me. She kept asking me how could I do something like steal and she wouldn't let me explain.

"She left me. But you didn't even ask if I did it."

"I need to know everything you know about how this could have happened. Pretend that you're a crook. How would you go about embezzling millions of dollars??"

"That's what I can't figure out. We have so many fire-walls and security programs. I never believed anyone could hack into the bank's computer system. Well, let me take that back. I know there are a people good at hacking, but our system is state-of-the art, or at least I thought it was."

In the computer hacking world, there's a woman known as the Gypsy Queen. She's a legend. She could hack any system. Any system! She wasn't bragging; it was just the truth. I found it hard to believe Todd didn't know there's no such thing as a hack-proof system.

"Todd, you're not that naïve. You know as well as I do there people out there who can hack your computers. Can they tell where the money was sent?"

"Yeah, it went to a numbered account at a bank on Nevis Island, in the Caribbean I'm not supposed to know that, but I overheard the auditors talking about it."

"If you had to pick which of your employees would you say is the least likely to do something like embezzle?"

"You mean who I think would be the most likely?"

"No Todd, the least likely. Someone who, if I told you they did it, you'd think I was crazy. There's no way it could have been them. Maybe some little old granny who's only there on Wednesdays and doesn't even have an email account."

"Well... "

"Stop, Todd. I want you to think about this. Do you have a place to stay?" He shook his head. "Okay. You can stay here. Since we're seventy stories up, I don't have to worry about somebody driving by and seeing you in the window. But I have to ask you not to leave this apartment for any reason. If you got caught, we'd both be in big trouble."

"I understand. Matt, I just don't —"

"Todd, stop. I believe you're getting screwed. And I want to know how they did it. Look, I have to leave for a while, but I'll be back later. We'll have dinner here. If you're hungry, there's food in the fridge. But under no circumstances are you to leave this apartment. Do you understand?" He nodded. "And don't call anybody either. Nobody! Not even Carol."

"Okay. Just watch the tube or read."

"Okay."

"Since Mary Ellen knows you're here, I'll ask her to take the dogs out later."

I went down to the garage and sat in my car thinking, and decided I needed to cover my ass. If it somehow got out I'd harbored ol' Todd while he was a fugitive, I could be in deep do-do. The best thing for me to do was to go straight to the top. I needed to talk to my childhood friend, Jeff L. Davenport, who was also the commissioner of the Seattle police department.

CHAPTER ELEVEN

I called Jeff L. from my cell. "Jeffers, Matt here."

"Hey buddy, it's been a while. How's it going? How's Florida treating you?"

"Great. Florida is nice. You need to come and visit."

"That sounds great."

"Look, the reason I called — I was wondering if you had a few minutes sometime today? Sakol too?"

"What's this about?"

"It'll be easier to explain it in person."

"Can you be here in forty-five?"

"Done."

Forty-five minutes later I was sitting in Jeff's office with Sakol sitting next to me. Jeff smiled and asked, "Okay, what's so important?"

"Do you know who Todd Hoss is?"

Jeff frowned. "Let's see... he beat up two of my boys and the FBI wants his ass and rumor has it Zampuchini the mob guy wants to talk to him, and I heard a rumor some South American drug cartel is looking for him too. Yeah. I know who he's."

"I knew most of that, but the South American cartels is new. You seem to know a lot about this."

"Yes, I'm sorry to say, I know more than I want to. Why do you ask?"

"He's a friend."

"And?"

"What if I told you he's innocent? That there's no way he would embezzle money."

Jeff's laugh sounds like a bark. "Ha! Bullshit, Matt. What have you been smoking? There's proof he moved the money. We've read the file. He did it. His fingerprints all over it."

"If he had done it, wouldn't he have tried to hide what he did? Isn't this a little too obvious? Besides, why would he hang around waiting to get caught?"

"Who knows? That's somebody else's problem."

"Do you know where the money is now?"

"No, why?"

"Well, I do."

"Where is it?"

"It's in a numbered account in some bank on Nevis Island in the Caribbean."

Jeff scowled at me. "How did you come by this information, Matt?"

"Todd told me."

Jeff had been leaning back in his chair and he sat up. "He what?"

Sakol piped up, "Excuse please. You say Mr. Todd tell you? You in contact with Mr. Todd?" Sakol liked to talk as if he'd learned English from Charlie Chan movies. He actually speaks perfect English with a slight British accent. When he questions suspects he talks to them as if he doesn't speak English very well. The suspect relaxes and will babble, thinking this stupid Oriental doesn't have a clue. Eventually Sakol asks, "Excuse please, thought you say..." And suddenly the suspect realizes the man sitting in front of him is not some dumb Oriental but actually a very intelligent individual. And by then it's too late. The trap has been sprung.

"Yes, I am." I answered.

"You want be arrested?"

"Not really."

"You never stupid before. Why now?"

"Sakol, I've known Todd for a long time. I'd bet my life that he's innocent. There's no doubt in my mind he never embezzled any money. And if that's the case, which it is, then somebody else stole the money. I want to know who."

Sakol shook his head. "Not your job, find who. You play stupid game."

"Look, both of you, Todd came to me and begged me to look into what happened. I know it doesn't look good." I had an idea. "Sakol, remember when you were talking to Senator Buck Markel and something wasn't right?"

"Yes. That not breaking law."

"True. But you knew something was wrong. Todd came to me because he needs help. I'm coming to you and asking for your help. I don't want to do this behind your backs. That's why I'm here. Look, if you insist, I'll bring Todd in. But for now, I'm asking you to trust me. Let me look into this. I'll keep you updated every step of the way."

Jeff shook his head. "Matt, you're putting us in a tough position."

"I'm willing to listen to any ideas the two of you may have."

"Damn it, Matt, you're breaking the law. Now that I know, I'm supposed to arrest your fat ass." We sat there for a moment glaring at each other. Finally, Jeff asked, "What are you going to do next?"

"Do you remember the Gypsy Queen, Melissa?"

"How can she help?" Jeff asked.

"Let's see, the number one computer hacker in the world who owes me a favor — a very large favor, I might add. Gee, I wonder if she can help."

"Okay, okay. Don't get smart with me. What else?"

"I want get into Todd's office. I want to how easy it would be for somebody to waltz in and find his passwords. There has to be an answer to this puzzle."

"Matt, if you say he didn't do it, that's good enough for us... for the time being. I'll admit, neither of us are happy with the way things are right now. I'll give you forty-eight hours and then you have to bring him in."

"Give me ninety-six hours."

"Forty-eight."

"Seventy-two?"

"Remember, if Sakol or I tell you to bring your boy in, you promised you will. Don't screw us over."

"I not happy. No screw up. Okay?" Normally Sakol has a cheerful countenance, but today he was scowling.

"Deal." Even as I made that promise, something inside of me said I would wish I hadn't made it. Well, too late now. I needed to find Melissa.

CHAPTER TWELVE

I needed to get into Todd's office, and I wondered how I could do it. If I could, I'd definitely have questions for him and there was currently no way to call him. I'd taken his cell phone and pulled the SIM card to disable anyone tracking him. So, I picked up a bunch of burner phones at a local gas station.

I returned to my condo and gave him a phone. I warned him again not to leave and cautioned him not to call anybody but me. I said it so many times he exclaimed, "I know Matt. I know. I'll stay here and I won't call anyone."

His attitude pissed me off, "Todd, the commissioner of police is breathing down my neck and he wants your ass in jail, now! If you leave, I promise I'll turn you in so fast you won't have time to buy coffee. Don't screw with me!"

I went upstairs to have a chat with Mouse. As always, he was happy to see me. He led me to his study and asked, "To what do I owe the pleasure of your visit?"

"I wanted to let you know I've got Todd Hoss stashed in my condo. But mainly I wanted to pick your brain. I'm looking for a way into the bank. I want to get into his office."

Mouse motioned for me to sit. "Who does their custodial work?"

"No idea. Just a sec." I called Todd on the new phone. His voice was frightened. I'd forgotten to give him my new number "Todd, who does the custodial work at the bank?"

"Berg Building Maintenance Service. Why?"

"I'll explain later. Thanks."

I relayed the info to Mouse, and he grinned at me. "What?" I asked him.

"I happen to have a small ownership in Berg. Denny Berg and I are old friends. Give me a second." Mouse made a brief call. After he hung up he told me, "Tonight, go to 2036 Eastlake and find a guy named Bob Carity. Carity is in charge of the crew that does Todd's bank. I need to warn you, he's not the friendliest person, but you aren't looking for a drinking buddy. Can you make it tonight?"

"Yeah. I'll make it work."

"Good. I'll call him back and explain you're doing me a favor. I have a new account and I need somebody to run the crew. I'll tell him I want you to watch what's going on and look around — get a feel for it — and that he should act like you're not there. Okay?"

"Mouse, you never cease to amaze me."

Mouse said, "I'm a little concerned, Matt. You're hiding a fugitive. I know he's a friend, but is it worth it? You could do jail time for what you're doing."

"Mouse, I'm positive this guy is innocent. If I'd embezzled that kind of bread, I'd be gone. That kind of money will buy you a lot of freedom in several countries. If he's good enough to have embezzled that much, he's smart enough not to get caught."

"I admire you, Matt. Your loyalty to your friends is extraordinary."

"You mean like going up into the mountains in the middle of a snowstorm and rescuing a sweet friend of yours? Like saving Jade."

Mouse grinned at me. "Yeah, something like that."

~ ~ ~ ~ ~

Bob Carity really was a nasty man. When I stuck out my hand to shake his, he looked at it like it was covered in dog crap. He turned around and called over his shoulder, "Follow me."

Carity led me to a dressing room with a rack of shirts. "Pick one that fits." I found one and was told to get in the van sitting at the curb. In a few minutes, Carity came out and got behind the wheel.

As we drove away, he said, "I don't appreciate Mr. Fox checking up on me. If he has a problem, he should come and talk to me."

"You have the wrong idea. Mr. Fox has a new account he wants me to handle. I don't know where you got the idea I was some kind of spy."

"So you say. I'll be watching you."

Well, that told me where I stood with ol' Bob. I was lucky I only had to spend one evening with him.

He pulled into the bank's parking lot and parked in the back. Inside, he said, "Follow me." He led me down a hall and to the lady's restroom. He explained that they started with the restrooms and one of his crew started cleaning. He unlocked a door and the other cleaner started on the teller cages. Then he abruptly excused himself and marched back outside, talking on his cell phone. I slipped down the hall and found Todd's office. It surprised me to find the door unlocked. Once inside with the door closed, I sat behind his desk and looked around the room.

Nothing seemed out of place, but a vent directly across the desk caught my eye. I stood up and scanned the ceiling. There was another vent behind Todd's desk and I reached up and ran my fingers across the screws. They were painted over. I crossed the room and checked the screws on the first vent. They had been painted over as well, but the paint seal was broken. Someone had taken the cover off this vent. Unless you actually felt the screws, you'd never know someone had tampered with them. I thought it was strange that whatever had happened, it happened in the vent across from the desk instead of behind it. It seemed more logical someone would want to look over Todd's shoulder.

I heard footsteps coming down the hallway. I grabbed the wastepaper basket and carried it out of the room. Bob stopped me. "What were you doing inside of that office?"

I held out the wastepaper basket. "Getting the trash."

His voice was surprised. "Really? Well, okay. But it's probably best if you just do what I tell you."

"Sure, no problem,"

"Well dump that basket. There shouldn't be much in there — that guy's not here right. There's a warrant out for him."

"Wow, how come?"

"He stole a bunch of money. And when they tried to arrest him, he shot a cop and now he's somewhere in the South Pacific."

I wondered where Mr. Carity got his information. I knew exactly where Todd was, or at least I sure hoped I knew where he was. "What do you want me to do next?"

"Get the trash from each office and dump it in the large can sitting on that dolly." He pointed to a large rubber garbage can.

What a stroke of luck. I wanted to look in each office and check out the vents. Now I had a reason to be in the offices. The vent's in the office next to Todd's also had the paint on the screws disturbed and one of the vent corners showed where the screwdriver had slipped and removed a little paint, nicking the metal. Out of the next five offices I checked, three had signs someone had tampered with the vents. I was wondering why. Todd's vent I understood. I figure somebody had put a camera in the vent and had been getting information from his computer. Perhaps there was still a camera in there? The vent was too high for me to investigate; I needed a ladder or a chair to stand on. I pulled a chair over and then climbed up on it. I could kind of see inside and it looked like two wires were lying on the bottom of the vent, but there was no camera.

I was just getting off the chair when the door to the room opened, Carity stopped and was glaring at me. "What the hell do you think you are doing?"

"I was wondering if the vents ever got dusted. I would guess there's a lot of dust inside and I was checking to see if I could tell and how hard it would be to remove the vents."

"They don't pay us to check the vents. Now get down and finish what I told you to do." He snarled.

"I've gathered all the trash. What do you want me to do next?"

"Go get in the van, I'll be right there."

I turned and headed for the back door. Something told me to go back and check on Carity. The door was still slightly ajar, and I watched as he climbed up on the chair and looked into the vent. He took something out of one of his pockets and poked it into the vent. Finally, he jumped down, and I hurried down the hall. I was leaning against the van when he came out the back door. "Why ain't you in the van like I told you?"

"I didn't know if you might need me for something else."

"Well, I don't. Now get in."

We rode back to the company's storage area in silence. I got out of the van and as we walked away; I asked him, "What time to you want me back tomorrow."

"Ah, tomorrow is a slow day. I don't need you." I guessed when he caught me looking into the vent something had tipped him off and once more I'd become some kind of spy checking up on him. Now I really had to find a way back into some of those offices. But first I needed to check on Todd.

~ ~ ~ ~ ~

As soon as I walked into the condo, Todd complained about how bored he was. Again, I made him promise he would not leave the condo. "Todd, I understand you're bored. But if you leave here, who knows who might find you. You have the police looking for you, you have the FBI involved and I believe the people who grabbed you and roughed you up could be mafia types." I had my suspicions on who might be behind things, but I would not share that with Todd. "If you walk out that door, I'm done with you. You're on your own. Don't come back! You either trust me and do what I say or leave now and we're done. What's it going to be?"

"I'm sorry. I appreciate your help. I just wish I could do more. Sitting here doing nothing is so frustrating."

"Are you working on what I asked?"

"What's that?" He looked bewildered.

"You're to be figuring out who is the least likely person in your office who'd do something like set you up."

"Oh, that."

"Yes that! Todd, it's important. I want you to make a list of every person in your office. Then go through the list and rate how likely you feel it is that they might be the culprit. That's important. Now do it now." I left him sitting at the dining room table working on his list. If nothing else, it would give me a list of the people in his office.

I went upstairs to see Mouse. I got an enormous hug from Jade and when I set her down; she went off to find Mouse.

Mouse came striding into the room with his hand outstretched. "Matt, how d'you do?"

"Great. Thanks' for your help getting into Ted's office."

"Was it profitable?"

"Yes, and no. That's the problem, I need to get back in there."

"I'll call Carity and set it up."

"No! That's part of the problem." I explained how I'd looked into the vents and what I'd seen. I told him about getting caught by Carity and after I was to leave, I'd seen him looking into the vents. It made little sense. Mouse agreed. "Give me a few hours and call me. I'll see what I can arrange.

CHAPTER THIRTEEN

I left and headed for the basement to retrieve one of my cars and as I opened the door leading down to the garage, Marshall Wells, head of security, hollered at me. "Matt, what are you doing?"

"Getting one of my cars."

"That's what we are supposed to do." Marshall came over.

"I hate to bother you guys. I'm perfectly capable of getting my vehicle."

"It's more than that, Matt. I want, no make that I have to know who comes and goes in my garage. Remember the other day when I told you I got a compliant somebody thought they saw a person lurking in the garage?"

"Yeah, I know who it was."

"You do? Who?"

"I can't really tell you, but I have handled it. And I'm sorry you're upset. I promise you I'll make sure you know when I'm in the garage and I'll ask before I remove any cars."

Wells laughed. "I guess that will do. While I'm thinking of strangers lurking about, do you remember when two

Mafia Soldati were hanging out across the street some time back and you had a chat with them?"

"Yeah. You and I took them up to Mr. Fox's place, and we had a heart-to-heart talk with them. Why do you ask?"

"One of them is across the street again."

"Are you kidding?"

"Nope. I planned to tell Mr. Fox, but now that I see you, I thought you could take better care of it."

"Thanks."

I slipped out the back door of the lobby and exited. I walked down the alley and turned the corner. When I got to the street, I looked across at the entrance to the building across from The Olympus. Sure enough, I saw Guido standing there. Guido worked for a mob boss named Sal Zampuchini, but during an altercation I'd ended up jumping on his right hand and busting it up badly. Now I wasn't sure who he might work for as I was reasonably sure he wasn't able to be a hit man anymore.

Crossing the street, I remember when I'd asked Guido his name and when he told me; I told him I didn't believe him. He assured me it was his name since they named him after some great uncle from the old country or something. Guido had a friendly face and looking at him you would never dream at one time he was one of the most feared hit men in the Mob. He smiled as I walked up to him and I extended my right hand. He put out his left as he held up his right and I could see it was badly deformed from when I'd stomped on it. I shrugged my shoulders and gave him a rueful grin, "Sorry about that."

"Not to worry. I had it coming."

"Perhaps, but you also caught me during a poor time in my life. I was still dealing with a lot of pent-up anger from a mission I did in the Middle East and you were unlucky enough to taste some of that anger. What are you doing over here?"

"I'd like to chat with you, do you have a few minutes?"

"Sure, what you need."

"Not here. Let's have a cup of coffee or a drink."

I motioned at a bar just down the street. He nodded his head, and we headed for the bar. Inside I ordered a beer from their on-tap selection and Guido ordered the same. We took a table in the corner and after we sat down, I asked him, "Okay Guido, what's up?"

"I've always felt I owed you."

That was something I didn't want to hear from an ex-mafia hit man. "How so? The hand?" I asked tentatively.

"No. Like I said, I deserved that. It's more than busting up my hand. When you sent us back to Mr. Zampuchini, you'd made a deal with him preventing him from retaliating for us screwing up. Mr. Zampuchini was so pissed at me he wanted to kill me on the spot when I got back. But as you can see, he didn't. I feel I owed you for that. So, as kind of a way to repay you, I'm here to warn you."

"Warn me, why?"

"The banker fellow."

I couldn't help it, my face showed how stunned I was, and I blurted out, "Todd Hoss?"

"Yeah. Mr. Preston, Todd Hoss. You need to leave that alone. You need to cut him loose."

I wondered how the news had got out so quickly. I just got Todd stashed away. It hadn't been that long since Hoss had come to me and asked for help. What Guido was telling me was not marvelous news. "Why do you think I have him?"

"Mr. Preston, please give me a little credit. I know things. I'm not without resources."

"Okay, let's say maybe I know where he's, I can't just walk away and leave him cold. I can't do that to a friend."

"Even if it means you might get wacked if you don't."

I didn't know how much Guido might know about Sal's demise up in Alaska, and I felt I needed to tread softly. "I assume you're here on the family's behalf?" Guido nodded. "I don't understand why your people are interested in Hoss. What's it to them?"

"Well, to start, I know of three hundred and forty-seven million reasons."

"Come on, that's like chicken feed to your people. Why are they so interested?"

"Well, a lot of that bread was The Family's, if you catch my drift? But actually, it's more like several of the family's heads want to know how he did it."

"He didn't do it." I insisted.

"Mr. Preston, please. Don't take me for an idiot. I've heard his fingerprints are all over the deal. It was his bank, his computer, his passwords. Everything points to the Hoss dude. You ain't that stupid. You must know he's done it."

"Guido, how do you fit into this?"

"You know I was on the carpet for the screw-up with you and then the little dude?"

"Yeah."

"At one point, Zampuchini needed a big favor, and I took care of it. Don't ask questions. I don't want to have to lie to you." I nodded my head. I understood exactly what he was telling me. "Because I helped him and because of this," he held up his hand, "I am now 'Messaggero'."

"Messaggero? What's that?"

Guido chuckled. "Few people know what that is. My job is to function as a liaison between all the families. I lessen the need for sit-downs of the Capos when they need to meet and that limits the exposure of all the bosses being in one place for law enforcement." Guido held up his damaged hand, "Because of this, the other families trust me. They know I'm no longer a button, or soldier. Because of what I do, I'm considered 'untouchable'. Any retaliation against me by any of the families would be quickly dealt by the rest of them. Messing with me is like committing suicide.

"All the families consider me 'Borgata', which means I'm one of their family. I'm not a member of any one family, but I'm a member of every family. Therefore, all the families trust me. And I have you to thank for this position. I make more money than I'll ever need, and I don't have to worry about getting whacked by one of the families, or that I might get busted by the fuzz. At the time when this happened," Guido again motioned towards his hand, "I didn't realize what was happening would turn out so well. But thanks."

"You work for the various Godfathers."

"Oh Mr. Preston, you watch too many movies. Nobody calls any of the heads of the family, godfather. You have the various families with their Capos, the heads; the Boss but there's no such thing as The Godfather. That was a movie."

"Well Guido, I'm pleased for you and your position, but this still doesn't explain how you fit into everything."

"I'm acting on the behalf of all the Capos. This comes from the top. Okay?" I nodded in understanding. "Everybody wants to know how this bank fellow pulled it off. How did he do it and what's preventing it from ever happening again? Some families know you and I have a relationship." The idea that Guido and I had any kind of a relationship was frightening. "The rumor on the street is you know where the bank dude is hiding. That means you have access to him, and you also might know how it was done, or at least you can get the info on how it was done. I'm the first person to contact you and request you help us."

"I take it from your comment, if I don't tell you what happened, I'll be getting another visit from somebody who isn't as friendly as you?"

Guido smiled and nodded his head. "Very perceptive of you, Mr. Preston."

I sat for a long time nursing my beer. Guido waited me out. "Guido, I'm not saying I know where the guy is, but I know him very well. He's been my personal banker for many years and when I tell you this, I swear on my mother's grave I'm speaking truth. Because you came to me and thought enough of me to warn me, if I had something to tell you, I would. Okay? I wish there was a way you could know this fellow as I do. Guido, this dude is so straight arrow it's almost embarrassing to tell people I know him. I believe he teaches Sunday School at his church, not that doing that can keep him from stealing from his bank. But please trust me." Guido nodded.

"This banker dude as you call him could no more embezzle that money than fly. I know for a fact, well not for a fact, but I swear to you he did not embezzle one dime." As I said the words, I hoped I was correct. "For what it's worth, and you know I'd never lie to you," He nodded, "When I learn how it was done, I'll sit down with you or whoever you want me to talk to and cover exactly how, and who pulled this off. I promise you."

Guido took a long sip of his beer. He played with the coaster for a while, then finally looked at me. "Okay, I'll go back to the families and tell them what you just told me. However, just between us, I have a very hard time believing you. But I trust you.

"And, I'm also warning you some families will not like what I tell them. I'll make sure nobody gets some crazy idea to come after you. I can always point to Louie and what you did to him if anybody wants to come after you. Because it's you, I believe what you've told me, kind of." I started to speak and Guido held up his hand to stop me. "As far as the banker dude doing the deed or not, I have a hard time with that. Everything points to him."

"Guido let me ask you one question. If you had three hundred and forty-seven million dollars, are you going to hang around town? That kind of bread will buy you a lot of cover. If he had that money, he'd be living in some banana republic with the dictator in his back pocket. Think about it. Nobody is so stupid to stick around after that kind of heist."

Guido continued to play with his coaster. He drank the rest of his beer and looked at me. "I'll give you that. If the cat is swift enough to do that kind of boost, he has to be smart enough to know he has to get out of Dodge. I'll take your answers back to the families. If this doesn't sit well with the people I have to speak to, give me a number where I can reach you and give you enough time if you have to hit the mattress."

I thanked him for his consideration and gave him the number to the new burner phone I'd just purchased. "I will give you my number, but don't let it get out you have it."

"I understand. I want you to know I'm impressed with you. For something that started out terrible, you've turned into a real stand-up guy." Guido bowed his head. We stood, and he embraced me and kissed both my cheeks.

"You've always been straight with me Matt Preston. Please don't disappoint me." We parted ways and as I wandered back to the lobby, I reflected about Guido. At one point he'd been in a terrible situation, but it had turned it into a beneficial situation for him. As strange as this sounds, I trusted Guido --- or at least as much as one can trust somebody like Guido.

CHAPTER FOURTEEN

After my brief chat with Guido, I wondered if having Todd staying at my condo was such a wise move. How long had Todd been there and already too many people knew he was there? After due consideration, I needed to find a better place to stash ol' Todd. I had an idea, and I called Scott, my real estate buddy and old poker buddy. "Scott, it's Matt."

"Hey ya old dog. I miss not seeing you. The poker games just aren't the same. Do you still have time to play?"

"Yeah, a bunch of the guys at the condo where I live play every week and I sit in occasionally. It's just for quarters, not the stupid stakes some of our games used to have. I'll admit, I miss those games."

"Ditto."

"I have a question."

"Shoot."

"Is your houseboat leased or empty?" At one point the houseboat used to be mine when I won it in a card game, but I recently sold it to Scott.

"It's empty. Why?"

"I want to lease it for a month. How much do you want?"

"Go to hell. There's no way I will take any money from you. It's yours as long as you need."

"Thanks Scott."

"What are you going to do?"

"Scott, it's best that you know nothing. Trust me, the less you know, the better off you are." Scott and I go a long way back and he's aware when I tell him to back off, it's what he needs to do.

"Matt, so help me, if this bites me in the ass…"

"Yeah, yeah. I know." We were both laughing as we hung up. I called Todd and explained what was going on. I finished with, "I will take you over to this place tonight around mid-night. I'll make sure there's plenty of food for you. Again, I demand that you stay put. Don't leave or you're on your own. I mean it buddy."

"Thanks for helping me out. I won't leave wherever you're taking me. I promise."

Next on the list was Melissa. I figured the best place to find her was with Randy Ralph. Before he and Melissa were married, Ralph was always on the make. Melissa finally trimmed the boy's horns… a little! I called the private number I have for Ralph on my regular cell phone. When he came on the line, his voice was tentative, "Matt?"

"Yeah."

"Wow. This has been a long time. I wasn't sure it was even you."

"Yeah. It's me."

"What can I do for you? Or did you just call me for shits and giggles?"

I had to laugh, "No Ralph, you're correct. I need to get a hold of Melissa. I don't have a number for her. Do you mind if I chat with her?"

"Hell no. She will be ecstatic to hear from you." He gave me a phone number to reach her, and we rang off. I called the number and there was no answer. I left a message on her service that I was trying to get a hold of her.

It had been a while since I'd talked to Lois and I wanted to hear her voice. I called her. "Hi babe. I miss you."

Silence. Finally, I heard her sigh, "What do you need Matt?"

"Honey, I got myself in a situation out here. I can't talk about it much on the phone, but I hope to have this resolved in a day or two and then I'm headed back. I miss you."

There was another lengthy pause before I heard her sigh again. In an indifferent tone of voice, she told me, "Call me. Maybe we can talk." And I heard the phone call end. I was keeping score, and this was one more thing Orchard owed me for; one really upset girlfriend.

Or was it ex-girlfriend now?

I noticed Melissa had called back while I was on the phone with Lois. I called her and on the third ring, she picked up, "Hello, this is Melissa."

"Melissa, hello. This is Matt Preston."

She squealed, "Matt. This is wonderful. I'm so pleased to hear your voice."

"Hello Melissa. It's good to hear your voice as well."

"It's been a long time, Matt. How are you?"

For the next few minutes we played the catch up game until finally she asked, "I know you didn't just call to shoot the shit. What's up?"

"Okay, got me. A friend has asked me to look into why he's being accused of embezzling some money. All signs point at him, yet I know he didn't do it. If you knew him, you would understand why I feel this way."

"Tell me how this happened?"

"They did it at his workplace and they used his passwords, and his terminal too."

"That's easy to do. I know of a lot of ways to do that. How much money are we talking about?"

"Three hundred and forty-seven million dollars."

Silence. An interminable silence and then in a soft voice, she whispered. "How much did you say?"

"Three hundred and forty-seven million dollars."

"That's what I though you said. How long ago did this happen?"

"Dunno precisely, several weeks ago."

"Why are you just now coming to me?"

"I was just told about it the other day. What difference does it make?"

"A lot. Every hour that goes by gives the thief more time to hide where the money is stashed."

"I know where the money is?"

"You do?" Her voice sounded skeptical.

"Yeah, it's in some bank on Nevis Island in the Caribbean."

"That is both excellent news and bad. Let me see, the reason you called is you want me to see if I can get it back?"

"More than that, I want you find out who did it and how. I think since we know where the money is, we can get it back."

"Gee Matt, I'm busy right now. I wish I could help you, but I just don't have the time to do this. I'd like to help, but…" her voice trailed off.

I waited a few moments, I kind of thought she might not want to help right away, and I had a plan in mind.

"Yeah, I understand Melissa. You have a reputation to uphold. You can't look into something like this and then fail. It wouldn't look good for you. This could really tarnish your reputation. My bad, I should have known you wouldn't be interested in working on a problem this difficult. I guess this is pretty sophisticated. Probably a bit over your pay grade."

Her voice snarled, "Matt, get bent. I know what you're trying to do."

"Gee, what am I trying to do?" My voice the sound of pure innocence.

"You're trying to guilt trip me into helping you."

"Oh Melissa, you hurt me. Why would I do that? What is there to guilt trip you about? Oh wait, you don't mean how I saved your life and Ralph's, and how I got you out of a shitload of trouble and helped you and Ralph end up together, and how I squared things with our government, and a few others. Melissa, you don't owe me a thing."

Melissa was laughing, "Matt, you're a bastard. I'm sorry. I was wrong. I owe you. Big time. And I'll try to help you all I can."

"Thanks. I hoped you would see it my way."

"When can we meet? I want to see you in person to explain this."

"You seem to feel time is of the essence, you tell me when we can meet."

Since I was still in Seattle, we decided tomorrow evening would work. I picked a spot in the north end in a neighborhood called Lake City. As soon as she told me yes, I had an idea. "I'll be there around mid-night and then we're going for a ride."

"Are you serious?"

"Yep. There's somebody I want you to meet. I want you to hear a story, but I need for it to come from him. Okay?"

"Pick me up tomorrow. You know where I'll meet you."

"Will Ralph be okay with this."

"Trust me. A little kinkiness on my part and the boy is eating out of my hand or maybe he'll eat…" She giggled as she stopped but I swear I must have been beet red. "Later Matt, see you tomorrow at 11:30."

We rang off.

I wanted Todd to tell her his story. I knew she'd have questions, and it was best if the two of them were face to face. Now the trick was to get Todd to the houseboat without being seen and provide Melissa with the opportunity to question him.

Thinking about Todd and his office made me think of Mouse. I called Mouse. "Matt, I'm glad you called. I'd like to see you tomorrow evening. Can you come up and see me?"

"It'll be late." I warned him.

"Like, define late."

"After midnight, sometime early in the morning."

"That works just great. It's dark by then. Tomorrow evening you and I will do some breaking and entering."

I protested and then I realized I was speaking to an open line with nobody there.

Break and enter.

Shit Mouse.

What's next?

~ ~ ~ ~ ~

I waited until it was dark outside before I took Todd to the basement of the condos. I had him crawl into the back of the dog van and covered him up. It has tinted windows, and I hoped if anyone was watching they wouldn't notice me. I drove over to the houseboat and Scott was waiting in the parking lot. Carefully I checked the area, and I felt I didn't see any strange vehicle that I felt was out of place. I opened the side door and let Todd out. When Scott saw who I had in the van, his eyes grew enormous. He handed me the key to the houseboat and bid me a good evening.

Our feet drummed on the deck as Todd and I strode down the dock to the old houseboat. Some time ago I'd won the thing in a card game. After it was mine, I found out that the space it occupied wasn't mine, but I got the problem solved. That's a story that's already been told and it's Scott's headache now.

I got Todd to the houseboat and showed him where to locate everything. Again, I stressed that he needed to lie low. He said he understood and for me to cut him some slack. I explained that I'd see him in 24 hours with somebody who may help with his dilemma. On that note, I left.

CHAPTER FIFTEEN

The following night, I took Melissa to the houseboat and introduced her to Todd. I told Melissa to call when she was ready to go.

At Mouse's pad, (I know, I heard the groan. But I had to use it once!) I parked my truck and took our elevator up to his floor. It was 2:15.

When I saw Mouse, my jaw dropped. Until now it had always been a suit with a vest, French-cuffed shirt and well-tied tie. Tonight, it was a dark gray pants that had a lot of room in the legs, and a matching military-style shirt. His athletic shoes were gray as well. My eyes must have popped out because Mouse smiled and said, "Surprise! I own something besides a suit."

"Why dark gray?"

"Dark gray is harder to see in the dark than black. I thought you knew that."

"Now that you say that, yeah. Damn. I wish I'd thought of it."

"Funny you should say that." He handed me a neatly folded stack of clothes. Mouse never ceases to amaze me.

The clothes, down to the matching sneakers were a perfect fit. In the garage, he led me to a — you guessed it — a dark gray Subaru.

"Don't you think you're carrying this grey thing a bit too far?" I asked.

He laughed. "You think so? I saw this car for sale online and it spoke to me. It looks stock, right?"

I walked around the car. It looked like a plain old Outback except the tires were wider than normal and it sat closer to the ground. Mouse opened the hood and nestled in the engine bay was as much motor as could be crammed into the space with a Paxton blower on top.

Mouse climbed in the driver's side. When I settled into my bucket seat, it seemed to wrap around me. The seat was firm, but also well padded. I noticed the seat on Mouse's side was well forward and he sat a little higher. He pushed a button on the dash and the motor exploded with a roar that shook the little car. The sound was pure poetry.

He slipped the gearshift into reverse and backed out of the stall. As he slipped it into first, he told me, "Six speed tranny, disk brakes all around, run-flat tires and it lowers three inches. I can put it almost on the pavement."

On the ramp to the freeway Mouse slipped the car into second gear and stomped on the gas. The acceleration pushed me deeper into the F-1 seats. When we merged onto the freeway, we were doing eighty, and he'd just shifted into third.

"How fast will this thing go?"

"I've had it up to almost one sixty, but then I chickened out."

I was stunned.

We wound our way through North Seattle and parked two blocks from Todd's bank. When we reached the bank, I asked him how we were getting in. He held up a finger, pulled a key from his pocket and unlocked the door. As soon as the door opened, I heard the soft beeping of an alarm.

Mouse disarmed the alarm. "It helps when you know the codes," he said.

I had to ask, "You didn't happen to steal three hundred and forty-seven million dollars, did you?"

"Are you kidding? That's chump change." I had no idea if he was serious or not. There was no way to know his total net worth, but he might very well be serious.

We went into Todd's office. I had stopped in the maintenance area and gotten a step ladder. Mouse climbed up and felt the screws that held the air vent in place. "You're right, somebody has removed this screen since the last time they painted it."

I waited as he produced a screwdriver and unscrewed the screws. Once the grate was loose, he handed it down to me and climbed off the chair. "You go up and look."

I climbed up and shown the flashlight into the opening. The wire was still there. This time, I could see a plug. I said as much to Mouse and he told me, "It's for a camera. If you look real close, you can see two holes, one for the video and one for sound. Whoever put that camera in here could also listen in to any conversation your friend had."

I put the screen back over the vent and replaced the screws. In the vent behind the desk, we found the same set-up. There had been two cameras in his office.

We moved to the adjacent office, and I checked the screws. They hadn't been removed since the vent had been painted. The next office was the same. The vent in the last office's screws had been removed. I removed the screws and looked inside. There was no wire, the dust in the bottom of the vent had been disturbed. Mouse told me to put the screen back on and go. I did and returned the ladder to where I'd found it. We slipped out the back door after we set the alarm and headed for the car.

When we were about to cross the street, a car came around a corner a few blocks down. We stepped back into the shadows and waited for the car to pass. It was a police car. It surprised me when Mouse stepped back into the light. The cop behind the wheel saluted Mouse with two fingers. Mouse returned the gesture and the cruiser sped up and disappeared around another corner.

"What was that about?" I asked.

"I have friends on the force, too. Not as highly placed as yours, but they come in handy. He was watching out for us."

~ ~ ~ ~ ~

The next morning — I should say, later that same morning — I woke up with the sun shining in my face. One would expect that if one lived on the east or south side of a building, but since my bedroom faced west, I must have overslept. I wondered about the dogs and threw on some clothes and went looking for them. I found them in the kitchen along with Jade.

"Good morning sleepy person, or should I say good afternoon?" Jade smiled at me.

"Have the dogs been out?"

"When I heard Mouse come in early this morning, I thought you might not wake up to take them out. I took them out early and Marshall sent someone up about an hour ago. They are happy campers."

"Thanks. How's Mouse?"

"He's just gotten up. Did you find what you were looking for last night?"

"We found wires in one of the ducts, and evidence of more. I don't understand it. They went to the trouble of removing one wire, why leave the rest?"

"Why don't you have some coffee? Come up when you're done."

"Will do." I went in search of my disposable cell and called Todd. When he answered, he started complaining right away. "I keep hearing strange noises. I don't like it here. Every time a boat goes by this thing moves. Houses aren't supposed to move!"

"You need to stay."

"I don't like it."

"Tough! How did it go with Melissa last night?"

"She made me tell my story a bunch of times. She says she wants to talk to you sometime. Do you really think she can help?"

"I don't know, but it's worth a shot. Now listen to me. Stay there. Remember, you came to me and begged me to help. That's what I'm trying to do and I'm tired of you bitching about it. I'll bring you some food later."

He hung up, but I could tell he wasn't happy with the way things were going. Well, I wasn't all that happy either. I didn't want to be dealing with his shit. I called Melissa, but she didn't answer. I called for the dogs and we headed up to Mouse's. As soon as we walked through the door, the dogs took off in search of Jade. She was becoming one of their favorite people.

I found Mouse in the front room. I asked, "What do you make of what we saw last night?"

"My guess is that the wires in that vent went to a device controlling the other two cameras."

"Yeah, but they went back and took the cameras out of Todd's office and when they were there, why not removed the wiring? It still makes little sense."

"Sorry Matt, I have no answer. Are you going to stay for dinner?"

"I have to take care of something and then I'll be back."

"How safe do you think Todd is?"

"How did you know I would see Todd?"

"Matt, please. I know you and I know what's going on. I don't know where Todd is at but I sure hope it's a safe place."

I could see no reason not to tell him, "I stash him at that old houseboat I won in the stupid poker game a few years ago. Do you think it's safe?"

"Does he know he's not to leave?"

"I've told him over and over. I have no idea if he will do what I tell him. If he leaves, all bets are off. He is on his own. Basically, I wash my hands of the entire thing."

"One thing I like about you Matt, you believe in something and then do everything in your power to make it happen."

"Well, I still can't see Todd boy stealing a bunch of money, but what we found last night makes me wonder what's up. Why were people spying on him? What did they learn? I am so confused. I need to speak to Melissa."

CHAPTER SIXTEEN

When I got to the houseboat and let myself in, I got a bad feeling. The place was way too quiet. The boat isn't that big, and I went room to room. It was deserted. I was both bummed and pissed. Bummed because he lied to me and pissed that I'd tried to help.

On my way out, I saw a car pull into the parking lot. Todd got out. When the dome light came on inside, I could see a woman behind the wheel. I doubted it was Carol, since she'd been so angry at him.

Todd walked around to the driver's side, leaned in and kissed the woman while fondling one of her breasts. Todd patted the woman's cheek and the car pulled out onto the street. Other than the car looking fairly new, I had no idea what the make and model was. Briefly I reminisced about when you could tell every make and model of car at a glance because they were distinctively different. Nowadays, they all look like jellybeans, and they come in really barfy colors.

I hid in the shadows until Todd was two steps past me and then stepped out behind him. I didn't have to work on sounding pissed, because I was. "What part of do not leave didn't you understand?"

I was pleased to see him jump, and he whirled around. "Shit, Matt, you scared the hell out of me."

"Good. I'm glad something does. Didn't I tell you if you left, I was washing my hands of you?"

"I needed to see somebody."

"Well, I know it wasn't your wife in the car. I'm telling you, there's no chick in the world who's worth getting killed over." Lois crossed my mind and I wondered if she might be the exception to that rule.

"How did you know it was a woman?"

"Because I have eyes. I saw her in the car when you opened the door. I saw you kiss and grope her. Unless you changed religions on me, it had to be a woman. Who was she?"

"Nobody."

"Listen Tod, you think Carol's angry now, wait until she finds out about your little bimbo. Talk about pissed."

"Don't call her a bimbo."

"Fine. Call your nobody to come back and pick you up. You can go stay with her. Let her figure this out. I've had it. Everybody I know tells me I'm an idiot for believing you. Go! Let her take care of you because I sure the hell ain't!" I turned to walk away.

"Matt, I'm sorry. You don't understand."

I turned back and tried to keep my voice down. "Damn straight I don't. Your freedom is hanging by a thread and you can't keep your pecker in your pants for five minutes. Who was she?"

"I can't tell you."

I started down the pier. "Keep thinking with your dick, buddy. Good luck. Maybe I'll see you around."

"Wait, where are you going?"

"Away from you." I snapped. "And when I get to my truck, I'm calling the police commissioner and telling him where you are. If you're lucky, maybe he'll pick you up before the Mob finds you. Do you have any idea how many people are looking for you? Do you?" He shook his head. "I'm not sticking my neck out for you anymore. You're on your own."

Todd came after me and grabbed my arm.

I snarled at him, "If you don't want to end up in the lake, you'd best take your hands off me, now."

"Matt, please don't leave. I'm sorry, I'll go back to the houseboat and stay there. I promise I won't leave again."

"Whatever." I tried to decide what to do. "Go back to the boat. I don't know what I'm going to do. You need to understand I was in the middle of something and getting involved with your problems was the last thing I needed. Right now, I need to leave the city for a while. If you stay here, you're safe. I'll arrange for food and you have books and television. When I figure out what I'm going to do, I'll let you know if I'm still willing to help you. Stay here. You're playing with fire and I don't care to get burned by your stupidity."

I was way too angry to be out and about, so I returned to the Olympus. When I got to my condo, I made a small but nourishing and curled up in my favorite chair. The dogs climbed up in my lap and I just sat there, drinking and petting them until I remembered dinner with Mouse and Jade. I changed into a fresh shirt and ran a brush through the silver locks. I use the word silver because it sounds better than gray.

On the way up I was thinking over what I'd witnessed, and it really bothered me. I was so positive Todd didn't embezzle the money, but I also would have staked my life that Todd would never have an affair. I didn't catch them doing the big nasty, but what I saw was very incriminating, at least to me. And it made me doubt myself, maybe he stole the money. Was the straight arrow image just a front? Still, if he embezzled the money, why the hell was he hanging around Seattle?

Dinner at Mouse's dinner was catered by the excellent restaurant downstairs. Towards the end of the meal, Jade asked what was bothering me.

"Why do you ask?"

"You're here with us, but you're not here, with us. Tell us what the problem is."

"Tonight, before I got here, I checked on Todd. He wasn't at the houseboat. When I was leaving, he drove up with a woman who wasn't his wife and he kissed her pretty passionately. I didn't think that was in his character. Now I wonder if he's innocent. I don't know what my next move is going to be. After what I saw tonight, I might be better off if I cut Todd loose, just as quickly as I can."

I didn't tell them about Melissa. But until I heard from Melissa, there was nothing to keep me in town.

Later, I called Henry. I could tell he was speaking to me from the plane. "Whatcha ya need, Matt?"

"Anything in town soon?"

"Where do you want to go?"

"Back to Fort Myers."

"Boeing Field tomorrow morning. Say elevenish. It won't be me, I have another plane headed your way."

"Thanks. I'll have two dogs with me."

"I'll warn the pilot to wear boots."

I laughed.

Briefly, I thought about Todd. Let the idiot stew for a few days.

More to ease my conscience than anything else, I'd ask Scott to stop by and check on him. Since I would be out of town, there wasn't much Jeff could do to me. I was so angry at myself for getting involved.

When am I going to learn?

CHAPTER SEVENTEEN

Considering my dogs have little flying time, I was happy at how well they did. Shortly after we were airborne, they curled up together on a couch and fell asleep. Getting off the plane they both stayed close to me for which I was grateful, since I didn't have leashes. When we arrived at the condo, Martha was waiting for us. The kids greeted her and as they bonded, I told Martha she was in charge and went to shower.

I was halfway through when Martha knocked on the bathroom door. "Mr. Admiral on phone. He wants talk with you."

"Tell him I'll call him back." I finished, dried off, got dressed and fixed a 'small, but nourishing' before I returned his call.

Lois answered and when she heard my voice, it was obvious I was still in deep-do-do city. She put me on hold without a word and I checked my phone for frost bite.

John picked up and snarled, "You sure took your sweet time checking in, Preston. What the hell happened up there, anyway? How'd you let things get so out of control?"

"Hey!" I barked. "Do you want me to hang up?" I had no intention of taking any shit over what happened in Alaska. I did exactly what he asked of me. It wasn't my fault it went south.

He sighed. "But I've been waiting to talk to you for days. You had to know I wanted to talk to you."

"Look Apple, I didn't see any reason to call you until you had time to go through the video—and then you'd know more than I do. Remember, I was the guy trying to fool everybody into thinking we were fishing."

"Don't call me Apple," John snapped.

"Then don't give me any shit about what happened up there. I'm just as shocked as you."

We discussed the details, including the attitude of the sheriff's office which didn't surprise him. Then we got to the part that mattered most to me.

"How much does Lois know?"

"She knows better than to ask, she's a professional."

"How much can I tell her? She's pretty mad about this."

He thought for a moment. "Do as you see fit."

We hung up, and I called back. When Lois answered, I quickly asked, "Can you come down and see me this weekend?"

Her reply was snotty. "Gee, can you break away from all your important things? Do you really have time for little old me? Do you have John's permission?"

"I don't need John's permission and if you're going to act like that, don't bother. Spare us both the misery."

"Fine."

I tried again. "Lois, please don't do this. I'll explain everything when you get here, in person — not on the phone. Please come down."

She sighed. When she spoke, her voice had mellowed. "I'll come down." Then she added, "I missed you."

"I missed you too. Trust me, I haven't been out having a great time without you. I'll explain everything when I see you."

~ ~ ~ ~

I called Henry and I couldn't believe my luck. They had just finished servicing a newly purchased plane and it was due to head to D.C. with two very spooky characters. Spooky was Henry's term. Once he dropped the two weirdos off, he would be free to bring Lois down. I asked Martha if she wanted some time off. She told me she really adored my dogs, but she was happy with time off too.

"I'm not sure how long Lois can stay, but as long as she's here, we'll be okay." I told her.

"Mr. Matt, Miss Lois needs to stay long as you need. You take care of her now. She's good for you. You need her. Dinner will be in the fridge and I'll leave some things in freezer."

~ ~ ~ ~ ~

I cut it a little close when I drove down to Page Field, and I barely had time to park my car before the plane landed. The Porsche I'd given Henry was parked by the hangar and it reminded me I had to get more of Snooker's cars over to an auction. With all the crap going on it had slipped my mind. I made a mental note to call my buddy Digger and see if he was available to help.

The plane taxied up to where I was standing. Lois got out and walked over to my car. There was no hug, no hello, no I'm glad to see you.

Before we even got in the car I said, "I can see you have something to say. Let's have it."

Lois got right to the point. "I want you to know, at first, I didn't intend to come down. I was hurt and angry when you left without telling me what was going on."

I wasn't going to let Lois chew me out for something that was John's fault.

"Lois, I think you should go back home."

"What?"

"You heard me, go. Get on the plane and go back to D.C." I leaned into the car and honked the horn. When Henry looked at me, I held up one finger signaling him to wait.

"But…"

"Go! Go on! Lois, I'm not taking any more crap for this. I wasn't happy about the way things happened, either. John ordered me not to tell you anything."

"He didn't say a damn word to me either!" Her voice softened, "And I want to stay, please. Can you tell me now?" I motioned to Henry it was all right to leave and we got in the car.

On the way home, I told her what had gone down in Alaska. When I got to the part about Jessie her reaction was?

"You were up there with a woman?"

I didn't appreciate her tone of voice. I was already close to blowing my cool and this wasn't making it easier. I pulled over to the side of the road and turned the motor off. There was no way I could spend a weekend with her acting like this.

"Lois, I'm serious, the plane is still at the airport. If you're going to get jealous, or have an attitude, I'm taking you back to the plane. I did nothing wrong. Not a damn thing! For a lot of reasons, the last couple of weeks have not been great. I invited you down because I wanted to see you, not because I wanted to deal with a hissy fit. That's just not happening.

"I didn't do anything wrong and I sure as hell am not letting you beat me up. You need to change your tone of voice and that attitude." She stared straight ahead with her arms folded across her chest.

"Oh to hell with it," I exclaimed and leaned forward to start the car. Lois reached out and pulled my hand away from the key.

When I looked at her, there were tears sliding down her cheeks. "I'm sorry. Matt, I love you so much. My feelings are so intense, and this is all new for me. I don't know how to react sometimes. I've never been involved with any man I cared for as much as I care for you. Please let me stay."

I leaned over and kissed her forehead.

She smiled and said, "Now, tell me what happened. I promise, I'll behave."

"What you think may, or may not have happened, is a long way from fact. Seeing how you acted just now, I understand why John didn't want me to say anything to you.

"I want you to know I thought about you a lot while I was gone. I even told her about you. Being there with her, in that situation, made me miss you even more. I couldn't act like a newlywed and that was our cover. If you can't, or don't trust me we need to stop seeing each other. I love our physical relationship, but it's so much more than that. I have feelings for you I can't even put into words."

"Please Matt, there's something I don't think you understand."

"What?"

"When I said the feelings I have for you are something new to me I meant that. I've never had feelings for anyone like I do for you. I'm just like you, I love our physical relationship, I crave it. But I love what we have along with that even more. The idea you were with another woman makes me jealous. I'm sorry. My job has always been my life — that is, until I met you. I love you. I'll try to be better, but I ask you to understand how I feel."

I pulled the car onto the road and continued my story. "You have nothing to worry about, I promise. Her name is Jesi Carson. Now, try this on for size. She's heavily tattooed on both arms and her chest and she has a "tramp stamp on the butt. She has a nose ring. Her nipples are pierced, and her clit has a gold ring though it."

Lois' eyes got enormous. "I know who she is. I knew about the nose ring, but you're putting me on about the rest."

"Nope."

She narrowed her eyes. "And you know about the gold rings how?"

"Remember we were posing as newlyweds. We knew someone had bugged the room, so one night she undressed, and we pretended to have sex. She wanted us to actuality do it, to make our cover more solid. The biggest reason it didn't happen was because I'm so in love with you I just wasn't interested."

That made Lois smile.

"I also discovered I don't like women with ink and I really don't care for a woman when she's pierced... anywhere! Especially down there!" I pointed at her crotch. "By the time it became an issue, we had to take off."

I described for her what had happened in Alaska.

Lois interrupted me. "You are shitting me! Sal Zampuchini, head of the Family, is dead?"

"Yeah, I saw it happen."

"And this Abdulaleem fellow as well?"

"Yes. I told you it wasn't a very good two weeks."

"Oh, my God. No wonder John has been such a total bitch lately. Sorry, what happened then?"

I told her the rest, including our narrow escape.

When I finished, she said, "Really?"

"The whole truth and nothing but," I agreed.

"Get me home, now!"

Lois was hardly through the door when she was attacked by the dogs. Both of them were putting their paws on her legs begging for attention. She stooped over to pet them and they tried to lick her face.

She was laughing so hard she could hardly speak. "Who are these vicious animals?"

"The one you're petting now is Max and the one dancing between your feet is Beanie. Her real name is Brenna, but we call her Bean or Beanie for short."

"They're darling." Finally, they settled down.

Lois took my hand and we headed to the bedroom. Once we were there, I took her in my arms and caught the zipper on the back of her dress. I pulled it down and slid my hands inside.

"Now, please shut up, take off your clothes and make love with me. I've missed you." I told her.

She apologized for being such a bitch at the airport.

And then she agreed to my request.

CHAPTER EIGHTEEN

As always, when I'm with Lois, Mondays arrive too soon. Martha had agreed to stay with the dogs while I went back to D.C. with Lois and I was happy to be spending the week with her.

Henry was our pilot on the trip to D.C. and he invited me to take the second seat in the cockpit. We had a splendid chat on the way up to D.C. Harry asked me about Alaska. After I told him my tale, he commented, "I'm surprised to hear al-Zaman would even consider leaving the safety of the Middle East. From what I know about him, he doesn't travel very often and never that far from the Middle East."

"How much do you know about Abdulaleem?" I asked. "Do you know what he looks like?"

"I don't need this to get around, but yes, I believe I know what he looks like. I met whom I believe was the real al-Zaman once. On later occasions I met men I was told were al-Zaman. Two of them were totally different people. Once it was the first man I met — the real Abdulaleem al-Zaman."

"If I got a picture, would you be able to tell me if it's al-Zaman?"

"I guess so, why?"

I asked him to give me a minute and sent Jesi a text. In about five minutes, some fairly decent pictures came through on my phone. I showed Henry the bearded man in the turban whom I'd seen assassinated.

He nodded his head, "Yes. That's one of the men I've met and whom I believe is Abdulaleem. These pictures from Alaska?"

"Yeah, why?"

"Do you have more?"

"Let me ask."

I texted Jesi again.

When the next batch came through, I showed Henry a picture of the bearded man in the stocking hat.

He winced. "I know him. I have a scar from the bullet he put into me."

"This may might you feel a little better. I saw him get shot and fall off the end of a yacht into a bay. The way he went in, I'm positive he's dead."

"I know I shouldn't say this, but I'm glad to hear that. I hated that guy and there are very few people I really hate."

I showed him the picture of the bareheaded man who had stood behind Abdulaleem.

"Oh my God, that's Farouk al-Hashim. He's the second in command. The name they gave him at birth was Abubakar. That means father of a camel."

"Gee, I wonder why he changed his name." We both laughed.

"Now that I see these pictures, I'm pretty sure the man in the turban could be Farouk al-Zaman. He was climbing the ladder of the UIBA back when I met him. Now I am not so sure which one is the real Abdulaleem. You'd better make sure it never gets out that either of you saw either of these men." Tapping the image of Farouk, Henry remarked, "Fewer people have seen Farouk than have seen

Abdulaleem. He's believed to be the UIBA triggerman. He does the dirty work. Be careful. Having these pictures is very dangerous. Basically, possession of either of these can be a death sentence."

"I was with the person who took the pictures when all this went down. Sal Zampuchini got killed along with Abdulaleem."

"Are you shitting me?" Thank God the plane was on autopilot. "Salvatore Zampuchini, *Don* Zampuchini? How come I haven't heard about this?"

"It just happened a few days ago. We were at the right place at the right time."

"No, Matt! You were at the wrong place at the wrong time. Did anybody see you there?"

"Yes. The Middle Eastern guys saw us and one of Zampuchini's goombahs chased us."

"Matt, I know a lot of the players in this fuck up. You're not safe and neither is your friend. I wasn't kidding, having these pictures is a death sentence. You're in big trouble."

Henry's concern alarmed me, and I called John on his private line. It rang for a long time and when John finally answered, he barked at me. "What are you doing calling me on this line?"

"Chill! I've just learned Jesi and I are both in danger. Do you understand what I mean?"

"Yes, I do. I know the players, but I didn't want you to know."

"John. You're playing stupid games, and I don't like it. I did you a favor, and this is how you repay me?"

"I was hoping if you didn't know, you would be safer. This has really turned into a total cluster. I'm worried about you."

"I'm safe for now, but can you put somebody on Jesi?"

He didn't answer right away. When he did, what he said made my blood run cold.

"Matt, I wasn't going to tell you this either. Jesi is okay. The clerk at the fishing camp is dead and the camp's computer is missing. Someone tracked Jesi down and when my people went to warn her, there were men there to kidnap and probably murder her. It turned into a mess. One of my people had to go to the ER. We took out two of the kidnappers and the rest took off.

"The problem is, the people we killed aren't Zampuchini's, and they weren't Middle Eastern. They look like local talent. We are trying to figure this out. Jesi's in Florida now."

"Good. What about my housekeeper, Martha?"

"She's safe too and your dogs as well. They're all staying with a friend of yours, Sergeant Brian Polk from the Fort Myers police department. I've assigned two men to stay with Polk."

"I'm glad to hear they're with Brian, but I'm sorry to hear how close it got for Jesi."

"Everyone is. Where are you?"

"On the way back with Lois. Henry says we'll be there shortly."

"Come see me. We need to talk."

"I will."

I went to the back of the plane and told Lois what I had just learned.

"I take it you're in a lot of trouble?" she asked.

"I really don't know. There are so many unanswered questions — I don't know who to be afraid of. This has really turned into a major screwup. Whoever said a good deed never goes unpunished was right."

~ ~ ~ ~ ~

There was a limo waiting for us on the tarmac and to my surprise, John got out. He hadn't said a word about meeting the plane. He wrapped me in a bear hug and afterwards he looked at Lois. She raised her hand as if to slap his face and John closed his eyes, screwed up his face and winced. "You know you have it coming, right?" Lois snarled at him.

He opened one eye. "I'm sorry, Lois. I see now not telling you was a mistake."

I pointed at John and then the limo and asked, "What brought this on?"

He frowned. "I fucked up, old friend. I'm so sorry."

"Which fuckup are you referring to?" I knew what he meant, but I wanted to give him some grief.

"I mean I got you involved in something and now you're in danger. It appears you unwittingly witnessed the start of a war between Zampuchini and the UIBA. Do you have any idea why al-Zaman shot Zampuchini? At least, we assume it was al-Zaman, however, we do have information now it might have been Farouk. He is reported to be a hot head."

"I think your correct from what Henry told me."

"You knew Farouk was second in command of UIBA?"

"Yeah, Henry told me."

"I'll bet Zampuchini's people are going crazy right now."

"Did you know I'd met Salvatore?"

John asked, "You told me that once before, but you never told me any details?"

"Back when Albert Bradson was running for President, I was in Seattle to interview somebody. Do you know the restaurant called Hanney's Hideaway?

"Ahh, one of my favorite places in the Puget Sound area."

"Albert and I were having dinner and Mouse and Zampuchini were there, Mouse introduced us to Zampuchini. I also had a run in with Sal when I was in Vegas." John smiled. "Remember, I was also doing a favor for Bradson then? I had to get tough with two of Sal's people."

"Well, I think his people will want to have another chat with you now. They probably know it was you in the fishing boat. I don't think they mean you harm, but they sure want to know everything you saw, and what you know about al-Zaman and Farouk. If you can, my advice it to stay away from them."

"Are you telling me to please be careful?"

"Yes."

"You don't need to tell me twice."

CHAPTER NINETEEN

The next morning Lois had to go to work. I intended to stay until Friday noon and then the two of us would fly down to the condo. John gave her the next week off. I think it was to make up for almost getting my ass shot off.

After Lois left, I went around the corner to Starbucks to get a morning paper and a latte. After I got my drink I sat down, leaned back and tried to relax, but as I sipped my latte, I felt like I was forgetting something. Then it hit me — Todd! Oh damn!

I went outside to make the call. When Todd answered, his voice was slurred with sleep.

"Oh shit, Todd, I forgot about time difference."

"Where are you?" His voice was a little less slurred now.

"I had to leave town for a few days. Just stay where you are, and you'll be safe. Since I arranged for a friend to bring you food you should be getting fed."

"Yeah. When are you coming back?"

"I don't know. I'm still waiting to hear from Melissa."

"This is getting old."

"You came to me. I'm doing the best I can."

The phone went dead. I sent Scott a text, asking him to call me. Scott would see that Todd continued to get fed.

I took a sip of my latte and found it was cold. Cold lattes suck so I tossed it in the trash and when I went to go back for a fresh one two beefy men stopped me.

"We don't want to hurt you," one of them growled. "But our boss wants to talk to you. Our instructions are to do whatever it takes to get you to come with us, without hurting you. So, if you would please not make me hurt you, I'd appreciate it. I don't need no trouble with the boss. I'm even willing to put my pistol in your coat pocket if it will make you feel better."

I'd bet this was the first time he'd ever had to beg somebody to go with him. I knew I might be doing something stupid, but I was curious.

"Who's your boss?" I asked.

"We ain't allowed to tell ya. You'll understand when you see him."

If this button-man was willing to put his 'biscuit' in my pocket I was feeling reasonably safe. It was obvious he was a member of the 'Honored Society'. This whole thing piqued my interest. At least it was better than arguing with Todd. "Okay," I said. "I'll talk to your boss, but you keep your pistol."

"Yes sir and thank you for coming with us."

They drove me to Leesburg. We turned down a street lined with mansions which probably started at the ten-million-dollar mark and went up from there. We pulled into the driveway of one of the larger homes and stopped under a portico. The house was magnificent. The guy who'd "invited" me led me past stunning art and gorgeous woodwork, wallpaper that could only be described as lush and furniture that belonged in a museum. Eventually, we reached an elevator. I stepped in, he didn't.

"Aren't you coming?"

"Someone will meet you upstairs." The elevator was pretty swanky, too. And this was a first — the first time I'd ridden an elevator in a private home. Regular buildings, of course, but a home? Nope!

When the elevator stopped, I stepped into an extensive study. It looked like a stodgy private club. Subdued lighting in the room was nice and a thick carpet covered the floor. Bookcases covered two walls from floor to ceiling and another wall were windows covered with heavy drapes. The fourth wall had a brick fireplace with an elaborate mantle. Arranged around the fireplace were leather couches and a couple leather wingback chairs. A massive desk sat in one corner with an antique globe sitting next to it.

A lovely young lady was waiting next to the elevator and when I stepped off, she motioned for me to follow her. She led me toward the fireplace and a man rose from one of the leather chairs and extended his hand. The room started to spin.

It was Salvatore Zampuchini.

CHAPTER TWENTY

I extended my hand. It wasn't exactly trembling, but I doubt if I could have threaded a needle.

"Mr. Zampuchini? Sir, I'm stunned, but also pleased to see you're alive. I would have sworn in court you were murdered in Alaska."

Zampuchini gripped my hand with both of his. "Thank you Mr. Preston, for coming to see me. Very few people know I'm still alive, not even Guido. He's on his way here now.

"I needed to speak to you but after that fiasco in Seattle with Mouse, I was afraid you'd refuse to come. It's good to see you again, my friend. And how is our friend Mouse?"

I doubted very much whether Mouse thought of Zampuchini as a friend, but I'm not dumb enough to say so.

"He's fine. He got married, has a nice condo in downtown Seattle,"

"Well, I'm pleased to hear things are going well for Mr. Fox."

If Zampuchini knew Mouse's real name, they must be reasonably close. Very few people knew Mouse's name.

"Thank you for coming. I trust the boys didn't alarm you too much. Please sit down. Can I offer you a cup of coffee?"

Since the cup I had purchased got tossed, coffee sounded good. Sal asked the young lady to get us some coffee.

Sal said, "I love having beautiful things around me. Especially young women." I didn't disagree, but I said nothing. He pointed at a chair and asked me to sit.

Stepping over to the chair I looked the older gentleman over. His three-piece suit was well tailored. He was a very handsome Mediterranean looking gentleman with a touch of silver in the hair around his temple. If I did not know who he was, I'd never have guessed his profession.

After I took a seat, I asked, "Will you please explain to me what happened in Alaska? I was there when the video was shot, and it certainly looked like you were killed."

Zampuchini bowed his head. When he looked at me, his eyes were moist. "The man you saw shot was my younger brother, Tony. Anthony Zampuchini. Many people have thought we were twins. He's precious to me. He's not dead. Thank God," Sal crossed himself, "he was wearing a vest. He was injured from being shot so close, but we had him airlifted off the yacht. Right now he's in a private hospital in Vancouver B.C. We think he's going to make it." Zampuchini crossed himself again.

"What was he doing with the leaders of the UIBA?"

"He was negotiating the sale of arms to Abdulaleem al-Zaman, or at least that's what the towelhead was supposed to think. It was a sting. We were asked to set up a buy and promised certain outcomes in regards to some federal investigation involving my friends.

"From the little we've been able to get from Tony, something tipped the UIBA people off. We don't know very much because we've only been able to see Tony for a few minutes since they shot him. The doctors are keeping him sedated."

"So, are there actually any arms to sell?"

"The federal people provided us with a couple dozen different items we were told represented what was available. The man who acted as a go-between would handle the actual take-down."

"Who is this man? Do you know his name?"

"Well, I see no harm in telling you. He was introduced to me as Jacob McNaulty. Mr. Preston, are you all right?"

It took a moment before I could speak. "I know McNaulty. We have a very long history. You want to watch him carefully. I'm not trying to tell you how to handle your business, don't get me wrong, just watch him."

Sal smiled at me, held out his hands and then turned them over.

"I'm telling you, don't trust him. Before you shake hands, count your fingers and when you get your hand back, count them again. It would take a long time for me to tell you the stories I know about him, and things that have happened to me because of him. Believe half of what you see and nothing of what he says."

"Ahhh, sheds some light on the assassination attempt on my brother's attempted assassination. I refuse to call it attempted murder. Anyway, the plan was, we would sell arms to al-Zaman's people and when the deal was going down, any of the UIBA the police could get their hands on would be swept up. Tell me what *you* know about what happened."

I told him things seemed to fall apart after the UIBA people had examined the samples. "It was right after they examined the samples they shot your brother. It looks like something about them wasn't right. These were the samples from McNaulty, right?"

"Yes. Was it al-Zaman who killed my people?"

"I thought so at first, now I believe it might have been Farouk al-Hashim, the second in charge. He could be the one who shot your brother. The rest of the killing was from a shooter up in the hills. The camera person thinks there might have been two shooters." I had no idea how much Sal knew about Jesi and I wasn't going to give her to him.

"I understand most of what you're telling me, but if the merchandise was tainted, how did McNaulty hope to pull it off?"

"I don't think it mattered. I think he hoped things would turn out just like they did. Now the UIBA wants your people dead and you're after whoever it was for shooting your brother. McNaulty dealt a blow to your organization and for sure made the UIBA a lot more unstable. It was a win-win deal. For him, the problem was us filming the entire thing."

"Can you get me copies of the pictures of the men on the hill?"

"I'll try. Will you excuse me for a moment?"

Sal showed me to an adjoining room where I called Jesi.

"Jesi, were you able to get any pictures of the people on the hill behind that old stump cleaned up?"

"Yeah, kind of. But they still aren't too clear. Why?"

"Do you still think there was more than one shooter?"

"I'm positive."

"Why?"

"I have a picture of two shadows side by side, but like I said, the features aren't very clear. I'm working on them with software which cleans up the images a little, but it takes time. Why?"

"I don't want to say any names on the phone. However, one of the men we thought was killed was only wounded, and it turns out he's the younger brother of the person we thought was killed. Can you send the pictures?"

"Give me a few minutes. Oh, thanks again for sending John's people to take me to Sergeant Polk's."

Zampuchini and I had a cup of coffee while we waited. "There's one more thing I'd like to discuss with you." he said.

Oh boy, here it comes. I've been asked so many times over the years I know when someone's going to ask me for a favor. "Oh?"

"I'd like to ask you to keep me in the loop on this. From our chat, I can see that we were being set up. The question now is who was on the hill shooting. I understand you do some work for Orchard and his organization, but unofficially. Can you bend the rules enough to let me know what you find out along the way? As you can well imagine, I have a lot riding on the outcome. Actually, it might be my life on the line here."

Stalling for time, I took a sip of my coffee; it was tepid. I must have made a face because Sal barked at the young lady, "Tiffany, Mr. Preston's coffee is cold."

Before I could object, she whisked away my cup and replaced it with a new one. I took a sip from the fresh cup and it was perfect. I smiled at Tiffany and nodded.

"Mr. Zampuchini…"

He interrupted, "Please call me Sal. Okay?"

"Sal, I'll promise you this, I'll keep you informed unless it conflicts with my commitment to John. Between you and the Admiral. I have to side with the Admiral. We go back a long way. All the way to Nam. But anything I can, I'll share with you. I'll also be telling the Admiral of our arrangement."

"I understand. If the roles were reversed, I'd want the same from my people. I know that you're a lot more than just a veteran. I've heard stories about you. I'm asking you to use your talents and find out more about what happened up there. I know you feel it could have been the leader, but with those people, there still may be a question."

I shrugged. "Find out what you can. I'll pay for your time. People won't know you'd be working for me and you can get probably get more information than any of my people can. I don't know why, but I intimidate people."

I couldn't help it, I smiled at that.

He turned his hands over to show me he understood why I was laughing. "Will you do this for me?"

"I'm flattered. First off, I won't take any money for several reasons. I'm not working for you, I was there, and I got shot at too. I want to know who and why. I want to make my decision based on what I believe is right and good, not what is in your best interest. Do you understand?"

"You're everything I've heard. I understand perfectly. I believe whatever you find out and tell me won't be tainted. I want you to know you can tell me anything, even something that might upset me, and being on my payroll might inhibit that. Just keep in touch."

"Give me a number where I can reach you when I have something to share."

Sal pulled a card out of his vest pocket and handed it to me. "Please memorize that number. If you every have any difficulties, any problems, no matter how small, anything to report to me, call that number.

"There's somebody by the phone 24/7. They'll answer with the word, yes. You tell them 8099. Remember that number. 8099. I promise the longest you'll ever have to wait for a call back is thirty minutes. You'll hear from me or my people. If it isn't me, please be open and honest with person who calls so they'll know what to do. Fair?"

I laughed and quipped, "Is this my get out of jail free card?"

Sal smiled, "No Matt, it's a lot more than that. That number will protect you in more ways that you might imagine. Never hesitate to use it. I mean that, never hesitate! Mouse is not without his abilities, but he could never offer you the services that card can. You're one of very few people who have that number."

Sal stood and as he extended his hand, I felt a vibration in my pocket.

"Hang on, I think this may be something you want to see." I pulled out my phone and opened the message. Sure enough, one of the fuzzy images looked suspiciously like McNaulty.

"Do you recognize the man?"

"It's still pretty fuzzy, but they're working on it." I looked carefully at the image behind what I thought was McNaulty. That face was much clearer. I was positive I knew that face. But where?

Sal extended his hand again. "Matt, thank you for coming to see me. And thank you for your willingness to share what you learn with me."

"It has been a pleasure to see you again, sir. This meeting is much more pleasant than our last." Sal threw back his head and laughed.

"I'll stay in touch."

"Mr. Preston, one last thing."

"Yes?"

"Your banker friend?" I said nothing. "I'd like to talk to him. That money isn't his."

I started to speak, and he held up his hand.

"I know what you're going to say. You don't think he did it. But I'd like to sort this out, too. I want my money back."

I shook his hand. There was no way I was going to change his mind and right now I was having my own doubts.

Tiffany took me back out to the limo and the car whisked me back to the Starbucks where I'd started. It had been a most interesting couple of hours. I went into Starbucks and ordered a latte and settled into a comfortable chair to mull over what had just transpired.

The face of the man on the hill bothered me. I knew that face. But who was it? And when and where was it I knew this person? I needed to discuss the previous few hours with someone.

I needed to talk with Lois.

CHAPTER TWENTY-ONE

That evening Lois and I had dinner at John's private membership club. They seated us at a nice quiet table—the tables were spaced to allow for private conversations. Considering some of the things that were discussed in DC, it made perfect sense. Our drinks were served and we clinked glasses. I told Lois how lovely she looked and how much I loved her. I ended with, "Well, I had a very interesting morning."

"Really? Tell me about it."

"I had coffee today with Salvatore Zampuchini."

"What?" She almost dropped her glass. She set her glass carefully down and asked, "How exactly did you manage that? He's dead."

I told her about my morning. When I got to the point where the arms deal went south, Lois agreed with me—something about the samples tipped the Arabs off.

"Where did they come from?"

"From McNaulty."

"What are you planning to do?"

"I don't know. I also have a problem back in Seattle I need to deal with."

"What problem?"

I outlined the situation for her, including the fact that I'd run out the grace period Jeff L. had given me—by quite a bit.

"Are you going back to Seattle?"

"I don't know yet. Zampuchini offered me a job."

"What?" Lois' voice rose an octave. "First it's Sal and now you have a job offer?"

"Relax! He wants me to investigate what happened up in Alaska. I told him I'd let him know if I found anything."

After dinner, we headed back to Lois' apartment. John had given us a limo for the evening and Lois demonstrated what she expected to happen when we got back to her apartment. I was tempted to tell the driver to pick up the speed a little, but I kept my mouth closed. I was enjoying Lois' demonstration a great deal.

After we arrived at her place, we left a string of clothing from her front door to the bedroom. Dimming the lights in the room as I entered, I noticed her lovely white bottom as she crawled across the bed. She looked over her shoulder at me and said, "Come here, I want you."

I'll just leave the rest of the evening up to your imagination.

~ ~ ~ ~ ~

Later, padding through the front room, I picked up my phone from the coffee table and noticed I'd missed a call. It was from Scott.

I called him back.

"Matt, there you are. You sent me a text asking me to call you."

"Thanks for calling. Sorry I didn't pick up earlier."

"Yeah, I can just imagine what you were doing." He snickered. "What do you need?"

"Do you mind still checking in on my banker problem from time to time? My visit here has taken more time than I thought. He also needs for you to keep bringing him food. Is that asking too much?"

"No. I'll be glad to do it."

"Great, thanks. I wish now I hadn't offered to help. If I'm wrong about this, I'll never trust my judgment again."

"Matt, remember, the past year and a half has been kind of rough on you. You probably don't want to hear this, but you're still recovering from the beating you took in the Middle East. Is it possible you might be wrong this time?"

"I've had the same thought several times."

"Talk to you later, I got to check on your boy."

"Scott, he ain't my boy. He's just my problem."

Scott was laughing as he hung up.

Strange, I sure didn't find it that funny!

CHAPTER TWENTY-TWO

Bored, there was nothing to do during the days, — but the nights more than made up for it. However, I was glad when Friday arrived, and Lois and I could head for the condo. I wanted to rescue my dogs from Polk and to relieve Martha.

When Saturday morning came, I remembered I needed to get ahold of Todd, who had better be cooling his heels at the houseboat. I hadn't called him for several days. To be honest, I was still furious he'd ignored me.

"Hey, what's up Matt? I'm glad you called—it's been so long I was getting worried."

"Listen up, Todd. I'm going to help you, I don't know why, but will. I still haven't heard from Melissa."

Todd sounded a little unnerved. "Is she really that good?"

"She's better. If you need me, call. If I hear you've been out again, all bets are off. I'll call Melissa off and I won't help you anymore. And I'll call the police commissioner and tell him where you are.

"By the way, is Scott bringing you groceries?" He told me he was and thanked me again for helping him. I hung up.

Next, I called Jeff. His greeting wasn't exactly friendly. He growled, "It's a damn good thing for you we go back a long way."

"Why, hello Jeff."

"Where the hell have you been? I gave you three days. Where are you and more important, where's Todd Hoss?"

"Look Jeff, things are taking longer than I planned. I'm calling to check in."

He shouted, "Check in? Listen buddy, you were to check in a long time ago. Now listen to me, I want that son of a bitch in my office in an hour or I'm putting out warrants for the both of you."

"Ain't that redundant? There's already a warrant out for Hoss."

"Listen butthead, you know what I mean. Where are you, anyway?"

"I think I'll keep that to myself. Hey Jeff, I need to get going."

"Damn it, Preston! I want your ass in my office, now! Do you understand me?"

"Sorry old friend, no can do. I'm still working on what happened to the money. I'll be in touch. Ciao."

As I hung up, Jeff was screaming, "Don't you dare hang up. Preston—"

I turned my cell phone off. After I handed over the real thief Jeff would mellow, and we would be friends again. Or at least I hoped so.

Max was pestering me, he wanted to go out. I got their leashes. Back in Seattle they never had to wear leashes for their outings, and they were not happy about needing them now. I needed to keep them on a leash—alligators are a real problem in Florida. My dogs would make a nice snack for one of those junior dinosaurs and I'd seen a couple in the canal across the street from me.

~ ~ ~ ~ ~

Monday morning, I took Lois to the plane for her flight to DC. Orchard had several things going on and she didn't know when she'd be able to come back. I told her how much I'd miss her.

She put her hand on my cheek and then kissed my lips. "I'll miss you too," she told me.

I wanted to say something more about my feelings, but the words wouldn't come out. I needed to define our relationship, but I didn't know what to say. The look on her face told me she understood. The drive home was sad.

I hate an empty condo.

Later that week I noticed Bean was panting a lot, and she'd developed a cough I didn't like. I didn't know if it was the move or if there was something wrong with her. It was a lot warmer than the dogs were used to. There was a veterinary clinic just up the street, and I'd heard good things about them. Thursday morning I called the vet, Doctor Leslie Oldman, and asked for an appointment. She said if I could get Bean into the office as quickly as possible, she'd make some time and see her.

Dr. Oldman didn't look old enough to be a veterinarian. An attractive lady, tall and slim, with long blond hair pulled back into a ponytail I liked the way she took time to pet Bean and get to know her. Eventually she took Bean to the back and was gone for quite some time. When she returned, I could tell there was something wrong.

She showed me two X-rays. "There are shadows on her spleen and her lungs. I can't tell what it is. Ordinarily, I'd start with exploratory surgery—this afternoon, but due to her age, I'd really like to get a better look at this first. There's a new clinic that does ultrasounds. If you take her for a test, they can email me the results and I'll have a much better idea if we even want to do surgery."

"If you think it's a good idea, I'll do it." I was trying not to fear the worst.

"Give me just a minute. I'll see if I can get you an appointment this afternoon."

~ ~ ~ ~ ~

At the appointed time, I took Bean to the new clinic and a tech took her to the back. Much later a different person returned Bean. She made no effort to introduce herself, just handed me Bean's leash. She looked at a clipboard for a moment and then started talking, "Your dog has congestive heart failure. There are growths on her spleen and on her lungs which we believe are cancer. Her kidneys are failing and there's a tumor on her trachea, and it's choking her. That's causing her cough. We could remove the growth and medicate her for congestive heart failure, but because of the cancer and her kidney problems, we would likely only be able to extend her life a short time. What do you want to do?"

Her monotone recitation stunned me. Did she just tell me I needed new wiper blades or that my dog was dying? I was crushed I was going to lose my little girl. But what really blew me away was the flat, emotionless tone this attendant had used. Absolutely no compassion. She could have been telling me I ran over a nail and I needed a new tire. She was so incredibly blasé. Her bedside manner totally sucked.

I picked Bean up and held her in my arms. It took a few moments for me to gather my thoughts.

"Thank you for the information. I'd prefer to take her to my vet. Please email your findings from today's visit to Dr. Leslie Oldman. Do you have her email address?"

"Yes, we do. We'll send her the results immediately." The woman turned and left the room without another word.

What a bitch! I was having a hard time processing the information and the technician hadn't shown an ounce of compassion.

I went out and sat in the car for a long time thinking. To say I was devastated would be an understatement. I started driving back to the condo with tears in my eyes. I'd let Bean curl up in my lap, even though it's not a good idea to drive that way. However, in my defense, I stayed in the middle lane of the freeway and paid extra attention to my driving. This was a special case.

Instead of returning to my condo, I drove directly to Dr. Oldman's office. I picked up Bean and carried her inside.

I had to wait for a while until the doctor was free, but eventually Dr. Oldman's assistant took us into an examining room. When Dr. Oldman joined us, I told her what happened, and that the clinic was going to email Bean's information.

"What do you want to do?" she asked,

"As much as I don't want to put her to sleep, after hearing all the things that are wrong, it sounds like the right thing to do. I need to be fair to Beanie. This isn't about me, it's about her."

Dr. Oldman had tears in her eyes. She was a hell of a lot more caring than the bitch at the clinic.

"Ethically I'm not allowed to tell you what to do, but once you have decided, I can tell you how I feel about it. Let me look at the test results they're sending up. I want to make sure we're doing the right thing. Go home and I'll call you later. Okay?"

I didn't trust my voice. I nodded, with tears running down my cheeks. The clinic had a back door so I didn't have to walk through the waiting room. I picked up Beanie and headed out to my car.

When I got back to the condo, I called Lois.

"What's up lover?" she greeted me.

It took a moment before I could speak. "I took Beanie to the vet this morning."

When she spoke it was a whisper, "Oh God, no. Don't tell me…"

"There's an extensive list of things wrong with her and even though they could do surgery to fix some of the problems, the best-case scenario is I'd have her for a few months, maybe. It's not fair to put her though that just for a couple more months. the doctor is looking at the test results before she makes a recommendation."

"Oh, Matt… oh my poor baby. I'm so sorry. When?"

"In the next couple of days would be my guess."

"Promise me you'll call me when you learn something?"

"Promise."

"I love you."

"Thanks. That helps. I love you too."

I took Max and Bean for a brief walk and when we got back, Dr. Oldman had called. I returned her call. Her assessment was the same, but she broke the news with a lot more compassion than the bitch at the other clinic. It didn't make the news any more palatable, but at least she wasn't cold or indifferent. Dr. Oldman told me it was up to me when to bring Bean in.

When I called Lois back, I cut the call short. I really wasn't in the mood to chat. With anyone.

~ ~ ~ ~ ~

It was dark when a noise woke me up. I lay there trying to figure out what I'd heard and where it was. I heard the noise again. It was coming from the front of the condo. I checked the clock — 3:07. I slipped out of bed and retrieved my pistol. When I got to the door, Max was already standing, there growling softly. I gave him a pat, unlocked the door as quietly as I could and eased it open a crack.

Lois was standing there. I opened the door, and she wrapped her arms around me and kissed me. While she kissed me, Max put his paws up on her legs. He wanted his share of loving too.

"Where's Beanie?" she asked, and I led her back to the bedroom where Bean was curled up in her bed. I put my pistol away in its secure hiding place and for the next half hour my little dog got all the loving any dog could ever want.

Finally, Lois stood up and went into the bedroom where she removed her clothing. As she crawled across my bed she looked back over her shoulder. "Come on, I wanted to give Beanie some love first and now it's your turn."

It was definitely my turn.

~ ~ ~ ~ ~

The next morning Beanie was coughing almost constantly, and she could hardly walk to go outside. I called Dr. Oldman.

I took Max with us so he could be there when they put Bean to sleep. I wanted him to understand as best as possible what had happened to his lifelong companion. You can't have an animal for years and not care. I would miss my little Beanie for a long time. My one consolation was that she would be with Blackjack somewhere over the rainbow bridge. Each dog takes a part of your heart when they leave you, but they also give you part of their heart in return. I'll admit, there are times when it doesn't seem a fair trade.

Dr. Oldman cried with Lois and me as she put Beanie to sleep, and for what it's worth, it made me feel a little better. It was a sad, sad day for all of us.

~ ~ ~ ~ ~

That evening I sat in my chair on the lanai nursing a small but nourishing, looking out over the canal and I wondered, as always when these days come, why do I have dogs. But the joy and the love they bring into our lives makes it worth the inevitable pain. At least it does for me. I know I'll have another dog.

Lois came and took my empty glass from my hand. Extending her other hand, she helped me up from my chair. She led me to the bedroom where we curled up together. For a long time, I thought about my little dog while Lois held me. I don't remember falling asleep, but when I woke in the middle of the night, I was undressed and under the covers. I snuggled closer to Lois and as I slipped back into sleep, I decided I could get used to sleeping like this.

CHAPTER TWENTY-THREE

The next morning over breakfast I expressed to Lois again how grateful I was she came down to be with me, and how much easier it made dealing with the loss of Bean. She wrapped her arms around me and lightly kissed my lips. "I think one of the hard parts of losing her is the sense of the passing of time. Things have changed. Bean is gone and that is something I can never have back. A major change like that makes you reflect on things."

"Did Henry bring you down?" I asked. Henry also worked occasionally for the Admiral. We'd never discussed exactly what Henry did for Orchard, and it was understood between us the subject was taboo.

"No, this was a new fellow I've never seen before, and I thought I knew all of Henry and John's pilots. His name is Dominick. Very interesting man and a very good pilot."

"I've never met him. And speaking of John, how did you get away?"

"I called in sick. He doesn't know where I am."

"How long can you stay?"

"I'll stay a couple of days, but then I've got to get back. I don't want to piss John off. He needs me, but there's a point where he may tell me enough is enough." We both laughed.

"Are you so busy you can't come back next weekend?"

"Lover, I don't care how busy I am, come and get me at your airport Friday evening. Either Henry or I will let you know the time."

"If I have to, I'll come up and see you."

"You have a deal."

Lois stayed for the rest of the week and suddenly it was Sunday afternoon. I hated to see her leave. I stood on the tarmac for a long time watching her plane disappear. Returning to my condo, I found it was now a lonely place. With Lois and Bean both gone, it was depressingly quiet. I decided I needed a small, but nourishing; I needed a Scotch.

Later, I sat in my chair with Max curled in my lap looking toward the river. I'd lost count of how many of those small, but nourishing, I'd consumed. I was having a pity party and to be honest, I didn't give a shit how many I'd annihilated. I was toasting all the wonderful memories I'd made with Beanie. It was strange, she and Max were littermates, and he was going strong while she'd developed so many health problems. Why was one of them so healthy and I'd lost the other so early? It wasn't fair!

I picked up my glass. It was empty. Damn, those things evaporate fast. The ice bucket was empty as well as the bottle of Scotch. Decision time. Do I get the makings for another one? Or just sit and mope over how unfair life can be.

When my cell phone vibrated it startled me. I jumped and fished it out of my pocket. I didn't recognize the number, but I answered it anyway. "Lo' this Matt." I hoped I didn't sound as deep in my cups as I felt.

There was a moment of silence and then a woman said, "Matt? Is this Matt Preston? Are you okay? This is Doctor Oldman."

I laughed wryly. "Yeah, I'm okay. Just having a wee bit of the Scotch and re, re, ah… reflecting about my little Beanie dog. Ya knows, I really miss her."

"A wee bit? Matt, it sounds like more than a wee bit of Scotch." She was teasing me. "I know you miss her. And that's kind of the reason I'm calling you."

I didn't understand. "Huh?"

"Matt, the county sheriff is a very dear friend of mine and last night he busted a puppy mill. He took me with him, and my clinic ended up with forty-five puppies."

"What?" Hot damn, I was eloquent tonight.

"I have forty-five puppies. They're in various states of health. I'll probably lose ten of them, maybe more. Some of them are in such terrible shape there's nothing I can do. But two of them are a little older than the rest and they're reasonably healthy. Healthy enough to place in some kind of foster care. They're between six and nine months old, and probably kept to use for breeding. They're both parti mix, and very cute. I don't know if you're interested in taking care of another dog so soon after losing Bean, but..."

"Doc, I hadn't even considered another dog." Things were slowly getting to my brain. "Wait a minute, did you say you had forty-five puppies?"

She giggled. "How much have you had to drink?"

"Dunno. Lost count. Why?"

"Do I need to call you back later?"

"No, it's good. I'm sober as a judge. Let me see, you said you and a county Mountie busted a puppy mill. You said you had forty-five puppies but would probably lose at least ten. Oh, but two puppies are in good shape and very cute and need a home. How's that?"

"Very good Matt." Now she was laughing more at me. "Are you interested?"

"Interested in forty-five puppies? NO!"

Now she was laughing so hard she could hardly talk. "No Matt, just one of the two puppies I mentioned."

"When do you need an answer?"

"Well, I was going to ask you to come and look at them tonight. But from the sounds of it, you're in no condition to be out on the road."

"Bullshit, I'm sober."

"Yeah, right. If you drive, my sheriff friend will lock you up! Listen, I know where you live—you're not that far away from the clinic. You sit tight and I'll bring the puppies so you can see them. See if one of them is interested in you?"

"All forty-five?"

"No Matt, just two. We can see if either of them is interested in you. Are you into seeing them?"

I knew what she meant. The best way to get a new dog is to let it pick you. You don't just get a dog. If there's more than one, you get down on the floor and play with them. Trust me, one of them will pick you. Really. I've seen it happen too many times not to believe it.

"Yeah. I'm dressed and everything. Come on."

"On my way."

I put Max on the floor and went into the bathroom, ran the basin full of cold water and splashed water on my face until I felt a little alive. After I brushed my hair and put on a clean shirt, I did feel a little more alive. During my brief rush of activity Max had followed me to the bathroom and was sitting in the hallway looking at me.

I asked him, "How'd you like to have a new companion?"

He gave me one bark. I turned on the outside light in time to see an SUV pulling into the parking lot. Dr. Oldman waved at me. I started down to meet her and was pleasantly surprised by how well I was navigating.

The doctor went to the back of her car to retrieve her passengers. She reached in and when she turned, she held out the puppies. I was hooked. Oh, my God. They were cute.

No! let me rephrase that that. They were adorable. Two wiggling black, white, cream and tan balls of fluffy fur. I took one from her and we went upstairs. I offered her a drink. She declined and told me I probably didn't need one either. I agreed.

We went to the lanai end of the condo and sat on the floor. Max was on his best behavior. He gently sniffed both puppies and then came and lay down next to me. The two puppies gamboled over and threw themselves on him. He licked one and then the other and then settled down tighter against me. One puppy was mostly black with tan eyebrows and four white feet, and she curled up next to Max and fell asleep.

The doctor remarked, "I've never seen that before. He has better mothering skills than a lot of females. Look at how that one took to him so quickly."

The other puppy came to me and put her paws on my knee. She was tan, cream and buff with black-tipped ears. She had one blue eye and one brown eye.

"What happened to her eyes? Is she blind in that eye?"

"No, she's a merle. It's a recessive gene. More accurately, she's a black-tipped merle. Very rare and very valuable." The little puppy was trying to pull herself up into my lap and I picked her up and held her to my face. When she licked me, I realized she was licking tears. My tears.

Then she nibbled on my mustache. That's when I totally lost it. From that point, she could have been the ugliest mutt in the world, and I'd have kept her. I held her in my arms and rocked back and forth. The little critter took a deep breath, sighed and closed her eyes. It looked like Max had adopted one and I had adopted one. "Did you know I'd keep both of them when you brought them here?"

Leslie smiled and shook her head. "No. I hoped you might pick one. I've got so much to deal with now, if I can place a puppy in a good home fast, I'm going to do it.

"What these two need now is socialization. I'm not sure, but I suspect they're littermates. We could find very little paperwork when the place was raided. These two just need a stable environment and a lot of love. Looks like they might have both here. One thing I have to make clear: these dogs are from a puppy mill and we have no idea what health issues might crop up. I have no way of knowing if they're the product of too much inbreeding. Right now, they seem to be in good health. But I have no way of knowing if there are underlying conditions. I don't want you to take one and end up angry with me if something comes up."

"Doc, I understand you can't give me any guarantees. I can deal with that. I'm willing to take a chance. Can I have both of them?"

"Really?"

"Really."

The puppy had moved and now she was lying on Max's outstretched paws. Max's face was right next to little critter, and it was so cute. Talk about your calendar picture.

"I can come up with a place for them to sleep tonight. Tomorrow I'll get some things."

"Do you still have Bean's bed?"

"Yeah, why?"

"Well, it will have a good doggy smell—the puppies might like it. They've been sleeping on a thin towel spread over chicken wire so almost anything is a major step up.

"The sheriff's a friend of mine. The main reason he took me when they raided the place, was because as a vet, I'd be the best possible witness. It was sickening. Four vets went in with the sheriffs and every one of us was disgusted by what we saw. Between us, we took custody on more than two hundred dogs."

I did the quick math, "Are you serious? Two hundred?"

"There were more than that, but some were already dead when we found them, and several of them died being transported to the clinics. They were that sick. All the vets filmed as much as we could and our hope is we can throw the book at these people. The entire affair was revolting."

"Were all the dogs cockers?"

"No, there were several breeds. There were a few golden retrievers that were sweet." She dimpled. "That's my favorite breed. But as I said, the entire thing really made me ill. I've seen a lot of cruel and disgusting things, but this was one of the worst I've ever seen. I wanted to kill somebody; I was so incensed."

I went off in search of Beanie's bed. I shook it out and fluffed it up, then tucked it in a corner. I laid the puppy I'd been holding and picked up the puppy on Max. Max actually growled at me when I moved it. He's never growled at me! I was stunned.

I placed his puppy on the bed. Max got up and laid down between the two little ones. Both of them scrunched up closer to Max and all three of them settled into a ball of fur. My eyes were leaking again. Oldman also seemed to have the same eye problem I had. I extended my arms and she stepped into an embrace. I felt a hiccup and then I heard her sob. It appeared the past twenty-four hours had been as difficult for her as the last couple of hours had for me.

When she looked up at me, there were tears on her face, "Thanks Matt. Sorry, that wasn't very professional. I just wanted to see if you could take care of one of them for a while. I never thought for a moment you'd take them both, or that Max would care for them like that. Sorry, I lost it. I'm embarrassed."

I tightened my arms, "Don't you dare. You said we were more than doctor client. You're allowed to show feelings. I feel honored you feel comfortable enough with me you'd share your feelings. Thank you."

"Matt, I need to go. There's still a lot of work for me back at the shop. I can only ask the staff to do so much and this is beyond the scope of what they signed up for."

"Do you need for me to come back with you and help?"

"No, you stay here with Max and the puppies. Knowing these two are safe is a big help. Honest."

I walked her down to her vehicle and watched her van drive away. I couldn't get over it. I'd started the evening with one dog and shazam --- I had three. This was kinda cool. True, I didn't know what health issues I might be dealing with later. I felt if I was careful, who knows? Anyway, I found my funk over Bean was a little less than before.

Max had a habit of coming and pestering me around nine o'clock in the evening to go out and do his business. Tonight, when he came and nudged my leg, I noticed it was nine fifteen. There was also a parade of two puppies behind him. I had a leash for him, but nothing for the little ones. I wondered if I took them outside to do their business if they would stick around. I got Max's leash off the wall and put it on him. I picked up the puppies, and we headed downstairs.

I set the puppies down and when one of them started to wander off, Max quickly got in front of the little gal. Somehow the puppy understood Max didn't want her wandering off. I took a chance, and removed the leash from Max. He went to a bush, never once taking his eyes off the puppies. I didn't know where Max had learned how to herd, but I was watching him do it.

When they were finished with their business, Max led them over to the steps. He seemed aware the puppies were not big enough to climb the steps and he turned around looking up at me as if to say, "Come on dad, a little help here would be nice!"

I picked them up and only then did Max run over to a patch of grass where he usually leaves a present and did his business. Once finished, he bolted for the steps and ran ahead of me up the stairs. I decided I'd pick up his present tomorrow morning. After I set the puppies down at the top, Max took over herding them down the hall and then to the old bed where the three of them curled up and promptly fell asleep.

Watching the sight before me, I could tell my eyes were leaking again. I missed Bean, but the two little balls of fur were really helping me deal with it.

CHAPTER TWENTY-FOUR

The next morning, I decided to call Todd. He seemed to be in good spirits.

"Good morning. I'm so glad to hear from you," he said to my greeting.

"Is Scott keeping you well fed?"

"Yeah, he's been most helpful. Thanks for having him look after me."

"Hey, I have some news. Don't ask me how I know this, but it's a fact. The money boosted from your bank was the mob's money."

"Impossible."

"Think what you want, I know for a fact they believe the missing money was theirs. And it really doesn't matter if it was or not. What matters is what they believe. I had a friendly chat with someone, and they made it clear they want you. I told them you had nothing to do with the theft, but they didn't buy it.

"Anyway, they're looking for you and if they find you, I don't even want to think about what they'll do to you. I really hope I'm putting the fear of God in you."

His answer was very subdued.

I wondered if I wouldn't be better off to turn his butt over to Jeff and Sakol.

Next, I called Melissa. There was no answer, so I left a message.

~ ~ ~ ~ ~

The week sped by and it was Friday evening and time to pick Lois up at the airport. I hadn't told her about my new little family yet. I considered taking them when I picked her up, but I decided to surprise her instead.

The plane was right on time and when I saw her, my whole body experienced a thrill. She was even lovelier than the first time I saw her. She just grows lovelier and more desirable with time. We hugged, and she gave me a kiss that curled my toes.

"Come on, let's go home," she said.

"I have a surprise for you."

"What? What? What?"

"If I tell you, it won't be a surprise." I grinned at her.

"You're not allowed to use that phrase; it belongs to Henry." We both cracked up.

Lois pestered me all the way home, but I held out. When I opened the front door, two balls of fur careened down the hall and then threw themselves at her legs. She screamed and then laughed. Both of them were jumping up on her legs and dancing around demanding to be picked up. Max came slowly sauntering down the hallway and I would swear he looked grateful we'd shown up to relieve him. I bent down and scratched his ears to show him how much I loved him.

"Where did the puppies come from?" Lois demanded.

"It's a long story."

Lois tossed her bag on a chair and snatched one of the puppies off the ground. She settled herself on the couch and as she played with her, she asked, "OK, where did they come from?"

"A puppy mill."

"What!" she snapped. "Matt! Please tell me you didn't buy these dogs from a puppy mill!"

"Calm down! No, I said they *came* from a puppy mill, not that I bought them from a puppy mill! Last Sunday night after you left, Leslie came by with the two puppies—"

"Oh, It's Leslie now? Not Dr. Oldman?" When I looked at her, her smile belied her words.

"She told me to call her that. We seem to have gone beyond a doctor-client relationship."

"This I've got to hear."

I told her about the raid on the mill. When I told her how many puppies Dr. Oldman ended up with Lois eyes showed her surprise. Lois was very pleased I'd taken both the puppies. I told her the last time I'd spoken with Leslie she told me just three of the puppies had died this week, and she was happy she'd lost so few. She really thought she'd lose a lot more.

The entire time I was telling my tale, Lois was playing with the puppies. Finally, she put them down and picked up Max. As she stroked Max, I told her what an amazing dog he was and how he'd taken to the puppies and watched over them. "It's a hoot when we go outside. He won't let either of them to wander too far. He's like a mother hen the way he watches them."

"What are their names?"

"Well, Leslie tells me when they got to the farm it was pouring down rain along with lightning and thunder. It was a miserable afternoon and evening, weatherwise and dealing with sick and dead dogs. So, I thought I'd call them Lightning and Thunder."

Lois clapped her hands and exclaimed, "I love it. Perfect names. So. which was is which?"

I pointed at the multicolored buff girl with a white streak across her forehead. "That looks like a streak of lightning. I guess I could call her Harry Potter except she's too cute to be a Harry, maybe Harriet. Anyway, the other one is mostly black and makes all kinds of noise so she'll be Thunder. When it thunders, she wants me to pick her up and hold her. She hates the thunder."

Just before bedtime we took the three dogs out and Lois witnessed Max carefully watching the two puppies. She was also amazed at how Max minded them. We agreed Max was quite something.

While we were out on the lanai playing with the dogs I asked. "How long can you stay?"

"I think I can wait to Monday morning to fly back up instead of Sunday evening. Is that okay?"

"Yeah. We need to chat about this some more. I enjoy being with you. I'm glad we're on the same coast now. Makes things a lot easier. I want you to spend more time with me."

"I agree."

"Does John know you're down here?"

"No! He grilled me about last week until I finally told him about Bean and why I came down. I didn't want him to bother us this weekend, so I kept this to myself."

"Thanks. This seems to make it more fun, kind of like we're sneaking off. Parking up on lover's lane and hoping we don't get caught."

Lois liked my analogy. "Yeah, this is fun. At least I don't have to worry about John interrupting us."

My cell phone in rang. I swear Orchard must be listening in.

"Good evening John."

"Good evening, Matt. Listen, when Lois comes back to DC on Monday, could you please come with her? I need to talk to you."

I chuckled. "How did you know she was here?"

"Matt, come on, do I really look that stupid? Wait, don't answer that. I'm so sorry about your dog. I know she was special to you. I liked the way Bean would come to me and she wanted me to pick her up and hold her."

"Thanks John. And, yeah, Lois is here."

"Can you come back with her?"

"I won't be able to, I have to get back to Seattle for few days. But I plan on coming to DC before I come home. So, to answer your question, sure, I can come and see you. What do you need?"

He hesitated then said, "Do you mind if I wait to explain? This needs to be face to face."

"I won't go up to Alaska and fish." He grunted. "So, am I in trouble?"

"No Matt, you're not in trouble. I just need to talk to you, and I don't want to do it over the phone. You know how I feel about phones. That's all." I understood about discussing certain things over the phone. I'm not fond of talking about important things on the phone.

"Fine. Do you need to speak to Lois?"

"No. You kids have a magnificent time and make sure she gets back here on time on Monday morning. You go to Seattle and deal with your banker buddy and then come and see me."

"How did you know about Hoss?"

"I'm not telling you my secrets. Make sure Lois is back on time Monday."

"Yes, Dad. Do I need to ask what time curfew is?"

John muttered a vulgar suggestion that I do a physically impossible act and hung up. I wandered back to the lanai and told Lois about the conversation. We both got a kick out of the fact that John knew where she was. I asked her if she knew what was on his mind.

"I'm not aware of anything."

"How did he know you were here?"

Lois bowed her head. "I'm sorry, I think it's my fault. I told the pilot on the way down about Beanie last weekend and that I was coming to spend the weekend with you."

"Ahhhhh… one mystery solved. Since I have to be up to DC for a few days, do you know of a place I can stay while I'm there?"

"Gee Matt, I'll ask around. Maybe you can stay at the YMCA." She smiled and leaned over and kissed my cheek.

I followed her down the hall to the bedroom and we quickly disrobed. She gave a wolf whistle when I was naked.

Opening her arms, she told me, "I love you. I can't get over how much I love you."

"And I feel the same way."

Looking at her standing there, sans clothing, I decided I liked her outfit. You know, of all the outfits she has, I think I like that one the best.

And I told her…

And then showed her.

~ ~ ~ ~ ~

When we got up the next morning, Lois couldn't find her underwear. "I remember hanging my bra on the back of that chair and I thought I put my panties on the seat."

About then Lightning came trotting out of the kitchen, proudly dragging Lois' bra behind her. Lois started to laugh. When Thunder came in with panties firmly clamped in her mouth, Lois lost it. For the next few minutes, we tried to corral the puppies. Once we each had a puppy the next chore was to pry their mouths open and try to retrieve her underwear. After we finally retrieved the lingerie, we discovered her panties possessed a hole in the crotch. I kind of liked the location, Lois not so much.

When I pointed out the new opening was conveniently located and I rather liked it, she said, "Yeah, you would. Pig!"

She's not wrong.

CHAPTER TWENTY-FIVE

One thing I'd like to make clear is my feelings regarding Lois. Yes, we have an amazing sexual relationship, but there's a lot more to us than just the physical part. For instance, I never asked, nor did I expect her to come down and spend time with me after I lost Bean. Lois came down because she wanted to be with me, to comfort me. She knew I needed her to help me deal with my loss. To me that was a very special thing.

I can talk to her about anything. No subject is taboo. She's been instrumental in helping me deal with my anger issues. We have many things in common and we have great conversations. We both like the opera but neither of us like the ballet. We enjoy reading the same authors. Our taste in art is much the same. We rarely argue except when Orchard sends me off on some crazy mission and then forbids me to tell her.

Regarding her hunger for our physical part, I don't know if it's because she's lived alone for most of her adult life, and now she has a partner she can share her most intimate desires with. She tells me I've helped her feel comfortable opening up about many things. Every facet of our association is wonderful. I've known some fascinating women in my life, but none of them hold a candle to Lois.

Sunday evening Lois and I were playing with Max and the puppies. Doctor Oldman called.

"Hi Matt. Do you mind if I stop by?"

"You aren't taking my puppies, are you?"

She laughed, "No, Matt. You adopting those puppies was one of the best things that came out of dealing with that puppy mill situation. I'm so grateful."

"Come on over. Lois and I were just sitting here playing with the dogs."

"Oh, Lois is there." She sounded surprised.

"Yeah, but we'd love to have you come."

There was a pause before she said, "Okay, I'm on the way."

Leslie arrived, and we sat on the lanai with three ecstatic dogs.

The doctor said, "I'm so happy to see the dogs. They look great. An enormous improvement since the last time I saw them. This week's been very difficult for me. Seeing them doing so well makes me feel better. I lost two more dogs. We expected it, but it still breaks your heart."

We chatted for a while. Finally I asked, "Was there a specific reason you came over?"

The doctor blushed. "Well, this week was such a bear. And I was so depressed over everything... and I... well..."

Lois spoke up. "And you wanted to see Matt. You wanted to be with a friend?"

"Kind of like that, yes."

"And having me here has upset your plans."

"Oh God Lois, I'm so embarrassed."

"Why? You had no idea what our relationship is. I'm glad you see the same qualities in Matt that I do in. He's kind and very compassionate."

I piped up, "Ah, excuse me, but I'm here. I'm hearing all of this. I feel like a used car or something. The next thing I know you're going to start kicking my tires and checking my oil. Do I need to take out my dipstick?"

Both ladies laughed. "Leave your dipstick where it is," Lois told me.

Leslie said, "Lois, I hope you're not upset. I just wanted to be around somebody who doesn't want something from me and who I enjoy being with. It was a spontaneous visit and I'm really embarrassed."

"Stop. Matt is free to do what he wants. I don't own him. One of the things I love so much about him is his free spirit. You can visit him any time you like." Lois turned to me. "And you can do anything you want with the good doctor, even play doctor if you wish, but only if I get to watch." Lois winked at Leslie. Everyone laughed.

Leslie stayed while Lois and I tried to improve her spirits. I asked about the remainder of the puppies. Leslie said most of them were out of danger. "By the way," she added "did you know the story about the puppy mill getting busted was on the television news? All the local channels carried stories mentioning each vet center where the puppies were taken. What surprised us were the numbers of people who called and inquired about adopting a puppy. Usually, once people hear puppies come from a puppy mill, nobody wants one. If every call we got took a dog, we don't have enough. All of us are gratified for the demand. However, we tell them there are no guarantees."

Eventually, it was time, and we all walked down to the doctor's car. Lois gave her a hug and when I took her in my arms, I held her for a long time. When I leaned back and looked at her, I said, "I want you to know that you're welcome to come over any time. I'm pleased to have you for a friend."

Lois pulled her back into an embrace and whispered something in her ear I couldn't hear. When Leslie stepped back, there were tears in her eyes. She whispered to both of us, "Thank you."

~ ~ ~ ~ ~

As always, Monday morning came too soon. I made arrangements for Martha to watch my little family while I was in Seattle and told her I'd back as quickly as I could. She told me to take all the time I needed, ending with, "I miss the Beanie. She was sweet. But the puppies are special. They make me smile. And bring back lovely Miss Lois, soon. She good for you. You nice person Mr. Matt, but when she with you, you nicer person." I told Martha goodbye and hung up.

Henry had dispatched a plane for me and a second for Lois. My flight out to Seattle was a fast, quiet one. I'd been calling Scott daily to keep tabs on my problem banker. Scott told me twice he was positive he'd seen a woman leaving the houseboat. When Scott asked Todd who it was, Todd first told him there was nobody; he was seeing things. The next time Scott saw the woman, he demanded to know who she was. Todd told him it was just a friend. I think I knew who that friend was. I'd caught a glimpse of her before.

I called Todd from the plane. "Who's the woman? You're supposed to be hiding, not throwing parties."

"She's an old friend. And don't worry. She won't tell anybody about me."

Since there was nothing I could do, I let it ride for the time being.

After our plane landed, Dominick, the pilot, asked me how long I'd be.

"I don't know. Why?" I asked.

"Henry told me I should wait for you." I wondered how Henry knew I would only be in Seattle for a quick visit. What had John told Henry?

"You have time to wait?"

"Sir, I'm at your disposal. I'll get the plane refueled and be here waiting. When you're finished, come back and we'll go. Henry said you needed to go to DC from here."

"Don't call me sir! Yeah, I'm going back to DC. Do you want me to call when I'm on my way back?"

"No need Mr. Preston. I'll be waiting."

"Thanks. And it's Matt. Not Mr. Preston, or sir. That makes me feel old."

Dominick laughed. "Yes sir… ah, Matt." I thought about making a smart remark about the sir thing, but I kept my mouth shut. I retrieved my truck and drove through town, bemoaning how horrible traffic had become.

I got what I needed from the condo and called Scott on my way to the houseboat.

"Matt, where are you?" he exclaimed.

"I'm in Seattle and I'm on my way to check on our problem. How's that going?"

"No Matt. Not my problem. It's your problem. I think he's going out when I'm not around. New things show up on the boat, so he's either leaving or someone else is bringing him stuff."

"Great. Thanks for your help. I'll ask him what's going on."

When I parked at the marina, there was a car parked in the slot reserved for the houseboat. I walked out to the boat, enjoying the sound of my footsteps on the dock. I always liked this setting. I wondered if Scott would sell the houseboat back to me. I could stay here instead of the condo when I came to Seattle.

WAIT!

Living four thousand miles away from a temperamental floating money pit. Gee, what could possibly go wrong?

I knocked on the front door. It took a long time for Todd to answer the door. The door finally opened a crack and Todd peeked out. "Matt, what a surprise."

I stepped forward, but Todd didn't open the door. "Hey, I'm no door to door salesman, let me in." I shoved the door, causing him to stumble backwards. He was naked. "Todd, go put something on."

A tall, very handsome naked woman stood in the doorway to the bedrooms. I'd met his wife, and this wasn't her. The woman gave me a startled look and disappeared toward the bedrooms. I told Todd, "Go get dressed. I need to talk to you about your visitor."

When he turned, I quickly glanced out the front window. The view of Todd from behind was not at all exciting. Actually, it was rather gross.

When the two of them came out of the bedroom, I asked them to sit on the couch and addressed the woman. "I assume you know about Todd's problems?"

She nodded.

"I've told Todd time after time not to leave and not to contact anybody." I looked at Todd, "I'm ready to dump you. Give me one reason I shouldn't just walk out and leave you on your own."

"Matt, this is Kaye. She's an old friend."

I couldn't help it. "She didn't look old to me."

Both of them blushed, Todd said, "You know what I mean. You're right, she knows about the problem with the bank and she won't tell a soul. I was lonely, and she came over to, you know, keep me company."

Kaye wore her dark hair down and it glinted with golden highlights. She had big brown eyes and a pleasant smile., I'd already noticed what nature gave her in the way of physical attributes when she was in the hallway. Mother Nature had been generous to the lady. "How do you fit into this mess?" I asked her.

"What do you mean?"

"Are you like the girlfriend or mistress or…"

"I know Todd's married, if that's what you mean."

I nodded.

"I guess I'm the mistress. Todd's working on getting a divorce."

I could see no payoff in pointing out that was a line that men have been feeding their paramours since the dawn of time. If it made her feel better to believe it, fine with me. I knew better.

"Todd and I used to work together at the bank. I got offered a better position at another bank and I took it. Afterwards, we could see each other and not be violating bank rules regarding having relationships with other employees."

If they were having an illicit affair, why worry about what the bank had to say about it?

Todd spoke up. "I know it sounds stupid, married and so forth and worried about what the bank would say. But being manager and vice president, the bank would have loved to have made an example out of me. Even though we'd talked about having an affair, we didn't while she was working for me. Now it doesn't matter anyway."

"Yeah, you got that right." So I was feeling sarcastic. Sue me.

I asked Kaye, "How do I know you won't say anything about him being here?"

"I understand how dangerous things are. And I'll be in in danger too, if our relationship gets out."

I couldn't resist. "Honey, you don't know how much danger you're in. There's more than one bunch who, if they knew about you, would whisk you off to some deserted place and torture you until they were positive you had no more information to share. And then they'd just dump your body someplace." Kaye reached out and grabbed Todd's arm.

I turned to Todd. "I only came to town to check on you. Scott tells me you're leaving the houseboat." A statement, not a question.

"That's not true. I stay here. Kaye comes and visits me a lot."

I wasn't going argue with him.

"I try to come over as much as I can." Kaye told me.

"I need to ask, and think about it, is there any chance anybody knows the two of you have a thing going on?"

Todd shook his head. Kaye spoke up. "I swear I haven't told anyone. There's no way I'd ever tell a soul."

I should wash my hands of the whole thing. One more screw up and I promised myself I would cut him lose.

I got my truck started and was just ready to pull out when somebody waved at me. Guido was parked next to me. I got out of my truck and leaned towards his window.

"Hey, what's up Guido Sabbatini?"

Guido's mouth dropped open. "How the hell did you find out my last name?"

"My friend, you're not the only connected one."

"Whatever. I understand you had a friendly chat with Mr. Zampuchini. Were you surprised he was still alive?"

"Very. What about you?"

"For some reason, I just didn't believe he was dead. I didn't know how or why, but I was positive he was still alive. I was right.

"Anyway, we've been keeping an eye on the airfield. They figured you had to come back, eventually. I followed you from the condo."

"Okay, I'm impressed. Now what?"

"Matt, it doesn't take a rocket scientist to know the banker fellow is down there on one of the houseboats."

"I'm not saying yes or no. What do you want from me?"

"Can I see the banker?"

"No."

"Why?"

"I don't see any reason why you should. He knows nothing. I already have people working on finding out how it was done."

Guido raised his voice. "How it was done? How he did it, you mean. Shit, Matt. I know how you feel, and you know how I feel. This is going nowhere."

"Okay Guido. What are you going to do? Are you going to tell Sal?"

"Tell you what... I'll give you till Friday. Then I'm telling Sal. I have to. More to protect myself than any other reason."

"Look, I have to do something right now. I can't tell you any more than that. I need at least three weeks."

He didn't look convinced.

"Give me three weeks and by then I should know something. If I don't come up with anything, I'll take you to Hoss and you can interview him to your heart's content. Fair?"

"Two weeks! Tops."

"Okay. Yeah, I think that'll work. I have your cell number and I'll keep you up to date. Since you're working with me here, I'll sweeten the deal. If I find out Todd really did the deed, I'll call you and let you know. Fair?"

"Two weeks. And Matt, please don't make me come looking for you. I like you and I'm beholden to you, but that can only go so far. Eventually one has to look out for themselves. Capisce?"

"Capisce, amigo."

~ ~ ~ ~ ~

Once I was on the road, I called Scott. "Matt, what's going on?"

"If I had to move the problem, is there a Plan B?"

"Houseboat not working out?"

"Not as well as I'd hoped. Certain people know where the problem is hiding now."

"Give me a couple. Let me see what I can come up with."

"Done."

I needed to get Todd off the houseboat. I wasn't so much worried about him, but there were innocent people around him, and I didn't want anybody to get hurt due to my negligence. I'd just decided to go see Mouse when my cell rang.

It was Scott. "I have a place I can hide your problem. Do you want me to take care of it?"

"Not right now. He's being watched, and I don't want you involved."

"Like I ain't involved now?"

"Sorry about that."

"Call me when you need me to step in."

"Thanks."

While I'd been on the phone, somebody had tried to call. I hit the redial button.

"Hello Matt, this is Dominick. I have a problem."

"What's up?"

"There's a problem with the starboard engine. When I try to engage—"

I stopped him. "I don't need to know what the problem is. How long are we grounded?"

"They promise me we can be airborne by tomorrow afternoon. I know the shop's owner and he pushed our job ahead of others. I'm sorry about this."

"It this something you did on purpose?"

"Of course not."

"Then there's nothing to apologize for. Are you okay for a place to stay and all?"

"Yeah, I have a…. um, a friend here who I can stay with.'

"Good, I don't need to know any more. See you tomorrow afternoon."

"Yes, sir."

Again with the sir stuff. I need to break the boy of that
nasty habit.

CHAPTER TWENTY-SIX

I spent the rest of the day with Mouse and Jade, discussing possibilities. That evening we decided to have dinner at my favorite restaurant anywhere, Hanney's Hideaway. I called Mary Ellen and asked if she was free.

"Whatcha got in mind?"

"I promised you a dinner for your help patching up Todd. I'd like to pay my debt. Interested in dinner at the Hideaway?"

"I'd love to." She sounded excited.

"How do you feel about going with Steve Fox and his wife?"

"I adore Jade, but I don't know Steve very well. It still sounds like fun."

We set a time for her to come up and have a drink before we headed off. Reservations are just about impossible to come by because the place is always busy, but I didn't worry, Mouse owned a piece of it. We'd get a table.

At the appointed hour, Mary Ellen came up. She stunned me. I guess I'd never really looked at her. She looked great—brains and beauty, what more could you ask for?

I was complimenting her when Mouse came in. "Why do you look familiar?" he asked.

"4-G. I live here."

"That's right. Now I know who you are."

Jade came in and hugged Mary Ellen. We chatted over cocktails, then headed down to the lobby. Mouse had a limo waiting.

The ride to Hanney's was crappy, as always, these days. I was tempted to say something about the traffic but held my tongue. I didn't have to drive and I needed to keep still. When we got to Hanney's they seated us immediately at one of the best tables in the house.

For those who don't know about the Hideaway, think of an upscale 50's chop house but with today's amenities. With a piano bar and a live person playing old favorite tunes, white tablecloths and heavy napkins, a candle on each table, and small hidden spotlights in the ceiling, all assembled to create a seductive ambiance. Take a date there and trust me, the evening will turn out just wonderful. Our meal was sumptuous, and as always, I had a magnificent time.

When we were back in the limo, I got a call from Scott.

"Hey, let me call you back."

After we got back to the condo, I returned his call. The news wasn't great.

"Sorry to bother you, but we have trouble," Scott said.

"What's up?"

"I was checking on your problem again and there was a strange car in the back of the lot. The two dudes in the car didn't look like Mormons, or boaters, or people who lived on houseboats."

"Why do you say that?"

"Perhaps it was the custom sharkskin suits with vents in the jacket's side to make room for a gun. Or that they were driving a black Lincoln with blacked-out windows. One of them was standing beside the car smoking a cigarette and

I've never seen a person so out of place. The other one held his right hand strangely, like he'd injured it. I acted like I was making a U turn and I headed back the way I came. Because I know the area, I knew a place I could get on the hill and I watched for about an hour, until they drove off."

"I think we need to move our boy."

"Yeah. I was hoping to do it late, but I don't know if we have that much time."

"I have an idea."

"Lay it on me."

"I'll call Todd and tell him to get ready to move. You call me when you're two blocks away from the houseboat and I'll call Todd and have him meet you in the parking lot."

"I was thinking I'll get a couple of my buddies go to the parking lot and hang out. You remember the pro football player? Duke of Earl, the Duke of Defense?"

I remembered him. An old poker pal. The dude was immense. "Yeah"

"He owes me a favor. I'll call him and have him and some of his buddies drive down to the houseboat parking lot and hang around the dock. If those guys are back, I doubt if they'll mess with us. I'll have the Duke and his boys stand in front of their car when I leave. That should give me enough time to get away from there."

"Okay, let me call him now."

I called Todd and told him the plan.

"Do you understand?"

"Yeah."

"Hey, try sound a little more grateful."

"Sorry. I need to let Kaye know."

"You are not to call her. Do you hear me? We don't know if she's being watched and you don't want anybody to know where Scott's taking you. I don't even know."

"What if I get lonesome, if you know what I mean?"

"I know what you mean, and you'll just have to take your problem in hand and deal with it all by yourself."

"That really sucks."

"I'm tired of your shit. If you don't want my help, tell me now and I'll call Scott off. You're on your own."

"No! This is cool."

"And you will not call Kaye."

"Well…"

"You will not call Kaye. Say it."

"Ummm…"

"You will not call Kaye. Say it!"

"Oh shit, Matt. I won't call Kaye."

"So help me, if you do, I'll drop you like a hot potato."

"Okay."

"Todd, I may be away for a while. I'll call you just as soon as I get back."

"Where ya going?"

"Trust me, you don't want to know."

"Is this like that Middle East thing you got involved in?"

"I have to go. Get ready to move."

The transfer went off with only a hiccup. The Duke and his friends stood in front of the car driven by the guys watching for Todd. When they saw Todd get in Scott's car, they tried to follow only to find Duke and friends blocking them in. One punk rolled down his window and told Duke to move. When Duke didn't move, the punk made a colossal mistake. He called Duke the N word. Duke and his friends don't like to be called the N word. They decided the punk's car needed to be remodeled and removed the front doors without tools. The last Scott saw of the hoods, they were running down the sidewalk towards the lake.

At least I had Todd in a safe place. The question was, would he stay there?

Why can't I just walk away? I really need to learn to say no.

If you believe that, I have some swampland in Florida I'm looking to sell.

~ ~ ~ ~ ~

The next day I headed to Boeing Field, not sure if I was going back to DC or going home. I had to check in with John and see if he still needed me. I was debating seeing Lois or going to Florida, and cell phone rang. Melissa.

"Hey kid, nice to hear from you. Any news about my problem?"

"Yes, I need to see you."

"When?"

"Now, or soon as possible."

"I'm on my way to the airport."

"Matt, trust me, we need to talk. Tell me where to meet you."

"Do you know where I live?"

"The condo downtown? The Olympus?"

"Yeah. Will that work?"

"Yes."

"Meet me in the lobby, one hour." The phone went dead. She'd been so abrupt I wondered what she had to tell me. I didn't think it was wonderful news.

I called Dominick to let him know I'd be later than expected.

Traffic was normal. For Seattle. I'd use the F word, but let's settle for screwed up.

I arrived at the Olympus just as Melissa rolled in.

"I just have few minutes. Can we go up to your place?" she asked me.

"Okay."

In my condo, I motioned for her to sit and asked, "What's so important we had to meet like this?"

"I don't want anybody to know we're friends. I don't need it known I'm helping you with the banker. You know how many people are looking for him?"

I motioned that I did, and Melissa cut to the chase. "Matt, do you trust me?"

That surprised me. We're old friends, or I thought we were.

"I'm serious. Let's say I held up a piece of white paper and told you it was black. I swore to you it was black. Would you believe me?"

"I don't understand, Melissa. If it's black, it's black. Telling me it's any other color is crazy. Exactly what are you asking me?"

"I'm asking you if I tell you something, regardless of how difficult it is to believe, or how farfetched you think it is, can you trust me enough to believe me?"

"I don't understand where this is going, but yeah, I guess if you tell me something you believe is true, I believe that you believe it. I know you wouldn't lie to me on purpose or try to fool me."

"Good! Remember that."

"Why are you making this difficult? Just tell me what you have to tell me."

She put her hand on my arm. "Matt, your buddy Ted is guilty. That piece of paper is black as the ace of spades. Ol' Ted stole the money."

My voice rose several octaves. "What? That's impossible."

"See. I knew it! You don't trust me; you don't believe me."

"One has nothing to do with the other."

"Yes, it does. You asked me if I could tell you who did the deed. I'm telling you as sure as God makes little green apples, your buddy took the money."

"But…"

"No, Matt. There are no buts. I'd stake my reputation as the Gypsy Queen he took that money."

"You don't know Todd. If there was ever a bumbling, clueless person, it's Todd. I think the world of Todd, but an embezzler he's not. He's a white piece of paper."

Melissa's voice was disgusted. "Matt don't waste my time. I did you a favor. It took a lot of time. I looked into this very carefully. Now I bring you the answer you wanted, and you tell me I'm wrong. I'm not wrong. I have proof."

Melissa rose, indicating our meeting was over. I realized then I'd hurt her feelings.

"Please sit. I'm sorry! I'm trying to believe what you told me. Really. It's just, I was so positive he didn't do it. I staked my reputation on it. I thought the paper was white. It takes some getting used to when you tell me the paper is black."

Melissa settled back into her chair. "I understand. You're a loyal friend. When you believe in somebody, you go all in. I know that firsthand. But this time, you are so wrong. I can show you he was the one with just keystrokes."

"What?"

"Keystrokes. Everybody punches the keys differently. Just like fingerprints, no two people are the same. I found the entries when your buddy tried to make it look like somebody stole all his information and moved the money. It was him. I found the back door he left in his system so he could move stuff around without being caught. The back door has his fingerprints, so to speak all over it. He was good at hiding what he did, but he did it.

"I agree with you about Todd's character. He's not swift enough to pull this off. He had to have had help. I'm sorry if I burst your balloon. For what it's worth, I do think the money was the Mafia's."

"Why was in Todd's bank? It makes no sense."

"Listen, some Podunk bank in a faraway suburb is an exceptional place to put money. Open an account and tell them it's for some mail order business. Start slow, then deposit more money into the account. Keep dumping money suddenly there's a lot of money all hidden away in the nowhere bank.

"Your buddy noticed some of those accounts and started looking into them. I found his tracks from investigating what was going on. He thought he'd erased everything. But he's not the Gypsy Queen."

"Can you get the money back?"

"Kind of?"

"What does that mean?"

"I can set it up so that if he if he tries to move the money it will automatically get dumped into a numbered account—one that only you or I can access. The trick is getting him to move the money. He was smart enough to establish a relationship with a banker on Nevis Island. We need him to move the money—as soon as the transfer is initiated, it can be routed where you want it to go."

"Thanks Melissa, I guess. Now I have to tell Chief Davenport I was wrong. And after I made an ass out of myself swearing Todd was innocent. I just never thought he had the smarts, or the moxie to do something like that."

Melissa jumped. "Hey, I just thought of something. The name Kaye kept popping up in his emails. Several of the emails were quite juicy. Actually, I was getting a little turned on reading them."

"No offense, Melissa, but if the wind blows the right way you get turned on."

For that smartassed remark, she slapped me hard on the shoulder.

"I'm not sure who this Kaye is." she said. "I thought his wife's name was Carol. Sounds like there might be something there to look at?"

"It's his ahhh, mistress, his paramour."

"How did you find out about her?"

"I caught her visiting Todd at the houseboat."

"Oh! what did they say?"

"She was the one who said she was his mistress."

"What does she look like?"

I described her.

"Oh my God, I know her. Her name is Kathrine Marie something. She's a decent hacker, but I'm better. I wonder how she worked this."

"I broke into the office and found some wires in the vents. A friend said they were for cameras."

"That explains a lot. Kathrine Marie watched and told Todd what to do. When they finished, they took the cameras. I wonder how she got your friend to go along with it?"

"They're having an affair."

"I know how to push Ralph's buttons. Time tested methodology. Lead him around by his dick. With sex, I can get him to do almost anything."

"No offense, but for sex, Ralph ain't that hard to manipulate."

Melissa laughed and nodded. "Are all men so easily led?"

I wondered. It's been said that men think about sex a lot. Like anything else, some men are more focused on sex than others. But I maintain, if a man is being honest about it, sex is often on his mind. Does it control him? For most men, yes.

"Melissa, men do spend a lot of time thinking about sex. Just some are more driven to act. I have no room to talk, sometimes I let desire get in the way. Often I meet a woman and desire them. It takes effort to put that aside and look at the woman as a complete person and not just a sexual toy. How the hell did we get on this topic? Do you feel you get hit on a lot? Do you feel you are viewed as a sexual object?"

"Yeah, a little more than I like. I do wonder. It seems half the time when I meet a man, he talks to my chest instead of my face. I don't feel I'm that well-endowed, so I wonder what they're looking at!" I was not going to touch that comment. "Are you going to tell Hoss you know he stole the money?" Melissa asked.

"Oh yeah. I want to see his face when I tell him. I wonder what his next move will be?"

"Be careful. You don't want anyone to think you know more about this than you do. Todd is damn lucky to still be alive. You need to be very careful because I have no desire to go to your funeral. I look shitty in black."

"Yeah, I understand. I really hate wearing a suit and the thought of wearing one for eternity leaves me cold."

"Keep in touch. I'll let you know when he accesses that account. I'll have a trap set. Don't forget."

"Not a chance. Thank you for all you've done, I think."

CHAPTER TWENTY-SEVEN

Armed with new information, I called Scott. I wanted to surprise Todd and see what he had to say but I didn't know where Scott had stashed him.

"Scott, it's Matt."

"Hey buddy, what's up? I was just going to call you."

"Listen, I need you to tell me where you have Todd stashed."

"I thought you didn't want to know."

"Things have changed. I had a chat with Melissa."

"Yeah. Where did she find out?"

"I'm an idiot. There's no doubt Todd stole the money. She knows where it's hidden and how he did it and everything."

"Oh, shit, Matt. I'm so sorry for you. You were so positive he didn't do it. You almost had me believing it."

"You never told me you thought he did it."

"Matt, we're friends. You believed he was innocent. What I thought didn't matter. You were trying to find out who was guilty. You didn't need my opinion to work it out. Okay, now that you know he did it, what are you going to do?"

"I want to have a chat with him. Where's he hiding?"

"I can tell you where he's supposed to be."

"What does that mean?"

"I went over there this morning to make sure he was okay, but he was gone. I thought he'd gone off on a tryst. I guess not since he still ain't back. What do you want me to do?"

"Nothing. You've done more than enough. You need to take care of yourself. Stay away from this. I don't want anyone to think you might know something and kidnap you to get information from you. I've got to look for him. I had him and I let him get away. Oh shit, so many people are going to be upset with me. This is a good time for you to walk away."

"What are you going to do?"

"Trust me, you don't want to know. Actually, I don't know myself. I just hope when I find him I don't do anything too stupid."

"Have you told your cop buddy yet?"

"Nope, that's next on my list. Not a phone call I'm excited to make."

"Better you than me."

"Thanks, buddy."

I didn't think Todd would answer his cell phone, but I tried it anyway. After one ring it went to voicemail, which he hadn't set up.

So much for that.

~ ~ ~ ~ ~ ~

I was working up the courage to call Jeff when my phone vibrated. When I checked caller ID, the number was way too many digits. Weird. I answered it.

A heavily accented voice asked. "Hello. Is this Matt Preston?"

"Yes, May I ask who this is?"

"I would prefer not to say my name. If I say my name it would trigger an alert and this call would be recorded. Actually, it's being recorded anyway, but my name hasn't set off any alarms."

I wondered who the hell this was. "Can you give me a hint?"

"I was featured in video filmed in Alaska. You probably believe I'm dead." I almost blurted out his name but caught myself. "Sir, I saw you shot and fall off the end of a yacht. I know you're dead because there is no way you could have lived through that barrage of bullets."

"You saw my number two shot and killed."

"You mean —"

"Do not say names," the man on the phone barked. "His name will also set off alarms."

"Okay, let's say I believe everything you're telling me. Why did you call me? And how did you get my number?"

"Really Mr. Preston, you can't be that naïve. Getting your number was a... ah, how you say, piece of cake?"

"Fine. Why did you call me?"

"I understand you are helping Mr. Zampuchini look for some answers. I too want answers. I want to know how you found out to come and take pictures. I want to know how come we were showed garbage. I have had you investigated. I have many questions. I have a safe place in Amsterdam. I want to know why somebody like Zampuchini would ask a person like yourself to become involved, no offense. I know what you did in the military and that you still have some role..."

I interrupted. "That part is inaccurate. I'm not in any organization."

"Yet you carry cards from a black operations group." He had me there. "Will you meet with me in Amsterdam?"

"Can I call you back at this number?"

"Yes. But why?"

"Sir, look at it this way. A very dangerous man calls me out of the blue, in spite of the fact I believed he was dead. And he wants me to meet him in a foreign country. Even knowing who you are poses a threat to my life. Now I'm supposed to accept all of this with no questions? Sorry, but I don't think so. I need some time to think this over."

"You mean you want to talk to Admiral Orchard. I would ask you not to take too much time. Many lives are in jeopardy right now."

"I'll call you back in a day or so."

"I'll be watching for your call."

Holy shit!

I mean holy, holy shit!

I'd just received a call from somebody purporting to be Abdulaleem al-Zaman, head of the UIBA. First Zampuchini is still alive and now maybe al-Zaman. What is it with supposedly dead people calling me? My hands were shaking. Damn what was I going to do?

However, the first thing I had to do was try and make nice with my old friend, Jeff L. Davenport.

~ ~ ~ ~ ~

I've told you before about grandpa and what he said when faced with a tough decision, usually the most difficult choice is the right one. My choices were to call Jeff or not. Guess which one was the most difficult choice?

I needed to tell him about losing Todd. I dreaded doing it. I sucked it up, put on my big boy pants and called.

The conversation started with, "Listen, don't you ever hang up on me again," Nice greeting. "I didn't want to get an arrest warrant for you, but we need, no let me change that, *you* need to do something now, bring Hoss in. You've had enough time to work this thing out. I've been more than fair."

"Ahh Jeff, I'd love to bring him in. I want to do just that, but there's a problem."

Jeff's voice rose several decibels. "What the hell do you mean there's a problem?"

"Well, I don't know where Todd is."

"WHAT!" he screamed. "Damn it Matt, find him. I want him in my office. NOW! Right now. Do you hear me?"

"And I really wish I could produce him. I also just learned that I've been played for a fool."

"What does that mean?" Jeff screamed.

"Do you remember the Gypsy Queen?"

"Yeah. What the hell does she have to do with this and what do you mean got played for a fool?"

"It means Gypsy Queen proved to me Hoss did steal the money. Now he's flown the coop. I was wrong and I'm embarrassed."

"I don't give a shit how embarrassed you are. I want you to find him and bring him in. How did you lose him, anyway?"

"Sal Zampuchini and his people found him, so I had to move him. A friend of mine took him some food and he'd disappeared."

"Zampuchini? I thought he was dead. What the hell is going on, Matt?"

"It turns out that Salvatore's younger brother, Tony, was the one on the boat. I'm told they look a lot alike. Zampuchini is fine and the brother is going to pull through."

"And Hoss?"

"I'm looking for him. Don't worry, I'll find him."

"Well ain't that grand. What the hell am I going to tell Frank?" Frank is the mayor. He used to have Jeff's job.

"Tell him it's all my fault. Throw me under the bus."

"You can damn well bet I'm tossing you under the bus. Frank kept calling me, asking me where Hoss was, and I kept reassuring him you had it all under control. Shit Matt, I'd like to throw your scrawny ass in jail right now."

"If you do that, I won't be able to look for him."

"Find him. Find him. Now!" Jeff shouted.

Jeff hadn't really been as upset with me about losing Todd as I thought he'd be, but I was close to the line here. To salvage things with Jeff, I needed to find Todd, and I needed to find him fast.

Scott called a few minutes later.

"Matt, I think I know a way to find out where your problem is hiding out."

"Don't make me come over there and beat it out of you,"

"Wow, lots of hostility there."

"You bet! I'm tired of dealing with this."

"Call Gypsy and see if she can help you. It's a start."

"Great idea."

"See, now be nice to me next time."

"Thanks, I'm calling her now."

CHAPTER TWENTY-EIGHT

I had to agree, the best place to start was with Melissa.

I called her and when she answered, she was laughing. "Hi Matt, I was wondering when you would finally get around to calling me."

"What do you mean?"

"I knew after you accepted the truth, you'd ask if I can find him."

"Sorry I doubted you about Todd. I'll bet he'll claim he did it all for his mistress."

"You guys always seem to think with the wrong head."

"Okay, enough man bashing for now, can you find Hoss?"

"As a matter of fact, yes I can. When you asked me to look into this, I accessed all the computers at the bank as well as Hoss' personal laptop and his cell. I also had the number for the cell you bought him. Among other things, I left tracer programs on all of them. I can see him every time he logs on or uses his cell phones. Would you like to know where he is right now?"

"Are you serious? Of course."

"He's in Seattle, down in the South Park area." She gave me the street and the block. "I can't get any closer than that."

"Thanks kid, I owe you."

"Yes, you do, and I'll collect later." She was laughing again as she hung up the phone.

~ ~ ~ ~ ~

The neighborhood was seedy, and the night was dark. The feeble streetlight down the block kept it from being pitch dark. I was hiding near the mouth of an alley and getting bored.

I heard a sound and then the shadows in front of me shifted. A door was opening. Success! A shadow slipped through a doorway into the alley. I stepped out behind him. I had my pistol in hand and I was angry enough to use it.

"Todd, stop!"

He started to turn.

"My boy, stand still. If you so much as think about moving, I'll shoot you."

"Matt?"

"That's right." I cocked my pistol. "I'm not kidding. Make one move and it may be your last."

"Hey buddy, I've been looking for you."

"Bullshit. You've been avoiding me."

"Why would I want to avoid you? You're the only one trying to help me."

"Yeah, Todd. And that was your mistake. If you didn't want to get caught, if you didn't want anyone to figure out what you did, why come to me? Did you really think I wouldn't figure it out? Or did you think if I figured it out you could con me into keeping it buried?"

"Figure out what? You aren't making sense."

Todd was turning again, and I assumed he had a weapon in his pocket.

"Stand still, stop moving!"

Todd kept turning. I aimed at his feet and pulled the trigger. The silencer on my pistol did its job — the only sound was a soft cough. Todd screamed and dropped to the ground, grabbing one foot. I heard something metallic hit the ground, which I assumed was a gun.

"I told you not to move. You must really think I'm a fool. I believed you. I made a fool of myself in front of so many people insisting you were innocent. And you were playing me the whole time. Did you really believe I wouldn't figure it out? Did you really think Melissa couldn't figure it out?"

"Matt, what are you talking about? This is me. Todd. You know I didn't steal the money. Oh God, my foot, it hurts so much. I think you shot off one of my toes. Matt, I need a doctor right now."

"Melissa told me how you did it."

"But…"

"Shut up and listen. You have a choice. Either stop with the innocent routine or I'll shoot you again. You still have nine more toes. If you say you didn't do it one more time, I swear I'll pull the trigger and take off another one. I'm so pissed at you it's all I can do not to pull the trigger."

"Matt…"

"I'm warning you." To emphasize my point, I pulled the hammer back.

"How did you find me?"

"Melissa told me where you were."

"How did she know?"

"She has ways. You should have known better than to take off like you did."

"What are you going to do with me?"

"Why, turn you over to the mob. You took a lot of their money and they want to talk to you. I won't take a chance you might find a good lawyer and get off. Sal Zampuchini can take it from here."

"Oh God, please don't do that."

"Why not?"

"Listen, help me get away. You're right, I took the money. Help me and I'll give you half of it. Half of three hundred and twenty-seven million dollars. Think about it. You'll be set for life."

"Todd, you should have done your homework. I have more than enough money. You know what I'm worth. Why should your offer interest me in the least?"

"If you let me go, I'll tell how I did it."

I couldn't help it, I laughed. "I already know how you did it. My question now is why?"

Todd didn't say anything. and I tapped his outstretched foot. "I asked you a question."

His voice was so soft it was difficult to hear. "All my life, all my fucking life, people took me for granted. People think I'm such a putz. Because I'm big and look kind of slow, I must be honest. Nobody can imagine me doing anything illegal. They think I'm too stupid — just this big bumbling oaf. I'm not bright enough to pull off anything as complicated as ripping off the bank for millions and millions of dollars."

"You didn't pull it off. I caught you."

A pistol was cocked behind me. A woman's voice said, "I don't think so. Put your gun on the ground and then step away. I've learned from you. If you make any wrong moves, I'll pull the trigger."

I put my pistol down and stepped away. A woman moved out of the shadows and crouched next to Todd.

"How bad is it, baby? Can you stand?"

"I don't know," Todd groaned.

"Kaye?"

"You got it, buster. And we're leaving now. I want you to move further back." I hesitated and Kaye aimed the pistol at my head.

"I really don't want to do this, but considering the amount of money involved, I'll pull the trigger. You need to back off."

I moved back and Kaye helped Todd up. "Where did he shoot you?"

"My foot. I think one of my toes is gone."

"Do you think you can walk?"

"I'll try."

Todd leaned on Kaye and they shuffled down the alley. As soon as they turned the corner, I crouched down and started to look for my gun. I found it, picked it up and ran to the end of the alley. and peered around the corner. A car pulled away from the curb and took off down the street.

I was so angry with myself. I should have guessed Todd wasn't alone. I'd screwed up and let him get away. Again!

I should at least have had Mouse for backup. I should have called Jeff. Even having Guido with me would have been a pretty good idea. Ego! Todd had pissed me off — an affront to my precious ego. It hurt my feelings. Yes, I'm being a baby. But hey, I trusted him.

Guess I'm not as bright as I thought.

CHAPTER TWENTY-NINE

Among the many things I needed to do was decide what to do about Abdulaleem.

If the person on the phone really was Abdulaleem, I needed to deal with the situation that presented. I'd had enough of Todd Hoss. I was leaving that shitstorm behind, for now, anyway. I needed time away from Seattle.

It was time to get back to DC and bring John up to date. The phone call from Abdulaleem really rattled me. If it was legitimate, there were other organizations out there who would like to chat with me.

Damn, John had really put my nuts in the fire on this deal.

~ ~ ~ ~ ~

About halfway through the flight to DC I called Lois. "Hi babe. Can I see you tonight? I've really missed you."

"I've missed you too. John still wants to see you."

"Yeah, I know. Tell him I'm on the way."

"He's been asking, no, he's been badgering me about when you're going to be back in town."

"Okay. Tell him I'll come and see him first thing."

"I'm glad you'll be in town for a while. I miss you."

"Ditto, lover. Do I get to stay at your place?"

Lois suggested something we could do when we were together. I told her to keep it in mind and I'd try to take care of it.

~ ~ ~ ~

After we landed Dominick asked. "You want me to stick around?"

"There are a few things I need to take care of. Perhaps we might get away in a couple of days. I have your number; I'll call you when I can get away."

"Fine. Take your time, I have a friend I'd like to see."

"I thought you had a friend out in Seattle."

"Mr. Preston, one can never have enough friends. If you catch my drift?"

"Matt remember? When you call me Mr. Preston and talk like that about friends, you make me feel old."

Oh, to be young and constantly horny again! However, I can't complain. Lois does a marvelous job keeping me happy and satisfied.

When I got to John's office, he wasn't there.

"It was so weird," Lois told me. "John took a call in his office and I heard him yell something. He tore out of his office, putting his coat on. I asked him if he wanted you to wait and he said no, for you to go to Florida and stay there. He would contact you when he could. I asked him what was going on and he told me it was none of my business."

"He said that?"

"Yes, and you're to go home."

"Back to Florida?"

"Yes."

"When can you come down?"

"I promise, I'll be there as soon as I can."

I called the number I had for Dominick. "Mr. Preston?" He answered.

"I'll break you of that mister shit if it takes the rest of my life."

"Sorry sir. Where do you need?"

"Are you free to fly me?"

"Sure. When can you get to the airport?"

"I'm on my way."

"See you there."

All the way back to the airport I wondered what was going on. I was pissed. John summoned me to appear and then takes off with no explanation.

He'd better have a fantastic explanation along with a huge apology the next time I saw him.

CHAPTER THIRTY

I was back in Florida lounging in my favorite chair on the lanai with a small Scotch with Thunder curled up in my lap brooding over how wrong I'd been about Todd, when my phone rang.

"Matt, hello. It's Guido."

"Guido, what a pleasant surprise. How'd ya get my number?

"Matt, duh! Come on, you know the people I work for. That's a stupid question."

Thinking it over, I realized it was rather a dumb question. "What can I do for you?"

"It's something I'd like to do for you. I just heard something you need to know."

"Something tells me this isn't going to be marvelous news."

His laugh was a bark. "Sorry Matt, not really. Have you ever heard of the Addams Family?"

"You mean the stupid old television show from the 60s?"

"No, I mean the husband-wife assassination team."

"Bullshit, Guido. You're putting me on. There's no such thing as the Addams Family hit team. What kind of joke is this?"

"Sorry, Matt. There really is and they're very good. They won't touch a contract for less than two million with all the money up front. And they guarantee success or double your money back. And they've never had to give a refund."

"Okay. I believe you. Why do I need to know this?"

"A very large contract was just issued, and they picked it up. Would you like to know who the contract is for?"

"Not really, but I bet you're going to tell me anyway."

"Well, there's some photographer chick out in Seattle, your friend the admiral, your flyboy partner, Mouse, and then there's you. All five of you are due to get whacked."

"How large for the five of us?"

"Twenty mil."

Four million per person! I asked, "Who put out the contract?"

"That's the weird part. Sal swears it wasn't him. Sal's kind of been in contact with the Arab group who got popped up in Alaska, and they swear it ain't them. Nobody knows. But the contract is for real. Just wanted to give you a heads up."

"Well, thanks, I guess. Are you sure this isn't some elaborate hoax?"

"Mr. Zampuchini had me run down the rumor. Most of the families know about it, but everybody swears it ain't them."

"What are your plans?"

"To stay the hell as far away from you as I can. Right now, you is bad juju, dude."

"Thanks for the warning."

"Not to worry. Ciao."

That gave me a lot to think about, but before I could start, the phone rang again. It was the admiral. "John, where are you?" I asked.

"I can't tell you."

"Okay, why did you stand me up? You demanded I come and see you and when I get there you're gone. Why?"

"I can't tell you."

"Then why the call? What's up?"

"Do you know anything about a hit team called The Addams Family?"

Normally, I'd let him tell me, but I had a bone to pick with him.

"Yeah. They're a man and woman assassin team, maybe husband and wife. They won't touch a hit for less than two mill with a double your money-back guarantee, which they have never had to make good. And, they've picked up a contract for twenty mill that includes both of us."

"I won't even try to guess how you know. I see I'm wasting my time here. Bye, Matt."

"Don't you dare hang up."

He asked, "Does this duo remind you of anyone?"

"No."

"Think about it."

I wondered what he was driving at. "Sorry, I don't know where you're going with this."

"Think, Matt. A couple of killers — not a man and woman, but they were a *couple*, if you catch my drift."

The penny dropped, and it stunned me. Two gay guys I'd known back in Nam and then one of them was killed in my backyard and the other one I'd shot on an island in Puget Sound. "Price and Hollis?"

"And who was their handler?"

"McNaulty," I whispered. "You think the Addams are getting orders from McNaulty?"

"It wouldn't surprise me."

"Do you think it's like the Price and Hollis situation and there's more than one team?" During the events that had brought Price and Hollis into my life a second time, McNaulty had engineered three teams, all of them using the Price/Hollis name and reputation. When you used a team, you thought you were getting the real deal, Price and Hollis. All three teams were so good nobody suspected a thing.

"I have no idea. But my question is, who screwed up the Alaska operation, or who does McNaulty *think* screwed it up? Who did McNaulty maybe see out there in a fishing boat?"

The light bulb popped on and I realized what was going on. "You sent me up to Alaska because of something you overheard about McNaulty?"

"Yes. And I'm sorry about it too."

Right then, I could have killed Orchard myself, forget about a hit team. "And he probably had something to do with sending the samples that tipped off the Arabs. Which explained why the UIBA was so quick to shoot the person they thought was Zampuchini."

"It fits. Unless you can think of someone else who could have put out the contract." John said.

"That was my next question."

"I'm out of ideas. You agree that this has something to do with the Alaska debacle?"

"That's my first thought, but why Henry and Mouse?"

"Henry knows a lot of stuff and he hears everything. On top of that, he knows some key players with UAIB. I think his hit is collateral damage control.

"Nobody really knows much about Mouse and his dealings, just that he seems to be everywhere. And he's a good friend of yours. McNaulty is probably just covering all the bases. Have you spoken to Mouse?"

"I had just heard about this when you called."

"Call him."

"Yes, sir."

"If I learn anything, I'll call you. Let me know what Mouse has to say?"

"Yeah. Where are you?"

"Right now, that's on a need-to-know basis. By the way, what are you going to do about Lois?"

"Same answer. Ciao."

I hung up. The entire thing sounded like a joke.

A terrible joke.

I mean come on, The Addams Family? It was a stupid TV show, and it was a stupid name for a hit team. How much fear does a hit team called The Addams Family create?

I needed to get Lois to safety and warn Henry. I didn't worry about Jessie because she was still with my friends in Fort Myers and I was the only person who knew that. I wanted to see Lois, but I wondered if that would put her in danger.

I called Mouse. Two rings later he picked up,

"Matt, what a pleasant surprise."

"Mouse, I have a question."

"What's up?"

"Have you ever heard of The Addams Family?"

"Which Addams Family, the 60s TV show or the hit team?"

"The hit team. Do you know anything about them?"

"Actually, I do. Her name is Diane. And Matthew, that woman will make your timbers shiver. She's almost enough to make Henry change religion. I saw her once, and she's absolutely stunning. His name is Dick or David or Dwayne or Dude—starts with a D. Anyway, doesn't matter, They're good. Very expensive, but very good. I've also heard they're swingers. How did you hear about them?"

"I heard there's a contract on you and me, along with—"

Mouse cut me off. "I'll call you back." And he was gone.

I resumed staring at the canal. Eventually the puppy in my lap woke up so I rounded up the dogs and we went for a walk around the complex.

While I walked, I racked my brain for a safe place for Lois, not to mention me. But where? The best option was in Seattle close to Mouse. Considering the arsenal stored in his basement, it was the safest place I could come up with. I briefly thought about going off the radar at Walter's, but I didn't want to put his family in harm's way. I wasn't worried about Walter. If anyone messed with him, they were on their own. I send a text, warning him. The chances of anybody getting to his cabin without his knowledge were between slim and none. Mouse's place was the best.

I called Lois. Her phone rang for a long time before she picked it up. Her voice was brisk. "Not now, I'm busy. Just come and get me as soon as you can."

No time to answer, just a click.

I called Henry next. He was talking to me from a plane. "What's up, Matt?"

"I have a problem. I don't feel comfortable discussing it on this line. When will you be down this way?"

"You want to go to DC?"

"I'll tell you later. What's going on involves you, too. How long before you could pick me up?"

"Let's do this. Get yourself over to the hanger. Dominick will take you to DC. You go hang with Lois and I'll let you know when I'm on my way."

I didn't like it. I didn't want Lois in an insecure environment. "Henry, if I tell you to pick me up at hanger three, do you know what I mean?"

"Yeah, I know what you mean."

"Call me when you're close and I'll meet you there. Don't file any flight plans yet." I still had to warn him. "Henry, I can't tell you more, but you need to be very careful."

"I understand. I'll be in touch."

There was no goodbye. There wasn't much to discuss at this point. I cared a lot about Henry and I hoped he was safe.

CHAPTER THIRTY-ONE

I called Mouse again.

"Who did you piss off?" he asked in way of answering his cell.

"Evidently, the same people you did."

"Yeah. How quickly can you get out here? I can keep us safe."

"I'm picking up Lois as soon as I can. We'll call when we're headed your way."

"Be careful."

"Ditto, amigo."

~ ~ ~ ~ ~

Jesi was next on my list. I rounded up the dogs and went in search of a payphone. I found one, finally, and called Brian Polk who was still hosting the tattooed photographer. I gave him a quick explanation.

Brian was unfazed. "Not to worry, my friend," he told me. "I've got somewhere else to go."

"Where?"

"Oh, not too far away. My grandpa built this place in the Keys back when he and my uncle were running booze out of Cuba. He had the fastest runner in the Keys for a long time. He knew those islands like the back of his hand—he was born there."

"He was a rumrunner and you're a policeman. Interesting."

"What's more interesting is not only was my uncle a rumrunner as you call him, but he was the sheriff of Monroe County, which is all of the Florida Keys."

"What?"

"It helps to know where the Feds are sitting up a sting. The revenuers never caught my uncle or any of his friends. He was re-elected every time he ran." He laughed. "Anyway, don't worry about us, nobody knows about the house. Let us know when things have died down."

We parted company and I had to admit, I kind of wished I could go with them to the Keys and pull the plug on the rest of the shitstorm brewing out there. But I had to deal with The Addams family. And apparently, I had to resolve Sal and Abdulaleem's problem. As for Todd, if I knew where he was, I might just call Sal and let him solve that problem.

Naw! I'm just blowing smoke.

I needed to get Lois out to Mouse. She'd be safe there. Right now I needed to get myself to the airport. When I pulled up, Dominick was doing a pre-flight check. When he saw me, he called out, "I'm ready if you're ready."

"Are you taking me to DC?"

"Yeah. Henry will catch up with you later."

"Let me put the car away and I'll be right there."

I drove the car as far into the hanger as possible. Outside, I started to pull one of the big doors shut. This particular door was always getting stuck and as many times as I'd asked one of the crew to fix it, it never got done. I braced myself and pulled as hard on the door as I could. There must have been grease on it because this time, my fingers slipped off and I landed on my butt.

As I hit the ground, I heard glass breaking overhead, and a piece fell on me. I looked up at a fresh hole in one of the small glass panes. There had been no noise, but now there was a hole exactly where I'd been standing. Someone was shooting at me. Had I not slipped, that bullet would have been in me.

Another pane broke above my head and I rolled over as fast as I could and started a low crawl towards the plane. Dominick started to spool up the engines. Luck was with me because the hatch was on the opposite side of the shooter. I dove through the hatch and was closing it when the plane started to move.

I don't know what Dominick told the tower, but from the time we started moving until we were barreling down the runway, the plane never stopped. I got myself into the right cockpit seat. I picked up the headphones and slipped them on.

Dominick's voice immediately sounded in my ears. "Are you okay?"

"Just my nerves."

"Okay. Listen, I've got a problem. I need to find someplace to set this bird back down. Soon!"

"Why?"

"A slug pierced the fuselage and hit me in the upper thigh."

"What?"

"I don't think I can make it all the way to DC. I'm bleeding a lot and I need to set down while I can."

Thinking quickly, I said, "I think I can keep this thing steady for a few minutes, do you want to check your leg out?"

Dominick pushed himself out of the number one seat leaving a pool of blood on the seat. When he tried to take a step, his leg gave out. He caught himself on the doorway and slid down to the deck.

"How well can you fly this thing?" he asked. His voice was weak, and he was mumbling.

"I've never flown this plane. I've done a little flying on a couple of the others, with Henry. I take it you can't get back up here?"

"No."

Panic City. I did my best to stay calm. Remember the duck? Calm on top of the water and paddling like hell under that water? Well, that was me. I needed help. I'd used the onboard systems enough to place a call.

"Admiral Orchard here, who's this?"

"John, it's Matt. As we were leaving Fort Myers somebody shot at me and hit the pilot in the thigh. There's a lot of blood on the seat, but he's still with us. When he tried to get out of his seat, he fell and now he can't get up."

"Where are you?"

Dominick explained where we were. About that time there was a crackle in my headphones, and I could hear Orchard talking, but there was a new voice too. The new voice told me not to panic. He told me he was in Pensacola and had been listening in on our call. Pensacola was the best and closest place for me to land. The voice assured me he would stay with me until I was down and safe.

The next few minutes were a terror-fueled blur. Dominick stopped responding, and I thought he might bleed out before we got down. I told Pensacola and they assured me everything was in place. Fire trucks and aid vehicles were already standing by. I didn't need to hear the part about the fire trucks.

The voice from the navy base asked me if the chase planes had found me. I looked and saw two F/A Hornets in Blue Angels trim flying beside me. They informed me they'd been training when they heard my mayday call and they were there to help me down. I had tears of gratitude in my eyes at that.

I could hear the pilots talking with the control tower at Pensacola. One of them reported mist coming off one of my wings. A bullet had hit something and I was losing fuel.

One of the pilots asked my name, then asked me, "How much flying experience do you have?"

"I've flown a little, but I've never had to take off or land."

"Okay. I want you to look at the bottom row of gauges. Starting on the left, tell me what the first two gauges say." I told him. "Look closely at the second gauge. Does it look like the needle is moving?"

"Yes. It's moving toward the E."

"Do you see a switch above the gauges?"

"Yes."

"Is the switch flipped to the same side as the gauge that shows you're losing fuel?"

"Yes."

"Flip the switch." I did. "It this gauge holding steady?"

"It seems to be, but it shows less than an eighth."

The pilot who had been talking to me said to the other pilot, "We need to get him down before he runs out of fuel." I was grateful he didn't mention what would happen if I ran out of fuel.

I'll never remember exactly how I got the plane on the ground. Between the controller in the tower and the pilot beside me giving me instructions, everybody was amazing. Their timing was perfect. The plane only bounced once when I touched the tarmac, and it wasn't much of a bounce. When the plane came to a stop, emergency vehicles surrounded it. Two burly EMTs came aboard and carried Dominick off the plane.

Two firemen hustled me away from the plane and the emergency vehicles started backing away. A pool of liquid had formed under the plane and it was quickly spreading. One of the firemen urged me to run. I wasn't far away from the plane when it exploded. The force of the blast drove me several feet forward and I landed my hands and knees, and I felt a hot rush of wind swept over me.

I must have hit my head on the tarmac because the next thing I knew I was in an ER.

The equipment monitoring me was loud. My first thought was, *Oh shit, a hospital.* I opened one eye and saw several people around me. My back was sore, but my headache throbbed with every beat of my heart. My hands throbbed as well. When I looked, they were raw and crusted with blood. My knees also hurt, and I assumed it was from landing on them when the blast threw me to the ground.

The thought kept running in my head, *Oh damn, here I am in a hospital.*

The movement of lifting my hand alerted the doctors I was awake, and they subjected me to pokes and probes while they asked how I felt. They told me nothing was broken, but my hands and knees were pretty torn up. There were two small blisters on my back, but they weren't anything to be concerned about. One of the ER personnel injected something into my IV and the room drifted away.

I woke up in a darkened room. The headache was gone, but I was sore all over. I looked at my hands which were bandaged and heard a sniffle. Lois was crying.

"Oh God Matt, I was so worried," she said.

"Baby, it's okay, I hurt, but I'm gonna be just fine."

Lois leaned over and I received the sweetest, most gentle kiss I've ever had.

"I love you. I'd be devastated if something bad happened to you."

"I love you too. How did you get here so fast?"

"Fast? Honey, the plane blew up two days ago. The doctors were afraid you might have a concussion. Everybody will be relieved that you finally woke up."

"The plane is totaled, I take it?"

She nodded. "The plane exploded. And even the pieces don't exist anymore. The plane was kind of a top-secret thing and Henry shouldn't have been able to get his hands on it. The admiral wants to have a chat with Henry to find out how he got it."

"What about Dominick?"

"You saved his life by landing as quickly as you did. The bullet had done some serious damage. Everybody says you're a hero."

"I'm glad he's okay."

"In the past two days, between John and a couple of other agencies, I've learned some interesting things about Mr. Dominick. Things even Henry doesn't know."

"Huh? I don't understand."

"It turns out Dominick is Russian by birth but holds several passports. His family owned an airplane service in Russia, and he was one of their pilots. Actually, he was a lot more than just a pilot. Without his family's knowledge, he smuggled arms and drugs in and out of Russia. He got caught by the wrong side and was scheduled to go before a firing squad. The admiral and Dominick's father are old friends. When Dominick was caught, he was doing a mission for Orchard and Ilox. They interceded and got him out of wherever he was being held."

Lois leaned over and gave me another big kiss. "Dominick's father, Orchard, and Ilox are extremely grateful to you for saving his life.

"Drugs? Arms? Are you serious? I thought he was just some pilot Henry picked up to fly for us. Is Henry safe?"

"Yes, and so is John. I don't know where John is, but he's safe. Henry is somewhere in Nevada. As soon as we can move you, we're going to meet Mouse."

"When?"

"Soon. For now, you just rest. I'll let you know when we can leave after I talk to the doctors." I closed my eyes.

My last thoughts were about Dominick.
Dominick? Who da thunk it?

CHAPTER THIRTY-TWO

Waking up, when I looked around the room I knew I'd go crazy if I had to stay much longer. I wanted out.

Out of the hospital.

NOW!

When Lois came to visit, I explained my dilemma and begged her to please find the resident floor doctor.

"Why?" she asked.

"Because if they don't let out of here by noon today, I'm leaving on my own."

"No!"

"Yes. Baby, I can't do another day here. I'm well enough to leave."

She returned shortly with a doctor who had seen me. He was the resident doctor for this floor. "Good morning. What seems to be the problem Mr. Preston?"

"Doc, release me, now. I'm a little sore, but I don't need to be here. I don't *want* to be here."

"Let me look at your chart."

"In about half an hour, I'm leaving. With or without a discharge, I'm walking out the front door."

"I'll be right back." The doctor called over his shoulder as he strode out the door.

I called Henry. "If you have any pity left for your partner, you'll send somebody and get me out of here."

"I'm making arrangements as we speak," he said.

"Where are you?"

"I'm in Nevada. Don't worry, I'm safe."

"Great. Now please get me a plane and get me out of here."

"I want to thank you for saving Dominick's life."

"I was saving my old fat ass, he just happened to be in the plane with me. Besides, if it hadn't been for me, he wouldn't have been shot."

"Dominick knew the risks when he signed on," Henry said. "This wasn't the first time someone shot at him but this time his luck ran out. You got him down safely so people could save his life. Thanks."

"Okay. You can repay me by getting me the hell out of here."

He laughed. "Just promise me you won't try to fly the plane. We'll run out of planes if you keep doing that."

I suggested he try something physically impossible.

"Temper, temper. Call me when you get discharged."

"That's gonna be in just a few minutes."

"Call me."

I started to tell Lois what Henry said, but she got a call. The ringtone was Orchard's. Lois stepped out of the room to talk. I didn't care what they were planning I was checking out. I'd had enough hospital!

When the doctor returned, followed by Lois, I had my pants and shirt and one shoe on. The pants were torn at the knees, but I really didn't care. He handed me a piece of paper.

"It would be better if you stayed another day. Try to stay off your feet, you're still concussed."

"Thanks, Doctor." I turned to Lois. "Are you going to give me a lift or do I need to call a cab?"

"Chill out! I know where the pilot is picking us up and you don't. Now shut up or I won't tell you. I don't know what they did to you here, but you've gotten ornery."

At least she laughed. when she said that.

~ ~ ~ ~ ~

Henry had gotten special permission for one of our planes to land at the base where I'd crashed. Lois had secured permission to drive out to our waiting plane. Limping to the plane, some of the ground crew started to cheer. Lois told me they were impressed I'd gotten the plane down considering it's condition, losing fuel and all. I climbed on board and before my seatbelt was fastened, we were moving and we were off to Seattle. I used the onboard phone and called Henry. I asked him if he was in a safe place and I heard the smile in his voice, "Yep! I'm very safe. Now stop worrying. Your pilot knows where to go."

"What?"

"Matt, it's all covered. You know I have several friends in the greater Las Vegas area. I'm with my friends and I'd going to disappear for a while. The Admiral said he expected to have this all resolved in two weeks. I'll let him know how to get ahold of me when this is over and maybe I might return."

"Maybe? What does that mean? You have a business to run."

"True, but there are at least three interested parties in purchasing our business too. I was gonna talk to you about it, but this thing with the Addams family cropped up and we never had the chance to talk. When this is over, you and I need to sit down."

I was not happy to hear he was interested in selling. But he was correct, this was not the time to discuss it. Mouse picked us up at Boeing Field. When we got to the Olympus, I introduced Lois to Jade.

Jade turned to me. "Matt, she's lovely. Why don't you make an honest woman out of her?"

Mouse barked, "Jade! That's none of your business."

For the first time, I saw Jade stand up to him. "Matt needs someone in his life. You've said so yourself many times. And I think she may be perfect. Now be still."

Then they were all looking at me.

"If you people think I'm proposing now, you're crazy. That's something I'd do in private."

Jade smiled sweetly. "Does this mean you're proposing?" She'd cornered me.

"Enough already. Leave it." I told her.

Mouse called Jade off. "Yes, leave it."

Lois put her arms around me. "I love you, regardless."

I kissed her. "Ditto."

That night, I held Lois tightly to me and kissed the top of her head. She asked me if I could make love. I told her she'd have to be on top, my knees couldn't take it. Later, as I was looking up at her, the words came of their own accord. Lois, will you marry me?"

She stopped moving. "Are you sure?"

"Someday, yes. I want you to be part of my life."

"Yes, I'll marry you."

You don't need to know about the rest of the evening. When I finally got to sleep, I slept better than I'd slept in a long time.

~ ~ ~ ~ ~

I woke to the sound of my cell phone chirping. I had a text message from Henry. "Landing BF 1300 hrs. Meet me. Important." Henry was flying into Boeing Field and he wanted me to meet him. I got dressed and called Mouse.

A staff person greeted me at the elevator door with a cup of coffee and took me to Mouse's office.

"Matt, how are you?"

"Fine thanks. Sorry for calling so early, but I need to talk to you."

"Never apologize. What's up?"

"I have to meet Henry at Boeing field today and I was hoping I could borrow your limo — it has bulletproof glass."

"Of course. I'll have Richard drive you down."

"I can drive myself."

"Nonsense. I don't use Richard nearly enough. Meet him at 12:30 under the portico."

"Thanks."

~ ~ ~ ~ ~

I watched one of our planes land and taxi over to the limo, and I met Henry on the tarmac. "What's this all about?"

"Does this airport have a bar?" Henry asked.

"Is that safe?" I was surprised.

"You'll understand in a minute. Bar?"

"I think so. Come on, let's find out."

Once we were seated at a booth with drinks in front of us, I asked, "Okay, why are you here? You're supposed to be in Nevada?"

"The reason I'm here is to tell you part of the Addams Family problem is resolved. I wanted to tell you face to face."

"What do you mean, *part*?"

He laughed mirthlessly. "The two of them thought attacking a bunch of queers would be an easy hit and just Mr.

Addams came to the ranch. The idea was to strike our compound and take me out first.

"We call it the ranch, but it's more like an armed fortress. A lot of us are ex-military and we've got some impressive safeguards. There's probably some way to get in without triggering any alarms, but you'd have to be damn good to pull it off. Mr. Addams didn't live up to his billing. He was not very good at forced entry!

"There are a lot of homophobic people in the world. The ranch is as safe a place as there is."

Henry was no slouch, but I didn't know he and his friends had established a safe house.

"We like buff, muscular men." Henry told me, "Most of us are fit and into looking good."

"Yeah, I know. Remember, I've seen you without a shirt and I'm jealous."

"Thank you. You know I'm gay, and you also know the training I've had thanks to Uncle Sam. Many of my friends have had similar training.

"I don't know how they found out where I was, but Mr. Addams tried to sneak into our compound two nights ago. Because of the threat on my life, we were extra vigilant.

"We caught him. He told us later the Mrs. was going after Jesi. Don't worry, I called Polk to warn him. He already knew. It turns out Jesi's had some of the training Lois had. Jesi injured Mrs. Addams. I don't know exactly how it happened, but Addams lost a finger. Unfortunately, she got away. If you ever see a stunning, dark-haired woman with her booger-picking finger missing, look out."

"Henry! That's gross," I exclaimed.

"What? You don't think gay men can be gross?" I had to laugh at that.

"What happened to Mr. Addams?"

"Do you really want to know?"

"Well, if you put it that way, perhaps not. Can you tell me if he's still alive?"

"I'll admit, he was a little worse for wear when he got on the plane, and I can swear he was still alive when he got off the plane. However, before he left us, he had something very interesting to share."

"What?"

"Who do you think hired them?"

"I have an idea."

"Who?"

"McNaulty."

"Bingo! I'll fill you in on the rest some other time. I've filled the admiral in."

"Am I to assume the airplane was not sitting on the ground when Addams exited the plane?"

"Remember, you don't want to ask questions."

"Okay. But why did come up here? You could have told me all that on the phone."

"I owe you. This was not a phone call conversation.

"Can I ask you a question?"

"That's a question. Yeah, ask. I might not answer it," he said with a smile.

"Does Dominick ride the same bicycle you do?"

"Let me put it this way. He likes to ride all kinds of bi-cycles. Does that answer your question?"

I had more questions, but I decided it was best to just leave things as they were. You know, sometimes too much information can be a dangerous thing. This was one of those times! "Where do you go from here?"

"That was another reason I came up here. There are three parties interested in buying the business. We've had some attractive offers."

"You'd mentioned this once before. How do you feel about it?"

"Well, I thought I'd see if I could convince you to sell. But now after more consideration, I think we need to hang on to it."

"Whatever you want to do, I'll leave it up to you. I'll admit, I enjoy having a plane when I need one."

Henry grinned. "And I really enjoy taking you places. Life around you is never dull. That may be a stupid reason to hold on to the business, but our little firm has done a lot of favors for some very important people with long memories. You've seen the books, we're in the black.

"Besides, I don't know if some of the people—Orchard for one—will even let us sell."

I hadn't ever thought about that, but he was probably right.

"You know, my friends and I talk about you." Henry smiled, "In the evenings we sometimes sit around a campfire. Everyone always wants to know what kind of mess you're in, what you did about it and of course, your love life."

That was a surprise. "What? I thought you guys weren't into women."

"That's not always true, but regardless, we all like a good story, and my God, you get into a lot of trouble."

Campfire. Gay guys. Stories about my love life?

"Whatever!"

CHAPTER THIRTY- THREE

Now that the Addams Family danger was over and according to Henry, things were safe, or at least as safe as things could be, it was time to return to some semblance of normal. We no sooner were settled at the Florida condo with all the dogs when Lois' phone rang. It was, of course, John. I could tell as she ended the call, I was not going to be happy.

Looking sad, Lois gave me the unwelcome news. "As I'm sure you realize, that was John. He needs me to get back to the office and hold things together. He didn't tell me where he is, but he said he couldn't get back to office for several days. Can you see if you have a plane going my way? I promise I'll come back just as soon as John is in the office."

Reluctantly, I phoned Henry and asked if we had anything available. Unfortunately, there was nothing going her way. So, I booked a seat on the first commercial flight available, leaving at 6 a.m.

It was a sweetly sad evening for all of us. Even the puppies seemed to know their humans were not in the same joyful mood as when they first arrive home. It's amazing how your pets pick up on your mood. Max and Thunder both crawled up in my lap and did their best to cheer me up by snuggling and nudging my hand for pets. Lightning did the same to Lois. When nine o'clock came, all three jumped down and headed for the front door.

"I can't believe it, all three of them knew it was time to go out." It amazed Lois.

"Yup, happens every night. I guess I've gotten used to it and don't think so much about it."

After taking the dogs out, we called it a night. We snuggled for a while, which, as you'd expect, turned into love-making. Our night was gentle and very special.

Every time I'm with that lady I fall in love with her a little more.

~ ~   ~ ~ ~

Since Lois couldn't stay, I decided I'd make good use of my time alone. Lois enjoys ballroom dancing and her favorite restaurant in DC has a great dance floor and a talented band. The next time we went to dinner, I was going to ask her to dance and surprise her. I'd taken some lessons and Stephen told me my rhythm was good and encouraged me to take more lessons. Stephen is the son-in-law of an old friend of mine who has since passed away. I'd helped him out of a scrape with the law and he was giving me free lessons. We were working on the Foxtrot and the Rumba. Even though it felt odd dancing with a guy, since I was learning something new it didn't bother me. Don't spread this around, but I was actually having a lot of fun. I gave Stephen a call and arranged for a lesson.

I heard somebody come into the studio, but I was too engrossed to pay any attention. Michael, an over-the-top gay man, and one of Stephen's employees, was also giving a lesson. When the dance steps brought me around, I was surprised to see Henry standing there with a grin pasted on his face. I thought he was on his way out to Vegas. What was he doing back so quickly? I wondered how much I was going to be teased about the ballroom dancing lessons and not incidentally, why he was here instead of Vegas.

Michael started over to greet him and I called, "Michael, that's Henry. He probably wants to talk to me." Michael ignored me and sashayed over to Henry. Something about the way Michael walked and stood while talking to Henry was so stereotypically gay. They said something to each other, and Henry started laughing. Michael touched Henry on the shoulder and then waved me over.

I excused myself from Stephen. For Henry to track me down and interrupt my lesson meant something important was going on. "Henry, I thought you were headed back to the Ranch. What's up?"

"I was but something came up. The admiral wants you, in person, now. He wouldn't tell me what it's about, just that I needed to get you to him, posthaste. Martha told me you were here."

"Let me say goodbye to Stephen." Michael was standing right next to us and I introduced the two of them.

I told Stephen, "Sorry, I'm not sure what's going on, but I have to leave immediately. Henry is my pilot who is here to fly me up to... well. I'm not even sure where."

Stephen's eyes widened. "Considering how you looked when you were dealing with my problems, I knew you were something special. I see now I was correct."

"Trust me, it isn't as wonderful as you are making out."

"Take care of yourself. I remember when you returned from the Middle East. You didn't look good. You still have a few more lessons you need to take." I remembered all too well the beatings I'd received on that little outing.

Michael touched Henry on his shoulder again before we left.

Heading out to the car, Henry asked, "Who was the yummy guy?"

"Why Henry, I thought you had a friend back in Vegas."

He winked at me, "One can never have too many friends."

I think I've heard that phrase before!

"I introduced you two."

"I know. And he's nice looking. Is he gay?"

"Are you kidding me? You couldn't tell? He's about as gay as you."

"Humm, I think I need to take ballroom dance lessons. Can you set it up?"

"Consider it done. Now what's got the admiral's knickers in a twist?"

"Dunno. I was ordered to return to Fort Myers, find you, and get you to him... like yesterday."

"Are we going to DC?"

"Can't tell you that."

The plane waiting for us on the tarmac was Henry's favorite. If there's such a thing as a hot rod plane, this is it. He told me one once about all the extra stuff on it, but I tuned him out after a while.

Two hours later we were on the ground. The plane taxied to a stop on the tarmac, the door opened, and an MP leaned into the cabin. "Mr. Preston?"

"Yes."

"May I see some ID?" I showed him my cred-pack. "Come with me please."

When I got out of the plane, I realized we had landed at a military base. A black Cadillac limo was waiting.

When I got in, I asked the driver, "Where are we?"

"Sorry sir, I'm not at liberty to chat with you. I've been told where to take you and ordered not to talk to you."

We drove somewhere else on the base and pulled up behind a sizeable brick building. A uniformed MP escorted me through the front doors and past a plaque that read Langley Air Force Base. At least I know where I am now.

He showed me to an elevator, leaned in, and pushed a button on the panel.

"Please don't touch the panel," he said.

The doors opened again on two MPs.

"Do you have any identification?" I showed my cred-pack again. It identifies me as a member of a federal agency which is totally fictitious.

The MP looked it over and handed it back to me. "Follow me, please."

It felt like we'd walked the entire building before we stopped in front of an unmarked door. The MP rapped twice, and a voice inside called out, "Enter!"

Admiral Orchard, President-elect Albert Bradson and two men I didn't know were waiting inside.

I extended my hand, "Mr. President, this is the first time I've seen you since the election. Congratulations."

"Thanks, Matt. But when we're alone, just call me Albert. We go too far back for you to call me anything else."

"For the time being, sir, you're no longer Albert. You're Mr. President and I won't diminish your standing. How's Maggie?" Maggie is his wife.

"Maggie is doing well, thank you for asking."

"Please tell her I asked about her and that I said hello. I think the world of that woman. You're very lucky to have her."

"I would have to agree. Right now I'd be lost without her. She's having fun with this president thing and I feel so sorry for her staff. She's really cracking the whip."

Bradson motioned to a heavyset man with salt and pepper hair dressed in a light grey pin striped bespoke 3-piece suit. "This is my chief of staff, Michael Bricker." We shook hands.

The other gentleman had a large red nose from too many steaks, too much booze and way too much of the good life. His hair was jet black which didn't fit the unshaved, lined face below the fake-colored hair. I don't know why some men color their hair. It doesn't fool anyone.

"This is John Mescher," Bradford said.

We had another John on our hands. There was no other introduction, no explanation who he was. He looked like he had slept in his grungy, dark brown suit. I extended my hand and he looked down at it like I was handing him a turd. I pulled my hand back.

I shook Orchard's hand and asked, "Okay, now why am I here? And why all the secrecy?"

The admiral motioned for all of us to sit. "I wanted you to come and see me, remember?"

"I tried, remember?"

"Yeah, I know. Sorry about that. The reason for the secrecy comes from the problems which have grown out of what I asked you to do up in Alaska.

"Many people believe this was an attempt on the two heads of the UIBA. Mouse and I disagree, we think Salvatore was the target and UIBA would be blamed."

"I thought the pictures proved it was McNaulty."

"The pictures are not sharp enough positively ID McNaulty."

That was bullshit. I sat there for a long time, mulling it over. There was also the phone call from somebody who had claimed to be the head of the UIBA. Did I want to share the information about the call? I mostly didn't want to get involved. I was still for so long the admiral asked me if I was still awake.

"Yeah, sorry. Just trying to wrap my head around all of this. I don't agree with either idea... not yet. But what I don't understand is, why am I here, now? Why is President Bradson here? And these other two gentlemen?"

Chief of Staff Bricker tented his fingers in front of his face and leaned back in his chair. He said, "Mr. Preston, if... let's say *if* it turned out a certain Italian crime organization had tried to murder two members of UIBA, or that the UIBA had tried to assassinate a high-ranking member of a large crime organization on American soil, I'm sure you can see there'd be hell to pay."

He paused, and I acknowledged his point.

"If this information were made public, there would be a bloodbath. Either way, this plays out, it has the potential to be major catastrophe.

"Any newly-elected president has enough to deal with when he takes office. Nobody needs a situation like this on top of everything else. There was a lot of bad blood during the election and the first thing President Bradson needs to do is ease the animosity. If he has those two groups trying to kill each other along with everything else, nothing will get done for a long time, if ever."

I interrupted. "But what do you want from me?" I had an idea where this was going, but I was hoping I was wrong.

Orchard said, "We want you to go to Amsterdam. Go to the UIBA there. Talk to them. See if you think they're being set up. If they were trying to hit the Family, try to find out why. Try to make peace with them. When you get back, get a sit down with Sal Zampuchini and reason with him. If they were hitting on the UIBA, find out if it's true and why.

"We need for you to resolve this before President Bradson is sworn into office."

"No!"

"Matt, listen—"

"No. Stop. I'm not getting involved."

"Matt." Orchard implored.

"What part of no don't you understand? I did a favor for you when I went to Alaska and look how that turned out.

The shitstorm from that is still ongoing. NO! A thousand times, no!"

President Bradson said, "I want you to—no let me re-phrase that, I need for you to take care of this."

"No!" I felt like a petulant child.

Mescher said, "Come on Preston, you already know most of the players in this dust up. You were there when the shots were fired. You have a better chance of fixing this than anybody else."

I didn't like being called by my last name and I didn't care for this person at all.

He added, "We already know the UIBA asked you for a meeting."

That stunned me.

"How the fuck did you know that?"

I turned to Bradson. "Excuse my language, sir. But how did you come by that information?"

Mescher said, "Part of the reason we're asking you to do this is because the UIBA wants to involve you. We also know you are, I hesitate to use the word 'friends' with Mr. Zampuchini, but you do have a relationship with the gentle-man and his organization." Mescher made no effort to ex-plain how he knew about the phone call.

I pointed at Mescher, "Excuse me but who are you?"

"It's none of your damn business," he snapped.

This cat was going out of his way to piss me off. I didn't care for his attitude at all. I addressed President Bradson. "I'm sorry sir, but I'm being railroaded into something."

To the other three, I said, "I did a favor for John going to Alaska. A favor that almost got me killed. I understand why you might think I'm the best person to handle this. But there's another player who knows more."

"Who?" they said in unison.

"McNaulty! John, I know McNaulty tipped you off about the meeting in Alaska. I don't care what you say, the pictures were clear. It was him. He's involved in all of this. Why not use him?"

Orchard said, "You're correct about McNaulty. We intercepted a communique, and the meeting was discussed. But we have him, ahhh... how should I put this... under wraps."

"What does under wraps mean?" I asked.

"Matt, please don't ask questions. That way I don't have to lie."

"I don't like that answer." I decided for Bradson I'd think about it. "Okay, I'll consider it. Consider, mind you. This is not a yes. But is McNaulty going to pop up along the way?"

"I doubt it."

I'd rather John had told me there was no way McNaulty would appear.

I asked Orchard, "Did you know McNaulty set the Addams family on us?"

"Yes."

"You heard what Henry and his ahhh... friends did?"

"Yes"

"Well, I hope I never see McNaulty again."

I wondered what I was going to do about Todd Hoss.

"When do I have to go to Amsterdam?"

"As soon as possible. Take Lois and go on a commercial airline. We want you to look like you're on vacation. When you get there, see what you can find out. You seem to have good luck working out some of these problems."

"I'll see if she's able to get away from the office. As I understand it, her boss is off somewhere, and she has to run the office. One thing I'd like to point out about luck...eventually it runs out."

The admiral said, "Ask Lois. I'll make sure the office is taken care of."

"Oh fuck! All right, I'll do it. But if I have any problems because of this, I'm coming after you clowns. And I'm only doing this for you, Mr. President."

"Thanks Matt," Albert said. "If I have to, I can always give you a presidential pardon."

"No offense sir, but I'd rather not have to cash that chip." Three of them laughed. Mescher didn't, he just sat with his arms folded across his wrinkled jacket.

I didn't laugh either. "I'll start this as soon as possible. But I have a problem I have to deal with back in Seattle first."

"You mean Todd Hoss?" John asked.

"Yeah. He really did steal the money. When I went to get him, he got away. As soon I can get away, I'll get Lois and we'll head to Amsterdam. Okay?"

John said, "You had him cornered once, but he got away?" That was an embarrassment I didn't need to relive. "Can't that wait until this is resolved?"

I explained, "No. Seattle's police commissioner is a friend of mine and I made him a promise in exchange for some leeway handling this. The clock is ticking and I don't intend to put him in a bad position."

President Bradson said, "I know Commissioner Davenport. Leave that up to me."

He tuned to his chief of staff. "Call Davenport and explain to him that I would consider it a personal favor." His smile was more of a grimace and I could just hear that conversation.

"Todd Hoss will still be waiting for you." Mescher added.

"I don't want to do this, but I'll see what I can do to help you. Again!"

At least Bradson had the grace to look embarrassed.

Mescher just sat there like a bump on a log and started at me. There was something about this cat I really didn't like.

I wondered who he was.

CHAPTER THIRTY-FOUR

There was still one other thing I had to deal with before I took off. I needed to make another call, one which I was dreading. Telling Zampuchini Todd Hoss was on the loose and that he was guilty.

I started with Guido and worked my way up, or down, depending on how you viewed it.

He must have had caller ID because he answered, "Matt, talk to me. What can I do for you?"

"Messaggero, I need to see you and I don't want to have this conversation over the phone."

Guido groaned, "When you start a conversation with 'Messaggero' I know it ain't gonna be good."

"Yeah, well, I told you I'd call you if I had news. Like I said, I need to see you."

"When and where?"

"I understand Sal's still where we had our last conversation? Correct?"

"Yessss," he said slowly.

"I'm coming up."

He asked me if I knew The Rim Rock Café just outside of BWI and I told him I did.

"Let me know when you're landing, and I'll meet you at the bar."

"Okay, I'll call you when we get close."

Henry was still waiting for me and he was unhappy he didn't get to push his hot rod plane to the max. We hardly got in the air and it was time to land. I called Guido just as the plane touched down.

I was seated in a far corner with a beer, mentally going over my conversation with Sal when Guido came in. He ordered a drink and after it arrived, he asked, "Okay Matt. What's up?"

"There's no easy way to say this. The bottom line is Todd Hoss took the money. I was wrong. The son of a bitch stole the money and now I look like an idiot. I was so sure he was innocent."

Guido had just taken a sip from his drink. He started to cough which turned into laughter. He got it under control then looked at me and lost it again. Tears were running down his cheeks when I finally told him to knock it off. "It ain't that funny."

"Oh yes, it is. Don Zampuchini told me if it turned out the son of a bitch stole the money he would have your nuts framed and then nailed to the wall."

My eyes got enormous, and Guido started laughing again. "I'm sure he won't do that. How did you find out?"

"I know a really good hacker. She proved to me he did the deed. Then Hoss took off on me and when I caught up to him, his girlfriend got the drop on me and they got away. I did shoot one of his toes off."

"You do that kind of thing a lot. You're going to get a reputation." He held up his hand.

"I know it may seem like that, but you know how skittish I am when I tell people to stand still and they don't. Anyway, I don't have a clue where they are now."

"May I make a suggestion?"

"Shoot."

"Let's go see Zampuchini right now and you tell him exactly what you just told me. He may be a little pissed at first, but not telling him would get you dead."

"Let's go get this over with."

~ ~ ~ ~ ~

When we pulled up in front of the house, a man in a three-piece suit opened my door. He leaned in and looked over at Guido. "Who is this?"

"He needs to see the boss. Please escort him in for me."

"You're not coming?" I asked.

"I think things will go better if it's just the two of you. Tell him the truth and you'll be fine. He likes you."

Just what I always wanted, to be liked by the head of a notorious crime syndicate. I watched Guido drive away, and for a second, I wondered if I'd ever see him again. The gentleman who had opened my car door ushered me to Zampuchini's office.

"Matt, good to see you again." Sal extended his hand. "Coffee?"

"Yes, please."

A different young lady handed me a perfect cup of coffee without asking me how I took it.

"What happened to the other girl?"

"She decided she'd rather be married to one of my boys. The wedding was two days ago and they're still on their honeymoon. This is Julie. Julie, say hello to Mr. Preston and then leave us, please."

"Hello, Mr. Preston." Killer smile and her looks made it obvious why Sal hired her.

I replied, "Please call me Matt. Mr. Preston was my father."

"Oh no, sir, I couldn't do that. At your age that would be disrespectful."

Sal laughed, I thought about suggesting he should perform an impossible act, but I decided against it.

When she was gone, I said. "Okay, Mr. Zampuchini. We need to talk."

"Sal, not Mr. Zampuchini."

"Well sir, at your age, that would be disrespectful."

He howled with laughter, then asked me, "Okay. Now why are you here?"

"Two reasons. The first one is Todd Hoss.

"You're convinced he's innocent. My mind is open, I want him to convince me."

"I caught him with a woman…"

Sal interrupted, "Matt, are you telling me you've never had a tryst when you were involved with a woman?"

"We're not discussing me. Sal, you don't understand how out of character it was for him to have an affair. This guy made boy scouts look bad. I've always viewed Hoss as a cross between The Lone Ranger and Dudley Doright. I've always trusted him. Sal, this is the guy who teaches Sunday School and is a deacon at his church. But he did it. He took the money."

Sal had been leaning back in his chair and he pitched forward. "What?" His mouth dropped open.

"Yes. He did it, I was wrong. He played me and I feel like a fool."

"Where is he?" he snarled.

"That's part of the problem. I had him but his girlfriend got the drop on me and he got away. I don't know where he is now."

"I'll put the word out. All of my people will be looking for him."

He made a call; the entire conversation was in Sicilian and I heard Todd Hoss mentioned several times.

At this point, I really didn't care what happened to Todd. Well, that's not entirely true. I was furious and embarrassed, but I don't know that I wanted Zampuchini's people to get their hands on him.

He hung up the phone. "You said there were two things you wanted to discuss with me. What's the other one?"

"I was contacted by the UIBA. I believe it was Abdulaleem himself. I don't know how he got my number."

"I got an email from him. No idea how he ever got my email address."

"Come on Sal, you gave me a hard time about getting an email address. You don't think these people have access to top talent as well in that area?"

"Yeah, well, that wasn't my point. They're asking for a sit down. They want to make nice and they apologize for what happened to Tony. They claim shooting him was a mistake. They want me to meet with them in Amsterdam. They swear I'll be safe."

I had a sinking feeling I knew where this was going.

"I was wondering if you'd consider going in my place?"

I wasn't about to tell him he wasn't the only one. "Are you fucking kidding me? Meaning no offense, but you can't be serious."

"I'm serious. Find out what Abdulaleem wants. If he's still trying to make a deal for weapons, tell them I'll do it in person. That you're there as my emissary."

"Look Sal, I'm flattered you'd even consider me but there are people in your organization much better equipped to handle this for you." Even if I wasn't already going for the President, I didn't want to represent Sal.

"Perhaps, but I trust you. You have no hidden agenda. You want to find out what really happened out there. And if that cache of arms really exists, you don't want those people to have them any more than I do."

"Mouse doesn't believe they exist. He has contacts all over the world and he's heard nothing about a boost that size. This is something you and Mouse would normally have heard of. He thinks it's a total scam.

"I think McNaulty made the entire thing up. And if McNaulty is behind this, I want no part of it. I swore I'd never let him get me on the back foot again. Sal, I just don't see me doing this."

"Will you at least see what set Abdulaleem off? Explain to him you and McNaulty have history. Don't try to make a deal, just find out why the last deal went sour."

"Can I think about it?"

"You mean you want to talk to the admiral about it."

"That too. You're asking me to take a colossal risk. I'm not wild about dealing with any of those crazies." The truth was I needed to make Orchard and the President were aware of what I was being asked to do and find out how they felt about it.

"Will you think it over at least? Please." Sal asked.

"I'll think it over. No promises, but I'll consider what you're asking."

"And will you also consider letting me talk to Hoss if you catch him?"

"Yeah. Let me catch him first."

"Thank you."

"Thank you for being understanding about Hoss. I sure called that one wrong. I'll let you know when I find him."

"When? Not if?"

"No sir, it will be when."

"Let me know what you decide and if you go, check in with me when you get back."

As I walked out to the car, the meeting had gone well, and I was relieved. I just hoped that the meeting with the UIBA went as well.

Guido was waiting and he whisked me back to my rental car. It was time to talk to Lois and deal with the next problem that needed to be addressed.

I wondered if I should get a real job so I could take a vacation.

I had one coming.

CHAPTER THIRTY-FIVE

When I asked Lois how she'd like to go to Amsterdam her immediate response was, "You're kidding!"

I assured her I was serious, and she told me she could pack in half an hour. I knew there was no way she could pack in half an hour, but I wisely kept my silence.

I arranged for Martha to continue watching the dogs and went on an emergency shopping trip. John had someone pull some strings and we had a direct flight to Holland, first class.

~ ~ ~ ~ ~

When the announcement to put our trays away and bring our seats to their upright position because the plane would land soon came, I smiled at Lois and took her hand. This was only the second time I'd flown first class, and I enjoyed the extra room and had been able to catch a little sleep. Flying commercial was a good idea. If anyone was watching for me, they wouldn't expect me to bring Lois or fly on a regular airline. You can thank old Todd Hoss for me not trusting anybody very much.

I'd stayed at the Luxury Suites in Amsterdam before and I'd made reservations and arrangements for them to pick us up at the airport. I didn't say anything about the hotel because I wanted to surprise Lois. After clearing customs with our luggage, I found the driver holding a sign that said *Preston.*

"I'm Matt Preston."

"Mr. Preston, my name is Erasmus. I'm from Luxury Suites. Is this all of your luggage?" I indicated it was, and he put it in the back of the van. It was a Mercedes Benz van and it still smelled of new leather.

For the next hour Erasmus gave us a tour. When we pulled up in front of the hotel, the managing director, Peter De Jonker, was waiting at the entrance. Other than discreet brass plaque next to the door, the building didn't look like a hotel. It fit the neighborhood.

De Jonker smiled and extended his hand. "Welcome back, Mr. Preston. So good to see you again."

"It's good to see you too, Mr. De Jonker. I'd like to introduce my friend, Lois." From the look in his eye, I could tell he approved of my friend.

"How was your flight?"

"Very nice. We're a little tired, but in good shape."

A lovely lady behind the desk took our passports as she apologized we were a little early and she was sorry, but our room was not ready. We told her we would take a walk around the neighborhood and return. Lois took my hand, and we set off to explore.

The hotel was next to a canal with several barges tied up in front of it. Two streets from the hotel we passed a diamond factory. A sign in front said they held tours daily, cut diamonds and produced jewelry. Lois informed me she wanted to go through the factory before we returned home. Dollar signs danced through my brain as they fled from my wallet.

I'd looked at maps before we left the states and I knew exactly where the hotel was in relationship to the UIBA safe house. I tried not to stare as we walked by. I observed a black plastic bubble at both ends of the block and also one above the front door. Three cameras were watching the front of the place. I tried to keep my face turned away from the cameras and concentrated on looking at Lois. After we turned the corner, Lois asked, "What was that building we just passed?"

"What building?"

"I'm not a fool. What was that building?"

I decided I needed to be honest. "That's the reason I'm here, babe. Abdulaleem is going to contact me and we're supposed to meet there. Amsterdam is one of the European headquarters for the UIBA."

"Why am I here?"

"Two reasons. Camouflage and because I wanted you with me. Actually, I wanted you with me more than I need you for camouflage." Lois squeezed my hand and rubbed her head against my shoulder.

"Excellent answer, boy. You're learning."

When we returned to the hotel a gentleman greeted us. "My name is Vladimir and I'm the concierge. May I show you to your room?"

We got on a small elevator. When I say small, I mean tiny. The three of us filled that puppy. He showed us to a room looking out front of the hotel and the canal beyond. It was like looking at a postcard of Amsterdam. Once we were alone, Lois turned to me and put her arms around me. I dipped my head and our lips met. The next thing I knew there was clothing strewn across the room and we had the covers pulled back on the bed. I took Lois in my arms and for a while we tried out the bed. We decided it was very comfortable and fell asleep.

I awoke to the sound of a shower. Glancing over at the clock, I realized we'd been asleep for several hours. I got up and padded into the bathroom. There was no shower door, so I just stepped in. Lois felt me behind her and stepped back. The feeling of her soft bottom against me woke things up. I murmured in her ear, "That feels wonderful. How about we get something to eat and then come back and take care of this?"

Lois turned and wrapped her arms around me. I got a big kiss and then she leaned back and asked, "Are you sure you want to stop now?"

I reached behind her and slapped her bottom. Being wet, it made a loud smack. She laughed and slipped from my grasp.

After we dressed, we headed down to the front desk. Vladimir was behind the counter and I asked, "Can you recommend a suitable place to eat?"

"What kind of food do you want?"

"Anything that ain't airline food." We all laughed.

"There's an Italian restaurant called Gusto. I promise you it will be wonderful."

Vladimir showed us on the map the location and we headed out. With just one minor mistake, we found the place. Vladimir had not exaggerated. It was amazing. I forget the name of the dish, but the waitress wheeled a cart up to our table with the largest wheel of Parmesan Reggiano cheese I'd ever seen. There was a dent in the middle and the waitress poured some marinara sauce into it. As she stirred the sauce, she would scrape cheese into it. Once the sauce was the consistency she wanted, she scooped everything out of the cheese and into a warming pan sitting over a small gas burner. On the bottom of the cart was enormous pot of pasta from which she ladled two sizeable portions onto two plates. She poured the sauce over the pasta and then scraped more of the parmesan cheese and added it to the top. I took a bite and I knew I'd never be happy with any Italian food again. If you ever find yourself in Amsterdam and want a good Italian dinner, you must visit Gusto.

With happy tummies, we started back to the hotel. We walked down an alley with several women sitting in the windows advertising their wares. I thought the lady I had was much more interesting! I whispered to Lois she was far better looking and a lot sexier. She kissed my cheek and told me, "Just wait until we get back to the room. I'll show you sexy." My pants were getting a little tight for some reason.

I must have had too much dinner.

As we crossed a street, a large Mercedes pulled up next to us. It was an S class, but it appeared larger than normal. Maybe the small streets made the car look larger. The back door opened and a dark complected man got out. He bowed slightly and said, "Mr. Preston? My name is Haazid. Would you and the lady be so kind and get into the car? There is someone who would like to speak to you."

I was briefly alarmed that we had been so quickly spotted. I was concerned for Lois' safety. "I'd rather the lady not be involved. Can you see she gets back to the hotel?"

"My instructions are she is to come with us. Please, get into the car."

I heard someone calling my name. It was Vladimir from the hotel. Somehow, he realized something was amiss and he called again, "Mr. Preston. Mr. Preston, may I see you for a moment?"

Without a word, I took Lois by the arm and we hurried toward Vladimir. The car door slammed behind me and the car quickly drove off. Vladimir asked, "Is everything all right? You looked like you were having difficulty."

"I don't really know what was going on. Thank you for getting us out of a sticky situation."

Vladimir smiled. "I can't let anything happen to you, you still need to pay for the room." He winked, making a joke. "Come, let me walk you back to the hotel."

"Do you do this for all of your guests?"

"Just the ones who look like they're taking up with shady characters. Do you have any idea who they were?"

"No. But I'll know by tomorrow morning."

He opened the door and Lois and I stepped into the lobby.

"Good night madam and sir." He glanced at Peter and the lady behind the counter. I speak enough German which is close to Dutch and I understood a little of what he was telling them about our rescue. He was also telling them to keep us in for the night. I didn't see that being much of a problem since we were tired from the trip and our walk around town.

After we were safely in our room, I called Admiral Orchard.

"Matt, what's up?"

"Our cover is blown. Lois and I were just stopped on the street by a gentleman who said his name was Haazid. He tried to get us into a limo but we were able to get away. Should I be concerned?"

"I didn't think so. Now I'm wondering. I'll make a few calls and get back to you. I suggest you stay at your hotel until you hear from me. Okay?"

Without saying goodbye, John hung up.

Tired from the time difference we lay down for a nap. There was a temptation to fool around, but both of us fell asleep. I was in the middle of a strange dream when I heard my cell phone. I grabbed it and without looking at who it was, I answered. A lightly accented voice asked, "Mr. Preston?"

"Yes, who is this?"

"My name is not important. I wish you had come with my servant, Haazid. We won't hurt you. We just want to talk."

His accent was very frustrating. It was familiar, but not. I'm good with accents, but this one had me totally confused. "Who's we?"

"I ask you to come and see us, we need to speak to you in person. It is regarding a fishing trip you recently took."

"And there are several people who didn't survive that fishing trip. Not to be rude, but I don't wish to find myself in a similar situation. So far, you haven't done much to make me want to come and see you."

"We wish to discuss what happened that afternoon and we would like you to take that information back to Admiral John Orchard. It is important that we have this conversation before you visit the UIBA. May I send a car for you?"

"You're not the UIBA?"

"That's correct."

"Who are you?"

"Not over the phone. I will explain everything when we meet."

"If I come, and I mean IF, it will be just me. My lady friend won't be coming." Lois started to say something, and I held up my hand to shush her.

"That's acceptable."

"When?"

"As soon as possible."

"Let me make a phone call."

"When you speak to your admiral, tell him not to discuss our business with Jacob McNaulty. I have said too much, but warn him about McNaulty."

"I'll call you back." I didn't give him a chance to answer, I just hung up.

I immediately called John.

"John, I just got a very strange call."

"That makes two of us. Who was yours from?"

"Whoever sent the joker to push us into the limo earlier. He wants me to come and see him. He said he's not with the UIBA and he assured me I wouldn't be harmed. He wants to discuss Alaska. Before he ended the call, he told me to tell you not to trust McNaulty or talk about any of this with him. I thought you already had him under lock and key. What's the deal?"

"Well, we did. Kind of. But he's escaped and is on the loose." Not something I wanted to hear. "My strange phone call was from McNaulty. He claims he's being framed. He said he's on our side and is still trying to bust the UIBA and Zampuchini's organization as well.

"I find it very strange that you got a phone call telling you to warn me about McNaulty at the very moment he's on the phone with me. What's your take here? Do you want to meet this guy?"

"Firstly, I'm not happy, Apple. You told me you had him under wraps. We're going talk about this at a later date. As for meeting the mystery caller, I say yes. I'm bound to learn something. Any information is better than none. It has to be a player, he knows too much not to be. Besides, if he intended to kill me he could have done it already."

"Don't call me Apple! I agree. Let me know when and where, and call me as soon as you can so we can sort this out."

I hung up and before I could call the mystery player back, Lois said, "I'm going with you."

"Sorry, doll. But no, you're not. I don't want to have to worry about you. Please respect my wishes."

"Darling, I've done things would turn your lovely silver hair totally white. I'm not some little girl. I'm trained and quite capable. More so than you know. I'm going with you. Please, let's not argue over this."

"I don't want you there. I need to keep my wits about me and when I'm with you, I don't think straight."

"You're a chauvinistic pig. I understand how you feel, and I love you for it. But right now, you need to put that away. You need me there."

"But—"

"Shut up. Who saved your ass from the situation in the Middle East? Henry and... that's right, me. I was part of that. And it wasn't the first time. I can be an enormous help to you."

I didn't want to do it. I was totally against the idea, but she was right, I wasn't viewing her as a whole person. She was a better than decent pilot and I was sure she had other skills too. We'd just never discussed them.

"This is against my better judgment; I want that on the record."

Lois wrapped her arms around me. "I love that you're so protective, it makes me feel adored and safe."

She kissed me and it took all of my willpower to push her away and make the call.

I called the mystery number back and said, "This is Matt Preston."

A deep voice replied in heavily accented English, "Please wait."

The voice from earlier came on the line. "Yes?"

"This is Matt Preston."

"Yes. What is your answer?"

"Lois and I will listen to what you have to say. Pick us up tomorrow morning at nine."

"Be outside of your hotel at nine. I will send my car."

~ ~ ~ ~ ~

Downstairs the next morning, Vladimir was behind the counter. I asked, "Can I see you outside for a moment?"

"Of course." he picked up a pair of sunglasses and led me outside. When the door closed behind us, he asked, "What can I do for you, Mr. Preston?"

"My ahh… my agency has asked me to go with the people you saw accost me on the street yesterday. Could you take a picture of the license plate, please?" I handed him a card with Orchard's private number on it. "If we're not back in an hour, please call this number tell them what I said and give them the license number."

"Of course, Mr. Preston. For the sake of discretion, I will have my assistant Maria pretend to be a tourist, taking pictures of the canal."

"Thank you. I know this is a little... unusual."

"You always make for an interesting visit."

"Trust me, it isn't planned. Just once, I'd like to have a nice, peaceful vacation."

"We will see what we can do next time." Vladimir smiled at me.

Lois and I stood outside the hotel and Maria waited behind a tree gazing across the canal. Lois asked me, "Who were you just talking to?"

"It was Vladimir, the concierge. You've seen him before."

"Bullshit! He's no concierge at any hotel. Since when does a concierge wear sunglasses with DE 380-17 technology?"

"What? What are you talking about?"

"DE 380 technology in his sunglasses—I would swear in court it was the 17 model. That, my friend, is the very latest technology. Front line troops don't have technology that good. They're still getting by with 14 or 15. He's more than just a concierge."

"What does this BS 300 something or other do?"

"It's DE 380. I shouldn't tell you because you don't have the clearance but I think you're pretty cute so I'll tell you anyway. Essentially, it's a camera. Ultra high-res recording paired with a multi-directional mic."

"In sunglasses?"

"Yep."

"You're kidding? Right?"

"No Matt. In Alaska Jesi had generation 13. The 17 is so new Orchard can't even get his hands on it. So, can someone explain how the concierge of some hotel rates a pair?"

"Sorry, I have no idea. I guess when we get back, you'll need to run a careful background check on this guy."

"You damn betcha I will. This grows stranger by the second."

Shortly, the Mercedes came around the corner and pulled up in front of the hotel. Haazid got out and opened the back door. As the car pulled away from the curb, Haazid turned and looked back at the two of us. "Would either of you like water or a soft drink? My religion prohibits me from drinking alcohol or from offering it to others."

"Thank you, no. We're good for now."

~ ~ ~ ~ ~

Many drivers of large cars on the small streets of Europe move quickly and easily through town. Our driver was no different. On the edge of town, we pulled up in front of a multistoried building. We entered the building and Haazid led us to the back of the building. We entered a room where a gentleman was standing at the window. When he turned, he smiled and extended his hand, "Mr. Preston, so pleased to meet you. My name is Glen Troutman. I trust Haazid took excellent care of you?"

"Yes, thank you." I turned to Lois. "This is my associate, Lois Tollifson. I hope you don't mind she came with me?"

"Of course not." Troutman and kissed Lois's hand.

I took the opportunity to look him over. Tan camo military-style jacket with nothing to indicate rank or service.

"Please take a seat," he said.

I didn't move, "Just so there's no misunderstanding, pictures of your car and license plate are already in Washington, if you catch my drift."

"Mr. Preston, if you'd like, call Admiral Orchard right now and give him this address. I have is nothing to hide. I merely wish you to share with me your interpretation of what happened in Alaska when you and your lovely friend here were filming Zampuchini's yacht." He smiled at Lois.

"Ms. Tollifson was not the person taking the pictures."

"I see."

"If all you wanted was to talk to me, why the cloak and dagger routine? Why not come to me and ask?"

"Please, sit, and let's have our chat." He motioned again to the couch. "I didn't know how you would feel about a meeting with me and I thought this was the best way to go about it. I see perhaps I was wrong; I apologize."

Lois and I sat down, and Troutman sat in a chair across from us. "Before we start, I have a question." I said.

"Yes?"

"Your accent. I can't place it."

"I'm Israeli."

"Mossad?

He tipped his head slightly in acknowledgment and said, "A Mossad Kidon, yes. But what's important to me right now is to determine what happened on that yacht in Alaska."

My internal radar was telling me something was odd about this guy. I decided the best course of action right now was to be cool. I wanted to see what he knew about the Alaska debacle.

I said, "If you tell me what you've heard, I'll try to fill in the gaps."

If he really was Mossad, he probably knew more than I did.

Troutman leaned back in his chair and studied us.

I learned from poker, whether you're bluffing or for real, keep still and let the other person decide if they want to play their hand. Running off at the mouth always gives away too much information. I tented my fingers in front of my face and returned his stare.

To my surprise, he agreed. For the next few minutes he outlined what he knew about my Alaska trip. There was no mention of the bogus samples.

I broke into his narrative and said, "There was a dispute over the samples. That's when Zampuchini was shot."

"I wasn't aware of that, thank you for the information."

I wondered if that was true or if he had chosen to leave that part out to see if I was being straightforward.

"Can you tell me who was shooting from the hill surrounding the bay?"

"Our assumption is they belonged to one or the other of the parties involved."

Lois broke into the conversation and said, "I have a question. why did you want us to warn the admiral to stop talking to McNaulty?"

"We, the Mossad, know a great deal about McNaulty. We don't believe he's a man who can be trusted. He does what he does for his own personal gain and cares nothing about anyone else. It's our belief he had something to do with the money the UIBA gave Zampuchini as a retainer."

"Nothing that man does surprises me."

"I have a question for you, Mr. Preston. What became the pictures you took with your young lady friend?"

"If you're asking me if I saw them, yes. I did. Where they are now, I couldn't say. I don't know, and I don't want to know."

"So, you have seen the faces of the leaders of the UIBA?

My warning radar went on full alert. "I've looked at the pictures of the men who were present that day. Whether they're actually UIBA, I couldn't say."

"To be blunt, Mr. Preston, having seen those pictures is a death sentence. I've met both of the individuals you saw up in Alaska and the dead body was introduced as the head of the UIBA.

"Are you aware the UIBA has a safehouse in Amsterdam?" I gave an affirmative nod.

"I also am aware of the arrangement between the Capo di Tuti Capi and UIBA regarding the sale of arms. I also know it involves your Colonel McNaulty…"

"Stop! He's not MY Colonel. Because of him I recently had a bad time in the Middle East."

"Yes, I heard about what happened. Also what you did for Ilox."

"You know Ilox?"

He smiled, but the smile didn't go all the way to his eyes. I could tell he was holding something back. "Anyway, we know Zampuchini claims he was acting on behalf of McNaulty in a sting operation. Zampuchini was setting up the sting in exchange for your government overlooking certain crimes is plausible.

"My principal concern is the arms. Do they really exist? If they exist, the Mossad will do everything we can to make sure the UIBA never gets their hands on any of them."

"I understand. I doubt if my government wants the UIBA to get anything either. For what it's worth, the cache doesn't seem to exist. What is your next move, if I may ask?"

"You may not," he said.

"Zampuchini is planning his own revenge on the UIBA."

"We are not concerned about the Mafia. How long will you be in Amsterdam?" he asked.

"Oh, a few more days, I suppose. A week, maybe." I didn't see any reason to detail my plans for him, either.

Troutman shook his head. "I fear for your safety. My advice is to go. Go back to the States and stay out of this affair. But it is apparent that neither of you will take my advice. Pity! Good luck, Matt Preston… And you too, Miss Lois. Both of you will need it."

He extended his hand. "I'll have my driver take you back to your hotel."

"Thanks, we'd appreciate that."

We'd been dismissed.

CHAPTER THIRTY-SIX

I woke to the feeling of a warm hand caressing me. I don't know how long Lois had been playing with me, but I was having a delightful dream and it flowed right into the feeling of her hands on me. I gathered her to me and kissed her. When I pulled back, I asked, "Have something in mind, did you?" Her response was a firmer squeeze and I figured out what she had in mind.

Hey, I'm not totally clueless.

Later, as she walked across the room to take a shower, I whistled and said, "I sure do like that outfit. Actually, it's my favorite."

She responded with a quick wiggle of her buns and I almost decided I needed to take a shower, but it was a decision between a cup of coffee or a shower and all that entailed.

The coffee won.

I stepped off the elevator and Vladimir greeted me, "Good morning Mr. Preston."

"Good morning. I'd prefer if you'd call me Matt. Mr. Preston makes me sound so old."

He laughed. "Okay. I'll call you Matt. I want you to know it's difficult to call a guest by his Christian name. But for you, I'll make the effort."

I gave him my best smile. "I'm off to get a cup of coffee. I saw a stand just around the corner."

"We have coffee here, but I understand if you want to enjoy a walk."

"Thanks. Lois will be down shortly, and I'll be joining her for breakfast."

"Would you mind if I joined you for a cup of coffee?"

I thought it was a strange request, but I didn't mind. "Of course not. Love to have you."

I'd been served and was sipping on a cup of excellent coffee when Vladimir joined me.

"Do you mind if I ask you a question?" he said.

"You just did." He favored me with a slight smile. "Sorry, go ahead," I apologized.

"Just exactly who are you? What are you doing in Amsterdam?"

I folded my arms over my chest, leaned as far back in my chair as I could and studied him. "You first," I said. "I'll tell you who I am after you tell me who you are.

"But you know who I am. I'm the concierge—"

"Stop!" I barked at him. "If you're going to play games, I'm leaving. I'm sorry, but a concierge does not wear sunglasses with DE 380 technology, especially the newest version. 17, I believe? Hells bells, our kids in the Middle East don't even have 15 yet. So, don't give me this crapola about you being the concierge."

Vladimir's face turned a little pink. "I apologize, Mr. Preston—"

"Matt!"

"Mr. Preston. You're more than I'd suspected. How do you know about DE 380? That information is classified. Most my unit doesn't know there's anything more than gen 14 and we invented it. So, again, I ask, who are you, Mr. Preston?"

I shook my head at him.

"Okay. I'll go first, I'm Mossad."

"Excuse me, but that's impossible."

"What? Why do you say that?" The surprise on his face was clear.

"Yesterday I met a Mossad Kidon."

"Really?" Vladimir replied with a skeptical look on his face.

"Yes!"

"Pray tell, what is his name?"

"Glen Troutman."

His laugh was a bark. "Ha! Glen Troutman is not a Kidon. He's not even Mossad. He isn't even Israeli."

"How do you know?"

"I'm the Kidon responsible for Abdulaleem, who we are told, has a safe house in Amsterdam."

"Who is Troutman, then?"

"His mother was from Jordan and his father was Iranian. He travels on a Syrian passport and nobody knows exactly what his true nationality is. For a while he had a Ukrainian wife, but they arrested her for arms smuggling. I believe that she was doing it for him, and he gave her up to get away.

"He was born in France, where his parents met. For a while we thought he was an active member of the UIBA. We've learned there is a 'Shahid' on him, which actually means martyr because whoever assassinates him will be considered a martyr if they were caught. He is the subject of a fatwah—your people would say there is a contract out on Troutman."

"Why did he tell me he was Mossad?"

"That I do not know. What did you discuss with him?"

"He had some questions about Alaska. I told him I didn't know any more than he did."

I debated for a moment if I should tell him anything else.

He said, "Okay, now tell me, who are you?"

"I'm an ordinary guy. Who's had the opportunity to do some not so ordinary things in service to my country."

He laughed at that and said, "Not so ordinary. We happen to have a mutual friend. I know more about you than you might expect."

"Oh? Who?"

"Mr. Ilox. You did him a great service. One he will never forget. So, is there anything I can do to help you?"

I shook my head. "Not right now. Lois and I are going to stick around and relax and wait for the UIBA to reach out."

"I take it she's special?"

"Very."

"Marriage perhaps?"

"I honestly don't know. I've tried the marriage thing. I'm not very good at it. But I may try it again for her."

"You two seem happy. Perhaps I'm just a romantic, but you two make me feel good."

"Speaking of Lois, I need to get back to the hotel."

"I'll walk you back."

We were chatting amiably about dogs—he has a Canaan Dog which I found interesting—when a black car came quickly around the corner in front of us. I thought it strange since the automobile windows were darkened which is not common in Europe. Because of the darkened windows, I also noticed the back window was going down.

As the car sped towards us, the passenger window continued down, and the gun barrel of a gun emerged. Without thinking I grabbed Vladimir's collar and yanked him to the ground as several holes appeared in the wall, right behind where he had been. The car squealed around the next corner and raced away.

Vladimir was leaning against the building holding his left shoulder.

"Are you hit?"

"Yes, but it's not too bad." I sat with him on the ground.

"Do you want me to take you to the hospital?"

Vladimir shook his head. "No. I don't want the police involved. There are people in the city who can treat my wounds."

Lois must have heard the commotion. I was still sitting on the ground with Vladimir when she appeared in front of me with a worried look on her face. I pointed at Vladimir.

"It's ain't me this time," I said, hooking a thumb at Vladimir. "He needs to be seen, and soon."

The young lady from the hotel desk was right behind Lois and she spoke to Vladimir in Dutch. I understood him telling her who to call. She didn't want to leave his side, and he had to tell her twice to go.

After she left, I leaned over and said, "Looks like someone thinks a lot of you."

"Yes, I know. And I've tried to discourage her, but it doesn't seem to be working."

"Why not let her help you?"

"I don't want her to get hurt."

"I feel the same way about Lois, and she doesn't listen either. Good luck with that."

"Thanks."

Peter De Jonker arrived with the young lady who had shown so much concern for Vladimir and helped him stand. The van that had brought us from the airport rolled up. Erasmus got out and with the help of the young lady, got Vladimir in the back. She got into the van and I wondered where they were headed.

Lois and I had breakfast and then went for a walk. I brought her up to speed. We agreed Troutman's activity was strange. Neither of us could guess what his game was.

"What's next?" Lois asked.

"I don't think there's any reason to stay."

She pulled my hand and said,

"Look! There's a tour of the diamond factory starting in ten minutes."

The tour was free and was actually very interesting. At the end, we were taken to a small room with two doors and an armed guard in front of each door. Our guide removed several trays of rings and bracelets. One ring was a beautiful shade of red gold. Lois picked up the ring slipped it over her finger. It fit perfectly.

There were loose diamonds in another tray and Lois pointed at one that looked like it had fire inside.

Our guide explained the diamond's particular cut was proprietary—only this house could cut a diamond this way. She showed us what the diamond would look like in the setting Lois liked so much.

I asked her if I could buy her the ring. She smiled.

"That's a promise ring," I explained. "I promise when all of this is over, I'm going to ask for your hand in marriage."

"I accept your promise to propose." She dimpled. "I'll accept your proposal, too."

As I paid for the ring, I remembered the vision of dollars flying away. It had been prophetic. But the ring looked great on her finger.

"What do you want to do?" Lois asked.

"Why not just fool around for a few days before we head home?"

Lois put her head on my shoulder and looked up at me. "Care to explain what you mean by fool around?"

"Let's get back to the room and I'll show you."

"I can hardly wait."

~ ~ ~ ~ ~

Later, in our room, I remembered the reason I was in Amsterdam. I made a promise to the President-elect. So, I dug out the phone number that was the contact number for the UIBA which Orchard had verified for me. It was an Amsterdam number and I wondered if Orchard had gotten the verification from Mouse.

I trusted Mouse more than Orchard.

I made the call and put the phone on speaker, then realized I had no idea what I was going to say.

Smart move, Matt.

The phone was answered on the second ring in a language I didn't recognize. Lois understands several Middle Eastern languages, but when I looked at her, she shook her head.

Oh damn, I was on my own.

"Hello. My name is Matt Preston. I'd like to speak with someone about an incident that happened in Alaska a few weeks ago."

I didn't understand the reply but the phone clattering on a table was unmistakable. I waited for what felt like hours, but when I checked, was just a little over five minutes.

"Who is this?" asked a voice with a heavy accent.

"My name is Matt Preston."

"Yes, yes. But who are you?"

"Do you mean why am I here?"

"No, who are you? Why do you call us?"

"This number was given to me as a contact for the United Islamic Brotherhood of Allah. I was in Alaska recently, the same time some of your brothers were killed. The new administration wishes to forestall any potential misunderstanding by the parties present and find a peaceful resolution."

"Do you represent your government?"

"When I can talk to somebody with some authority, I will divulge who I am and whom I represent."

"What organization do you represent?"

"I will divulge all of that when I meet with your people."

"Can we call you back at this number?"

"Yes."

Click.

Rather a rude ending to the call I thought. Those who know me can guess what I was thinking. A lot of coarse language was involved.

"What was that?" Lois asked.

"Typical terrorist paranoia I would guess. They expect us to wait for them. But I bet if we started fooling around, they'd call back at the climactic moment and expect us to ask how high when they said jump."

"Humm, fool around. You mean like this?" Lois put her arms around me and kissed me with a lot of fire and firmly rubbed her body against mine.

My toes curled.

You don't need any further details, but we finished with the fooling around and were down in the hotel bar having a drink before they called back.

The same voice as before said, "Go out the hotel front door, turn left and go two blocks. Cross the street and turn left, cross again. Walk down the right side of the street and we will meet you. Come alone."

"I'm bringing my friend."

"No. You will come alone."

"If she doesn't come, I don't come. We're a package deal."

There was a lengthy pause. "Very well. But you will not tell the concierge."

"Agreed. We're leaving now."

Lois and I were crossing the lobby when Vladimir called, "Leaving us?"

"Just getting some fresh air."

"It's a nice day for a stroll. Are you going sightseeing?"

"Don't ask. If you don't ask, I won't have to lie."

"I see. Well, be careful. It's dangerous when you cross the street on the right."

"That's just fine. We're going the other way."

"Very good. Enjoy your stroll."

As we walked away from the hotel, Lois said, "That was quick thinking."

We'd walked about half a block beyond the two blocks we were told to walk when a car pulled alongside us and stopped and a Middle Eastern man in a Saville Row suit got out and opened the back door.

"Mr. Preston," he said and gestured at the door.

We climbed in.

We drove past the nondescript building I'd scouted earlier, but we turned at the corner and again into an alley. The car stopped at a door just about where I thought the front door was on the other side. It opened and another Arabic man in a white Qamīṣ stepped out.

He led us to a set of stairs typical of Amsterdam. Basically, a ladder more than a set of stairs. We climbed up two sets and emerged into a large comfortable room. I was shocked to see at a window across the room was the man who I'd thought was Abdulaleem al-Zaman.

But here he was – alive! He smiled and held out his hand. He was wearing a short-sleeved button-down shirt with tan shorts and sandals.

"I won't try any subterfuge. You know who I am?"

I smiled in return as I took his hand. "It's my understanding that knowing who you really are can be very dangerous to one's health."

"Let us put those ideas aside. One should never believe everything they hear."

True enough.

"What did you have in mind?"

Al-Zaman motioned for us to sit on two large pillows. Mine was very comfortable. He sat in a chair resembling a throne.

"I've heard you are good friends with your new president," he said.

"In a way. Before we elected him, he was my attorney. We were, or guess we still are, good friends. I'll admit, I'm partially here on his behalf."

"And the rest of the reason you're here is because Don Zampuchini asked you to come."

"Yes. He asked me to find out why you shot his brother."

"I wish I hadn't. That act has opened a lot of hideous boxes. In my defense, when I saw the weapons Zampuchini was trying to peddle, I became angry. I thought he was trying to cheat us. I've since learned he was not the supplier."

"What markings? I know very little about this hypothetical cache of arms."

"We were offered the opportunity to purchase several hundred MPX submachine guns, manufactured, as I'm sure you know, by Sig Sauer, and some ten dozen M3 MAAWS, all diverted from your Army.

"What we were shown were inferior Chinese copies. Most of the weapons we've been told about are manufactured only in four countries. There are manufacture marks on each weapon and parts of the serial number indicate the country where the arms were manufactured.

"Arms made in Brazil are the most desirable, but ones manufactured in Czechoslovakia are acceptable. Those made in China or Viet Nam are not. The Chinese and Vietnamese are inferior and easily jam or have other issues. We had made it clear to both McNaulty and to Zampuchini's people we would not accept weapons from those countries. When Farouk recognized this instantly and warned me the serial numbers and the markings of the country of manufacturing didn't match, I realized we were being… how do you say, taken? I knew we had been lied to. I get angry quickly."

"I can tell you right now who lied to you."

al-Zaman grimaced. "McNaulty."

"Exactly right."

"You called the cache of arms hypothetical. You are saying the cache doesn't exist?"

"It depends on who you talk to. There's an actor who claims to be Mossad who believes they're real. Cat calling himself Glen Troutman."

"You have spoken to Troutman?"

"Yes."

"Where?"

"Here in Amsterdam."

"He's here now?"

"He was yesterday. Why do you ask?"

"Troutman is a liar. Do not trust him. He's not Mossad. We've had dealings with him in the past and now there is a price on his head."

"I'm aware of that. What's your opinion? Do you think this cache exists?" I asked.

"I'm like you, skeptical. Too many unanswered questions. Other times I wonder. We intercepted some intelligence documenting a large number of arms that were not where Army records said they were supposed to be. McNaulty claimed they were for sale. Where is your Mr. McNaulty?"

"Don't call him *my* Mr. McNaulty. I don't know where his is now. He was supposed to be in custody Stateside, but he's not."

"He escaped Admiral Orchard?"

"I can't answer that."

"And you don't know his whereabouts?"

"No! And for the record, the idea he's loose makes me very unhappy. But more important to you, he presents a threat to both you and Mr. Zampuchini."

"If he were to have an accident, would that be cause for concern, as you put it, Stateside?"

"Personally, I'd be overjoyed. He won't be mourned, I assure you."

Abdulaleem smiled. "As it happens, I have a very good idea where Mr. McNaulty has gone to ground."

I had no reason to doubt his claim.

al-Zaman closed his eyes for a long time. When he opened them, he smiled at me. When he smiled, it struck me what a handsome man he was. Today he was clean shaven, and his white teeth stood out against his coppery skin. He cut a most dashing figure.

I wondered where that thought came from. Was I turning into another Henry?

"Troutman, imposter or not, gave you good advice—the same advice I'm giving you. Stay out of this."

I laughed. "I'd like nothing better. Nevertheless, I have been tasked with finding a peaceful solution. Is there anything I can do to make that happen? What do you want?"

"Obviously we'd like the cache of arms," Ahmad said with a knowing smile.

"And if the cache doesn't exist?"

"Disappointing, but no surprise. From the start, it sounded too good to be true. Nevertheless, it was worth gambling on. Let me say this, we do not intend to exact retribution against your Italian friends. Both of us were losers in McNaulty's little game. I can never replace al-Hashim, he was my most trusted friend. This misunderstanding ends now."

Promising. I asked, "Can you give me your word none of your people will retaliate? If I ever prove who was shooting from the hills—though I'm positive it was McNaulty, I'll tell you. Will you give me your word as the leader of the UIBA to let this end here?"

"I'm not the leader, al-Hashim was the leader."

I smiled and shook my head. "Even if that were true, with him dead, you are the leader anyway. Correct?" That at least got me a smile. "As leader, if you assure me this ends here, I'll take your promise to Don Zampuchini."

On the way to what I thought of as the killer stairs, I said, "You told me not to say anything to the concierge, why?"

al-Zaman laughed. "Troutman is not Mossad, the concierge is. If you told him you were seeing me, he'd have stopped you. He's trying to protect you. The Mossad is furious because of his claims. They don't look kindly on false claims regarding their organization.

"Your hotel concierge is only here, temporally. Vladimir is scheduled to be transferred in a few days. He's been trying to protect you while you've been here."

I had believed Vladimir when he told me he was Mossad, but it was nice to have that corroborated by someone who was most certainly his enemy. I debated asking him about the attempt on Vladimir's life. I wondered just who I could trust. Talk about your wheels within wheels. I needed a scorecard just to keep track of the players.

"Thank you for seeing me and for being so candid. I have every hope that this matter is resolved."

We shook hands, and a man escorted Lois and me out of the building. We declined a ride back to our hotel. I needed to talk this through with Lois and there was no way of telling if or how many ears were listening in our hotel room.

I felt like Alice must have felt when she fell down the rabbit hole.

CHAPTER THIRTY-SEVEN

Vladimir met us in the lobby with his arm in a sling. He took me aside, "I see you are back in one piece. How did it go?"

"I could ask the same question. How are you?"

"I'll be fine. I wish I could say this was the first time I've been shot, but I can't. I did want to see you again before I go."

"I learned something that will be very interesting to you."

"Really? What's that?"

"The UIBA know you're Mossad."

He smiled at that.

"How long will you continue with this charade? I can't imagine being a concierge of a hotel with your knowledge and skill set is a good usage of your talents."

"Thank you for your vote of confidence."

"The other day when I just happened to be walking by you were being followed. I was watching you." Lois came walking up to the two of us. Vladimir smiled, "You were very observant to notice the sunglasses. I wouldn't have been using them had I known you knew what they were."

"I told Matt you were not who you claimed to be. I've seen some application of the software and I've seen nothing like your glasses. That's even above my pay-grade and I'm privilege to a lot of very interesting tidbits."

"I'm hungry. Can we go back to that Italian restaurant? Gusto?"

"I'd love to eat there again."

~ ~ ~ ~ ~

We sauntered down back streets as we made our way to the proper canal which would lead us to the restaurant. When we entered, the same waitress as before greeted us, remembering us. "Nice to have you back so soon?"

"We had to come back. Dinner was wonderful. We're hungry, please feed us." The waitress was laughing as she seated us at a table in front, looking out over the canal.

I didn't think it was possible, but that meal was even better than our first one. When the owner stopped by our table, we told her how much we enjoyed her restaurant. She thanked us for coming back. We'd enjoyed our walk to dinner, so we decided to walk back to our hotel.

As we crossed the street to walk back to the hotel, I noticed somebody fall in behind us. I don't enjoy having strangers in an alley behind me. I took Lois's hand and slowed down.

So did the guy behind us.

At the next street we turned left and stopped in front of a window. In the reflection, Glen Troutman came around the corner behind us.

Troutman couldn't know I was on to him, so I decided it was safe and started walking toward him. still holding Lois's hand.

"Mr. Troutman. What a pleasant surprise," I said cheerfully.

"Mr. Preston, I have a gun in my pocket. Stay where you are."

There certainly was something poking against his coat. The problem was, I didn't know if it was a real gun or his finger.

"What do you want?"

"I want you to go back down the side street we just came up. Don't try anything. Please don't make me shoot you."

Lois and I obeyed. When we turned, I caught movement in the shadows. Was it a person? I couldn't tell for sure. I made a point of not looking at the shadow when we passed.

We were a few feet past the apparition when a voice said, "Stop, all of you. Troutman take your hand out of your pocket, slowly. If you make any wrong moves, I won't hesitate to shoot you."

I turned to look back at who was behind us. It was Vladimir. I was really starting to like this guy.

Glen slowly drew his hand out of his pocket. He was holding a gun. For a moment, it looked like he might shoot.

Vladimir racked the slide on his pistol and said, "Don't do it, Glen. Just drop the gun and step back."

Troutman appeared to be thinking it over. Finally, he dropped the gun and stepped back.

"Mr. Preston, please pick up the weapon." I did.

"What are you going to do?" Troutman asked.

"First, Mr. Preston and his lady friend will leave us. Then, you and I are going to take a ride in the car waiting at the end of the block."

He addressed me. "Mr. Preston, I can't keep following you around and getting you out of trouble. Please return to your room and arrange to leave as soon as possible. Amsterdam is no longer a safe place for you. Now, please go."

I asked Troutman, "Why were you following us?"

"I was positive you would talk to Vladimir and if he told you who he was and who I am, I would no longer be safe. My attempt to kill him this morning failed."

A thought occurred to me. "Did you have anything to do with what happened to me in Alaska?"

A frightened look came over his face.

"Well, did you?"

"McNaulty set it up."

That was one mystery solved. "Well Mr. Troutman, I have a feeling I will never see you again. Good evening."

Troutman said, "Mr. Preston, I beg you, don't leave me here with this person."

I was having a hard time feeling sorry for the man. "Less than a minute ago you were pointing a gun at us. You shot at me in Alaska. This morning you shot at Vladimir, who was right next to me. How do I know one of those bullets wasn't meant for me? What were you going to do with us just now?"

Troutman was silent.

"And now you want me to... well, do what?"

"Don't leave me here with this man." He gestured at Vladimir. "You're leaving me to die."

"Did you really expect things to turn out differently? What did you think the outcome would be?"

"If you get me out of here, I can be a lot of help to you."

Vladimir said, "Troutman, shut up. You intended to murder Mr. Preston and now you expect him to help you?"

Footsteps coming up the alley announced the arrival of two enormous men. Troutman whimpered. Vladimir cocked his pistol. "Be still now!" The hotel concierge turned and looked at me. "Mr. Preston, you have your instructions. Leave now. Good night. Have a safe trip home.

~ ~ ~ ~ ~

286

And that was something I didn't need to be told twice. Lois and I turned and walked directly back to the hotel. As we passed the front desk, the young woman called, "Did Herr Concierge Schreiber find you?"

"Yes, he did."

"Oh good. Then you'll be checking out?"

"We're going up to pack right now."

From the room, I dialed John. When the admiral answered I went straight to business. "I need help."

"What's up?"

"We need a flight out of here as soon as possible. I'll explain everything when I get back to DC. How soon can you get us out?"

"May I assume that everything turned out well?"

"Yes. I have splendid news all the way around."

"Go now and call me when you get to the airport." The phone went dead.

~ ~ ~ ~ ~

Henry was dispatched to fetch us with one of our larger planes. We had lots of room and we even thought about some fun and games. But when we lay down on the large couch, both of us fell asleep before anything got started.

Within a few hours Lois and I were sitting in John's office with President-elect Bradson and Chief of Staff Bricker. John Mescher was wearing the same wrinkled brown suit. The remaining hair on his head was tousled and he needed a shave. I still had no idea what his position was, and I hoped he didn't have to interact with the public.

I covered everything that had transpired over the past few days and I finished with, "Both have agreed to let things end here. It would seem now the most important thing is to get ahold of McNaulty before he creates any more problems."

Orchard grunted. "He's back in custody."

"When did you get him?"

"That's all I can tell you. I can assure you that he won't be a problem for us again.

Mescher said, "I can't believe you had the opportunity to take out al Abdulaleem and you didn't do anything." His voice was sour.

Who was this guy?

John glared at him and snapped, "Will you leave it alone? That's not why Matt was over there. If you want al-Zaman so bad, why don't you and your people take him out?"

It was obvious the subject of the removal of Abdulaleem al-Zaman had been discussed before. I also deduced Mescher worked for an agency much the same as Orchard's but perhaps with conflicting interests at times. Interesting. I had a million questions. But I'd seen John in this kind of mood before. There was no point in asking him anything. He wasn't going to tell me more and if I pressed him, he'd get ugly. I decided to let it go.

John asked, "Are you ok with things?"

"Kind of have to be. Right?"

"Yeah. What do you think will happen to Troutman?"

The last time I saw Troutman he was between two large, brawny men. Vladimir told me Glen would be taken care of. I figured it was like McNaulty; don't ask questions. "I don't know, John. But I would imagine it's something like whatever happened to McNaulty."

Bradson stood and extended his hand. "I want to thank you for your efforts. It seems that once again I am in your debt. If you ever need me, let me know. I'll do whatever I can."

"Did you speak to Commissioner Davenport?"

The president laughed, "I had Bricker make the call. Your friend got very belligerent and it became necessary for me to call him myself. Jeff and I may be old friends, but after that conversation, it will be some time before things are back to normal between us. He's very unhappy that you had Hoss and he got away."

"I'm sorry the Commissioner is upset with you and I'm even more upset than Jeff that Todd got away."

"What you were doing is more important. Now you can go and catch a thief. Hey, that would be a good title for a book."

We all laughed, well, most of us anyway. Mescher scowled.

Mescher stood and without saying a word, left the office. From the look on Bradson's face I could tell he was unhappy with Mescher and his attitude. I still wondered who he was and where he fit into Bradson's administration.

John smiled. "Let's talk about that fishing trip you promised me."

"Let me know when you can get away and it's a done deal."

Look out Kip Gates, there are some fish with our names on them. For now, I wanted to go back to Florida, put my feet up and play with my puppies. I'd had enough of dealing with reality.

But there was still that damn Todd Hoss situation to resolve.

Whatever. I'm going home first.

CHAPTER THIRTY-EIGHT

Tuesday evening and it was poker night again. I was treating myself to an evening of playing with the guys from the condos. This was my first opportunity to play with the guys since our first evening. Jason wasn't playing tonight and I asked about him.

Dude replied, "He hasn't been back since that evening he wasn't feeling well. I wonder what's up?"

I felt bad to think I might have shamed him into not playing, so I decided to stop by his place and check on him. Besides the 144 condominiums, our Condo association also includes fifteen houses which are a lot bigger and more expensive. A lot of the residents call street where the expensive homes are located, Ka-Ching Strasse. Jason lives at the end of the street and his house was worth the most money because it's on the river.

When I got home, the lights were still on at his place, so I walked over and knocked on his door. Shortly Jason came to the door and when he saw me, I could tell by the look on his face he was surprised to see me. He invited me in and escorted me to a small office at the back of the house. He motioned for me to sit in one of the large over-stuffed leather easy chairs in the room. I sank back in the chair, engulfed in the smell of leather. "I'm pleased to see you Matt?" even though he was clearly surprised to see me, he'd invited me in and offered me a drink.

"It's nice to see you Matt, even if it is unexpected. Is there something I can help you with?"

"You weren't at the game tonight. The guys said you hadn't been playing lately. I was just wondering if everything was okay."

That seemed to trouble him. He looked down at his hands and said, "There are a lot of things going on right now. I don't know if you were aware, but Sarah isn't doing well. Her memory is failing faster than the doctors had hoped and I have to decide what to do—I have to find a place for her. I just can't take care of her the way she needs.

"The kids are insisting we move back to Minnesota so they can be with their mom and help me out. I'm not wild about going back. I really hate the weather, but it's not fair to the kids, or to Sarah, to keep her down here. This isn't the way I planned my retirement."

"I'm sorry to hear that. For what it's worth, I never expected to end up in Florida. At any rate, I hoped you weren't staying away from the game because of me."

Jason smiled. "Well, you definitely surprised me. I got your message. I want you to know I rarely stacked the cards. I don't do it for money, I just really like to win. I can't explain it. By the way, you handle a deck quite well."

I laughed. "You should have seen some of the guys I knew in the service if you think I'm good. There were guys who made me look like I had two left hands with all thumbs."

"Yeah, I was in the army and I saw a few of them too."

"What are you going to do about Sarah? How serious are you about moving?"

"I've looked into a place near where the kids live that specializes in dealing with patients that have memory problems. Our family owns several apartment complexes around Minneapolis, so I have a place up there to live. One apartment building is very close to where I want to put Sarah. The units are large and very nice. I know it would be best for everyone concerned. My biggest problem now is what to do with this place."

"Have you considered selling?"

"Yeah, I'm going to have to. But I hate having to deal with the sale and everything on my own. I'll need to take Sarah up north and then come back and clean the place out and deal with all the crap getting ready to sell."

"Do you mind if I ask what you'd like to get out of it?"

He named a price, which was reasonable considering where the house was located. I asked about the furniture.

"I'll ship some stuff back to Minnesota. Most of I I don't care about. Why are you asking? Are you interested?"

"I might be. The longer I'm here, the smaller the condo feels. Since this is where I spend most of my time now, I'd like a larger place.

"Tell you what Jason, when you decide it's time for you to sell, let's see if we can work something out. I think your asking price is fair. When you're ready, let me know. That way you don't have to deal with getting the place cleaned up for a sale. I really like the garage arrangement. I could fit a few cars in there."

"Thanks. If you you're willing to buy the house, that's a big load off my mind. Okay, I'm going to start the ball rolling to get Sarah moved and settled in. I'll get back to you in a few days."

"If I'm not around, don't worry. I'm dealing with several things right now, but I'll always be back. Go over and tell Martha you want to talk to me."

Jason extended his hand. "Thanks for stopping by. You've taken a huge load off my shoulders."

"I'm glad you're feeling better about things."

When I got home, I rounded up the puppies and Max and we all went outside. One thing I really liked about Jason's place was that part of the screened porch had a grass strip alongside. I could set it up with a doggy door and some kind of fence and then the dogs could get outside and do their business and still be safe. The house would be perfect for me.

CHAPTER THIRTY-NINE

Now that I was back stateside, it was time to find a solution to my other problem. Since Melissa found Todd before, I was hoping she could find him again and that's where I started. I gave her a call.

She answered the phone with. "Hello, Matt. are you back in the states?"

"Yes. How did you know I was gone?"

"You never called me back."

"What do you mean?"

"I was waiting for you to call because I knew you wanted to bring your boy in. After he snowed you and kind of left you holding the bag, I was sure you'd ask me to find him again."

"I'm sorry I ever doubted you. In my defense, I've had a lot going on, but you blindsided me. You know, he claims he did it for his girlfriend, Kaye, because she asked him."

Melissa laughed, "You men are all alike, you're always thinking with the wrong head."

"Yeah, yeah, all right, we're all horn dogs and only have one thing on our minds. Okay, now that we got that out of the way, any idea on how to locate Hoss again?

"Yes, I do. You know I left a trace program on his devices? I've been able to watch him any time he logs on. He's been very careful, but he logged on last night. Would you like to know where he is?"

"Are you serious? Of course."

"Right now, he's in North Fort Myers, Florida. I can't give you his exact address, but I can get within about thousand feet of his location."

"North Fort Myers? That's where I am."

"Then you should be able to find him. Right?"

"Damn. You're kidding. Where is he?"

"There's a string of motels on the Tamiami Trail, not far from you."

"I know where it is. I'll get a rental with dark windows and park so I can watch as many of them as I can. Would you do me a favor?"

"Of course."

"The next time he logs on, call me."

"Will do. Since I installed a better program, I think I can give you an actual address. I won't know the room number of course."

"Babe, if you didn't have Ralph, I'd marry you."

"Careful, I might take you up on that." There was a tone in her voice I didn't like.

"What's wrong?"

"Later. This isn't the time. I keep telling myself Ralph is just being Ralph, but it's getting old. Later, Matt."

"Thanks, kid."

I thought about Ralph and Melissa. They made a great couple, but it looks like even in paradise there can be problems.

Back in the day, as they say, there was a road called Tamiami Trail. The road stretched all the way from Tampa to Miami. Now I'm not finding fault here or want to put anybody down, but a lot of Floridians tend to slur their words.

I call it 'mush-mouth'. The word Tamiami originally was the road from 'Tampa to Miami'. Over time, it became "The Miami Trail" and then Tamiami Trail. Which is also known as US Highway 41. It was the trail down the west coast of Florida which over time became the major North/South road down the coast and just south of Naples Florida, the road cut east across the everglades on what became known as Alligator Alley. For years the road was littered with dead alligators. Even today they find a stray gator on the freeway now and then.

Highway 41 is no longer the major north/south highway. The I-75 freeway took it's place. The freeway circumvents Fort Myers and North Fort Myers. However, when US 41 was the major highway through the Fort Myers area, several motels sprouted up along the thoroughfare. Today many of the establishments are run down and rent by the week, the month and sometimes, by the hour. It made sense that Todd would seek refuge in something like one of those little dives. But my question is what brought him to the Fort Myers area. I assumed he didn't know it was where I'd settled.

~ ~ ~ ~ ~

Later that day I drove down Tamiami Trail passing several of the motels on the strip. I wondered which one Todd was using. Most of them looked rather seedy.

I was having a late lunch at the condo when Melissa called back.

"He's at 15494 Tamiami Trail. He's actually on his laptop right now trying to move some money that's gone. He's sent several emails to the president of the bank where the funds were stashed and he's livid."

"Are you in any danger of being found?"

Melissa laughed, "Matt, do you know who you're talking to? I didn't get the title Gypsy Queen for dancing around the campfire. It's virtually impossible for anybody to find me."

"Hold on to the money. Keep it accessible. I may need it soon and in a hurry. I'm headed out now to see if I can find Todd. Thanks."

~ ~ ~ ~ ~

The motel was a series of small buildings laid out in an L shape and at one time there had been a swimming pool in one corner of the property. Someone had filled in the pool with dirt, now covered with brown grass and in the middle were three sickly palm trees. It was called The Three Palms, and I assumed they named the motel after the three trees. My guess is the pool ended up costing the motel owners more to keep running than it was bringing in.

It was the cleanest of the motels on the strip, with a fresh coat of turquoise and pink paint. Where else but Florida are you going to find that color combo? The motel had seen better days, but the owners were trying. Six cars were parked in front of the cabins and I parked nearby. Using a pair of binoculars, I jotted down each license plate number. One car was backed into the parking space, but it was an out-of-state car and had plates on the front.

I called Brian Polk, my old friend on the Fort Myers police force.

"What's up?" he asked.

"If I gave you some license plate numbers, could you tell me if any of them are rentals?"

"Yeah, give me the numbers."

He called back five minutes later.

"Brian, whatcha got?"

298

"Your third plate is a Hertz rental. What's going on?"

The car backed into the slot. It figured.

"Did you hear about the bank VP in Seattle that absconded with hundreds of millions of dollars?"

"Yeah, what about it?"

"He's at the Three Palms motel in North Fort Myers."

"No shit?"

"No shit. There's a warrant out for his arrest and the FBI want to have a chat with him too. Can you come and help me?"

"Matt, that's out of my jurisdiction. Let me make some phone calls and I'll call you right back."

Right back was less than two minutes later.

"There are three county sheriffs on their way and I'm right behind them. You're going have to stay in your car until they've got him in custody and cleared the area."

"Okay." I wasn't excited about being told to stay in my car like a good boy. I really had a grudge to settle with ol Todd, but I also understood why I had to stay in my car.

I called Guido.

"Yeah." I love the way he answers the phone.

"Guido, it's Matt."

"What's up?"

"Todd Hoss is in a dive motel in North Fort Myers, Florida. Lee County Sheriffs are on their way to arrest him. They'll take him to the Fort Myers jail for holding. Will you call Sal and let him know?"

Guido growled, "Shit, Matt. I sure wish you'd called me first."

"I understand, but I also have to sleep at night. I have no idea what Sal and his people would do to Todd if they got him first."

He sighed. "Damn, damn, damn! Sal's not gonna be happy."

"Why? You guys have a lot of mouthpieces on your payroll. Have a couple of them get over to the jail and see if they can spring him. Or work a deal where somebody gets time to talk to him. That's why I called you now."

"Yeah. I'll check with Sal and see what he wants done. I don't like it, but I understand why you didn't call us first. You know, this call will go a long way to putting you tight with the boss. Ciao."

"Goodbye." Somehow the idea of being tight with the big boss didn't fill me with joy. I looked in my rear-view mirror and saw two sheriff's cars and a Fort Myers squad car with Brian behind the wheel pulling in behind me. It was time to bust ol' Todd.

Everyone gathered behind the cars. One of the sheriffs said, "How do we want to do this?"

"I have an idea," I offered.

"What's that?"

"Let me call him. I'll tell him he's surrounded, and the best thing for him to do is to just come out with his hands up."

The three sheriffs looked at each other and then at Brian.

Brian said, "He's okay. And it's a sound idea. If we can take him without a fight, that's best for everyone."

They agreed. Brian said, "Let us get set. We'll tell you when to call. But you stay here out of the way."

"Yes sir."

The sheriffs worked their way to the cabins on either side of Todd's. We were lucky and both were empty. Brian had gone behind the shacks and was now moving up alongside of Todd's unit. One of the sheriffs signaled me to make the call.

Todd picked up on the second ring. "Matt? Is that you?"

"Yeah, Todd. It's me. I have to give you credit. You didn't make it easy, but I found you."

"Where are you? What are you going to do?" His voice trembled.

"I'm outside your motel with a bunch of Lee County sheriffs. They're here to arrest you."

"Bullshit. I don't believe you."

"Three Palms Motor Court. You backed in your rental car, which you got from Hertz."

The curtain on the window moved slightly.

"How'd you find me?"

"Not important right now, Todd. You need to come out. Now! Just like the movies — come out with your hands up. When all this started, you asked me to help you. Trust me, I'm helping you. Come out now, or it's going to go bad. The sheriffs wanted to go in with force. I told them you were a smart guy and that you'd listen to me. This is your only chance. Come out now... or else."

"Just a minute. I'll call you right back."

"Five minutes and they're coming in after you. I can't promise you won't get hurt. "

"Five minutes."

Three and a half minutes later, the door swung open and Todd stepped out with his hands in front of him. He was still limping from when I shot his toe off and he stumbled. With no warning, several shots were fired from inside of the motel unit. Todd staggered then pitched forward to the ground.

"Who pulled that trigger?" I shouted.

"The shots came from inside," Brian yelled. "Whoever's in the room, come out now and you won't be hurt. If you don't come out, we're coming in. You don't want us to come and get you."

A woman's voice replied, "How do I know you won't shoot me?"

"You have my word on it," Brian said.

"Who the hell are you?"

The sheriffs had moved into position on either side of the door. Even though I'd been told to stay in my car, I was behind the sheriff on the left.

I called out, "Kaye?"

"Matt?" Her voice sounded unsure.

"Yeah. Listen Kaye, I promise you won't get hurt if you come out now. Come out with your hands in the air."

After a lengthy pause, Kaye called, "I'm coming. Don't shoot. I'm unarmed."

Kaye rushed through the doorway buck naked with a pistol in each hand and I had to give her credit. A naked woman jumping unexpectedly through the door was enough to startle everyone long enough for her to get several shots off. Kaye was excellent with a pistol. Her first shot clipped Brian. Her second shot hit one of the sheriffs in the forehead. She took off past Brian, firing two shots into him as she went by. He was wearing a Kevlar vest, but I had no way of knowing how effective it would be from that close.

She hit a second sheriff in the neck, and he went down. Her next shot was wild, hitting the last sheriff standing in the upper leg, and he wasn't standing anymore. He raised his gun.

Kaye aimed at him. Without thinking, I screamed, "Kaye, behind you!"

She turned and I dove. I was fast, but not fast enough. Pain blossomed in my right shoulder.

I heard three more shots, coming from behind me this time. The sheriff who'd been shot in the leg put three bullets into Kaye. She was just a few feet from her car. She'd almost made it.

I got up and started across the parking lot towards Kaye. She was still alive and reaching for her pistol, lying just a few feet from her hand. I beat her to it and picked it up.

She screamed, "Give it to me. Give me the gun."

I left her laying there.

The sheriff who'd been hit in the neck was still and when I felt the side of his neck, he was gone.

The sheriff with the thigh wound was holding his leg with one hand. He was trying to use his cell phone, but his hands were covered with blood and the phone kept slipping from his hand. I asked what number he was trying to call. I punched in the number on my phone and handed it to him.

"Are you okay," I asked him, and he nodded.

I went back to see about Brian. One bullet had hit his left hand, and his ring finger was missing. The other bullet went through his shoulder next to his vest, leaving more of a groove in the meat than an actual hole. I was more worried about his fingers and how much he was bleeding.

The sheriff who'd been shot in the head was dead.

I had to force myself to go over to Kaye. She was lying on her back and was having difficulty breathing. I knelt beside her and picked up her hand. "Kaye," I said softly.

One eye fluttered open, and she looked up at me. "I thought you were Todd's friend."

"I was until I found out he played me. When I found out he was guilty, that was it. I was through trying to help him. Why did you come to Fort Myers?"

"My brother lives in Cape Coral. He has a fishing boat, and a cabin down in the Keys. We were down there for a while. We came up to get the boat. We were going to go to Cuba."

"Why did Todd take the money?"

"He did it for me. I set it up. Bob Carity hid cameras in the vents so I could watch Todd. I did a couple of test runs and once I was sure it worked, I convinced Todd to do it. Carity was supposed to take everything out of the vents but I guess he didn't do a very good job."

"He left some cables left behind. Was he supposed to get a cut of the money?"

"Yeah. He had the idea I was kind of sweet on him. He thought when this was over, we would go off together."

"Why use Todd? You were able to move the money. Why not take the money and run?"

"I needed a fall guy, somebody to take the heat. He was such a dweeb he never knew what was happening. I made sure it looked like he did it so they'd go after him."

"But he didn't have to do it."

"Matt, you have no idea what you're talking about. I had him so pussy whipped, so addicted, he'd have done anything for me. His wife hadn't given him a decent screw for several years and all I had to do was fuck his little brains out a few times and he was mine."

She tried to laugh, and it caused her to cough.

"It's amazing what you men will do for a piece of ass."

She coughed again, and I told her to lie still.

"Why? I'm gonna die right here, lying naked in a fucking parking lot."

"Kaye, not to sound cold, but you chose this path. What made you think it would turn out any differently?"

It hurt, but I slipped off my shirt. My right sleeve was soaked in blood. It was running down my arm and dripping from my hand. I put it over her, covering her up as best I could. I felt it was the least I could do for her. "Thanks," She whispered.

"Why did you shoot Todd?" I asked.

"Calculated risk. I figured if I shot him and ran out of the room naked, I'd surprise everyone so much they wouldn't react in time. It was a gamble. I almost pulled it off."

I had to give her that. "Yeah, you almost pulled it off."

Sirens were coming from all directions.

If Kay lived, she'd get the death penalty anyway. Dying here would be a lucky break. Either way, justice had been served.

I left Kaye there. When I got back to Brian, I tried to kneel beside him and fell over. I guess I was losing more blood than I realized. I pushed myself up and took his hand in mine. He opened his eyes.

I squeezed his hand. "Dude, you can't die on me."

His voice was weak, but I could hear him. "Why?"

"Because if you do, Miss Doris will never forgive me. You have to make it. She's going to be mad as is, you dying will just make it worse and I'll be left here to deal with it. Don't you dare do that to me."

His weak laugh twisted into a grimace. "Oh shit, my chest hurts so much!"

I didn't doubt it, he had taken two shots straight into the vest.

"Damn it, Matt! I was almost retired. I thought I'd made it through with no terrible things happening to me. Over twenty-five years on the force. Not once have I been shot. This is all your fault."

I continued to hold his hand until two EMT's made me move so they could start triage.

I had to move to get out of their way, but I didn't feel good. I decided I needed to get out of the sun. I tried to stand, the world spun, and the ground kissed my face.

CHAPTER FORTY

The first thing I noticed was a hospital smell. Then the sounds of doctors being paged, and the beeping of a heart monitor entered my consciousness. I tried to move and found my arm was strapped to a board and there was a needle with a tube attached stuck in the crux of my elbow. A plastic bag was hanging over my bed which was hooked up to the tube in my arm.

The thought finally settled in. "Oh shit, I'm in a hospital."

Did you know I hate hospitals?

What was I doing in a hospital?

Then I remembered hitting the ground with my face. My shoulder also hurt.

Oh yes, Kaye shot me.

Okay, then I knew why I was in a hospital.

In the distance, I thought I heard Lois insisting, "I have to see Matt Preston. This is a matter of national security."

"Ma'am, you cannot go in there. You're not related to Mr. Preston."

"And I'm telling you Mr. Preston is a government agent. Here are my credentials. I'm authorized to see him. You're not cleared to see or know what his credentials are. Now, either let me in or I'll bring down the wrath of several government agencies on you and this hospital."

"Ma'am, I'm not authorized to allow you to go back there and see him."

As loud as I could, I screamed, "Lois. Help! I need you now."

Damn, that really set off my headache.

Note to self, don't do that again.

The next thing I knew Lois was by my side holding my hand. "Darling, it's okay. I'm here." Her soothing voice helped ease the headache.

The nurse appeared behind Lois and pulled on her arm. "Ma'am, if you don't leave, I'll call the police."

My cred pack was in my pants pocket. I could see my pants on a chair. "Nurse, nurse!" I snapped.

"What is it, sir?"

"Pants pocket. Please. Left back pocket. Get it, please."

"Why?"

I raised my voice. "Get it, damn it. Now!" That set off my head throbbing again.

When she stepped to the side of my bed again, she had my cred pack in her hand.

"What's this?"

"Open it and look inside. See, I really do work for the government in a classified capacity. This woman is my handler. She's here to make sure I don't accidently say something you shouldn't hear that would get you either locked up or maybe liquidated."

Her voice lost some of its authority. "What do you mean?"

John and I had given a couple of doctors a hard time in a similar situation. I decided to really lay it on thick.

"Nurse, I'm a GS 47 black operations assassin for the United States government. You had to know, but now you know too much. Unless Lois tells me not to kill you, I'll—"

"Matt! Stop!" Lois scolded me. "You're not authorized to tell her that."

"Do you want me to take her out?"

"Matt. Stay."

"Yes, ma'am."

The nurse fled the room whimpering, her face white with fear.

Lois was grinning as she laid a hand on my cheek.

"I'm glad to see you still have your sense of humor. And since when is there a GS 47?"

"She doesn't know that."

She caressed my face and asked, "How do you feel?"

"Like shit. What's happening?"

"I don't know. They won't talk to me since we're not related or married."

"Well, you have the ring, how about we get married?"

"If you weren't so stoned on painkillers, I'd take you up on that."

"I wish I was a little more stoned. My arm is killing me, and I have a headache like I've never had before. By the way, remind me to ask you when I'm not so stoned."

"You got a deal." Lois kissed my forehead. Gently.

"What if we called John? Can he pull some strings and get me out of here? I don't think there's any damage, just the bullet that went through my shoulder."

"Gee baby, I've never seen your degree in medicine. Should I be calling you doctor?"

"You know what I mean. Can't they just sew me up and let me go home?"

"Like I said, they won't talk to me."

The curtain was pulled back and a man in scrubs entered with our nurse behind him.

"Nurse Rowe tells me you've been giving her a hard time. You're claiming to be a secret agent or something."

I pointed to my cred pack, lying on the side table. "There's my ID. My associate here, Lois Tollifson, was trying to find out what my status was. Even after we identified ourselves, your nurse refused to cooperate. Just so you're both aware, we have to file a report on what happened this afternoon and the two of you will be mentioned prominently in that report. Now, what is my status and when can I go home?"

I had to give the doctor credit; he didn't bat an eye.

"You're scheduled for surgery in an hour. It's mainly to examine your shoulder more closely and then sew you up. Our initial exam showed no damage other than the two bullets—"

I interrupted, "Did you say *two* bullets?"

"Yes. Two bullets entered and exited your shoulder. The entry points are so close together that it's almost a single hole. Assuming no other major damage, well clean it up and close the wound."

"I understand."

Kaye had been one damn magnificent shot. What a waste.

"Why couldn't you tell Agent Tollifson that?"

"I'm sorry sir, but Dorie, I mean Nurse Rowe doesn't have that kind of authority. Actually, I don't even know if I have it either."

"Okay, when can I get out of here?"

"We'd like to keep you overnight."

"No. After you fix my shoulder, I'm going home. No offense, but I don't do well in hospitals. I've spent too much time in them over the years."

"When I was examining you earlier, I noticed several scars from past wounds. Are those all service related?"

"Most of them. What about the sheriffs? How are they doing?"

"Two of them didn't make it. The third will recover. He's scheduled for surgery later this afternoon."

"And Sergeant Polk?"

"One finger is so badly damaged it couldn't be saved. The bullet also damaged the finger next to it. It will be some time before he has full use of the rest of his fingers on that hand. His shoulder injury was superficial. His vest took two bullets, so his chest has a large bruise. I believe he should recover without any problems."

"The woman, Kaye?"

"She was DOA."

I knew she was dying when I left her in the parking lot to check on Brian, but I was still bummed it had to end the way it did.

"Has Sergeant Polk's fiancé, Doris Wentworth, been notified?"

"I believe Ms. Wentworth is with him now. He will be…" the doctor looked at his wristwatch, "No I take it back, he should be in surgery as we speak."

"Can I get a message to Ms. Wentworth?"

The doctor looked over at the nurse. "Nurse Rowe, please find Ms. Wentworth and bring her to see Mr. Preston."

"Thanks, doc."

~ ~ ~ ~ ~

Doris was crying when she came into my room.

"When they told me he'd been shot, I was devastated. I already knew I'd fallen in love with him, but when I thought I might lose him, it broke my heart. When he gets better, we're going to have to sit down and straighten things out. We've talked about a more permanent arrangement but he's afraid I might think he's after my money. Matt, you know I don't give a damn."

"Doris, he's is crazy over you. Trust me, you need to make him marry you." She gave me a big smile and squeezed my hand.

"I'll work on that."

~ ~ ~ ~ ~

I was back from surgery. I was pleased there was no pain. I let my mind wander back to the happenings of the afternoon. I felt bad about how Kaye died— her bullet-riddled naked body lying in a parking lot covered with my bloody shirt. It's not how anyone would want their life to end.

I found I was still astonished at her vulgar statements about her sexual relationship with Todd.

Lois and I share an unbelievable relationship, both physical and mental. I wondered just what I would do to keep our relationship intact. Would I rob a bank? Would I kill for her? I knew the answer to the last one was yes. If her life was in danger, I wouldn't think twice about taking somebody out. As for robbing a bank, I don't know if I'd do that. What Lois and I had was something special, but robbing a bank? Whatever Kaye was providing, ol' Todd was hooked. So hooked it got him killed. It was a sad ending for both.

Todd. He'd made a real ass of me, running around insisting he was innocent. I guess the old adage about still water runs deep was truer than I realized. In my mind, I always thought Todd looked how a bank vice president should look. He looked innocent; so trustworthy. Not that I knew exactly what a crook should look like, but I still didn't think they would look like ol' Todd Hoss.

I remembered Melissa, and I knew I needed to call her and warn her. There were some who thought the three hundred and forty-seven million was still in play. If anyone ever found out how instrumental she had been in catching Todd, not to mention that she knew exactly how he stole the three hundred and forty-seven mil and where it was, she could be in major trouble. Before I could make the call, I was asleep.

~ ~ ~ ~ ~

I had to wait an extra day to be released from the hospital. Somewhere along the way my wound had gotten infected and the powers that be were afraid the infection might spread. The floor doctor refused to discharge me. I argued, but to no avail. I could just get up and go, but when I got home, I'd have to endure endless hours of pointed remarks from Lois and probably Martha to boot. I just didn't want to deal with that.

Lois stuck around long enough to take me back to my condo and then she took off, but she promised me she'd be back for the weekend. The three dogs were overjoyed to see me, and the two puppies promptly climbed up in my lap and left a little excited pee on my lap as they licked my face. Martha was deeply sorry about the accident and she promptly picked them up and took them outside. When she returned, she apologized again for not taking them out sooner and it was all I could do to assure her it was not her fault. At least she was kind enough to help me clean up and change. Martha's help was appreciated since I found putting on a clean pair of pants with my damaged shoulder was a genuine challenge.

I went out to the lanai and curled up in my favorite chair and that sweetheart Martha brought me out a small but nourishing. I took a sip and it sure tasted good. Because it was hard to move, I asked Martha to please bring me my cell phone. I wondered if Jeff was still mad.

"Preston, I don't know if I want to talk to you. I'm pissed!" Jeff barked his greeting.

That answered that.

"Jeff, chill! When I see you, I promise I'll explain everything."

"Yeah, I really want to hear you explain about the President of the United States calling me and telling me to mellow out about Todd Hoss. In addition, telling me when you returned from some top-secret mission you were on, you'd bring Hoss in. How the hell do I argue with that?

"But wait, it gets better! I get a call from Bumfuck Florida and I learn that Todd Hoss is dead. I'm told his girl-friend, who is also dead, shot and killed Todd. You're in the hospital, recovering from your injuries. You being dead with Hoss in the hospital so I could arrest his fat ass would have been better."

"Take a breath, Jeff. You're going to have a coronary. Remember, I wasn't the one who shot Hoss. His lady friend killed him along with a couple of Lee County sheriffs. I know you don't care I got shot."

"You know that's not true."

"Jeff, you have my apologies for any problems I may have caused you. I'm sorry Frank got on your case about Hoss. I was so positive he was innocent. I was wrong and you have every right to be totally pissed at me. I can never apologize enough for that."

"Why didn't you bring him in when you found out he was guilty?"

"I tried! My ego got in the way and I wanted to bring him in by myself. But he got away. Then I had to go help President Bradson and... well, anyway, everything is over now.

"By the way call Mouse and get Bob Carity's address. He works for Mouse. Todd's girlfriend told me before she died it was Carity who set up the cameras in Todd's office so she could coach him. Since he knew exactly what was going on, at least you'll have one person to prosecute."

"Yeah, we'll see. Where's the three hundred and forty million?"

"I believe it's being transferred back to the bank from where it was stolen."

I needed to call Melissa and have her move the money back ASAP. Let the bank decide who actually has claim to the money.

"Matt, I don't know how you do it. You try my patience. You do the stupidest things and somehow you still come out smelling like a rose. I mean, how does one argue with the president of the United States? Damn, I was so angry with you that day. By the way, if I were you, I'd stay out of Seattle for a while. Frank is still pretty upset with you. I can only do so much."

"Goodbye, old friend. You need to come down and visit. I'm getting a new house—lots of room for you to come and visit."

"That's a deal."

"Who loves ya baby?" I was pleased things were back to normal Jeff. We go too far back to have issues between us. I felt much better now.

~ ~ ~ ~ ~

The next day I was sitting on my lanai playing with the puppies when it dawned on me there was another car auction coming up.

I had two big problems. I had done nothing to get the cars ready for auction. And I was in no condition to do anything now. Somehow, I needed to get several cars ready for the auction as quickly as I could. I grabbed my phone and called my buddy, Digger.

"Matt, you ol dog. How the hell are you?" Was Digger's greeting.

"Hey Digger, old buddy, great to hear your voice. What are you up to these days?"

"Don't old buddy me... what do you want, Matt?"

"Digger, you hurt me. Do you really think I only call you when I need something?"

"You mean you don't need anything?"

"Well, it's like this. I need your expert help to get the next batch of cars ready for the auction. I had a slight mishap a few days ago... and I umm... well, sort of got shot in the shoulder and I'm out of commission."

"Excuse me, how the hell do you get sort of shot in the shoulder? This has got to be a good one."

"It's a long story that I promise to tell you when you get here. Please. Just let me know when you can leave and I'll send a plane for you, okay?"

"Did I say I'd come and help?"

"Please. I'm serious, you know more than anyone else I know, and you do the best prep job."

"Slow down. You're laying it kind of thick, ol' buddy."

"Do I have to resort to guilt? I will if I have to."

"Oh fine, I guess I can help an old friend in need. Is it okay if Heather comes too? If she can't come, I can't come."

"So, it's like that huh? Of course, Heather can come. I see we're a little hooked on her?"

Digger made a vulgar retort.

"Well, I'm glad for you. Call me when you want the plane to come and get you."

"We'll be right down. Take care of yourself until we get there."

Digger showed up a couple of days later with his lady friend in tow. Heather, who I'd rescued from an abusive situation, was going to help out as well.

When Heather saw me, she carefully put her arms around my neck and gave me a gentle hug.

She whispered in my ear, "I can never thank you enough for what you've done for me. Digger makes me so happy. Thank you. I love you, Matt Preston."

I'd asked Lois to marry me in the ER. Yes, I was high on pain meds, out of my gourd. But I was serious. I needed to ask her again… when I'm in my right mind.

Don't even say it.

EPILOGUE

Burns Colorado was exactly as I remembered. A post office on a dusty, pitted road, out in the middle of literally nowhere, up in the Colorado mountains. Yes, that's all Burns Colorado has to offer. Not what one would consider a bustling metropolis.

Lois, John and I were headed for a fishing camp. The owner of the resort, Kip Gates, was driving his old mammoth Ford F-450. The three of us bounced around on the back seat.

After several miles of torture, arrived at the ranch, with spectacle of the Rockies spreading before us.

John said, "Kip, you have got to be the luckiest man alive, getting up every morning and looking at this. This is amazing."

Kip snickered, "Yeah, the hardest part of living here is not allowing yourself to get so jaded you don't appreciate it. You forget what the rest of the world is like. But occasionally we get somebody like you who reminds us of just what we have. I agree, this is amazing."

Dinner that night was just like I remembered, wonderful! The two things I remembered the most from my last visit was the excellent food and the view which rivaled the food. After dinner, Lois and I retired to our cabin and as we curled up together, Lois whispered. "I love you, Matt. Thank you for bringing me."

We kissed, and as usual, things heated up. Time passed and with our passions spent, we fell asleep in each other's arms. Between the clean air, the amazing dinner, and our intimate time together, we both slept through the night.

The next morning after breakfast, Kip showed up with three horses. Lois had expressed her lack of desire to fish from the back of a horse over dinner the previous night. Kip's wife had suggested Lois stay behind and they would do whatever it is that women do when their men go off and fish. This made it just John, Kip and me.

Kip led us up and down through the tall trees. We climbed a steep hill just before we came around a bend and there, spread before us, was the lake. The surrounding mountains reflected off the glassy-smooth lake. It looked like a picture postcard.

Kip dismounted and set up three poles. He handed one to John and one to me, telling us to follow him. The horses waded out into until the water was almost lapping against their tummies. Kip set John up and moved me further down the lake. John had no sooner flicked his fly out over the water when a beautiful trout leapt into the air and snapped at the lure. When the fish hit the water the pole bent and John had a proper battle on his hand.

John got finally got the fish close enough to net it. Only after he had the fish in the creel and a new fly ready to cast did the grin come off his face. It was obvious he was in heaven.

"Matt, thanks so much for bringing me here."

He looked over at Kip. "Do you have any cabins as monthly rentals? I wanna stay."

Kip wisely kept his mouth shut.

For the rest of the day we fished, and it felt like every other cast resulted in a hooked fish. John and I kept the first fish we caught, but from then on, we got very fussy. When we headed back each of us had a dozen beautiful rainbow trout wrapped in grass in our creels.

As we left, I looked back at the lake. This was a memory that would be with me for the rest of my life. I'd never had a day like this. I was one seriously happy camper!

After another fabulous dinner, Lois and I told everybody we were going for a walk. Kip warned us not to stray too far. When we asked why we were told about the bears. Needless to say, Lois and I stayed close to the ranch house.

Very close!

"Lois?" I said as we walked.

"This sounds ominous," she joked.

"No. There's been something on my mind for some time now. When I was in the ER, I asked you to marry me, and you have the ring I got you in Amsterdam. I was pretty out of it in the ER, but I was serious, and I'm serious now. I know you love what you do for John, and I know he'd be totally lost without you, so I'm not asking you to marry me now, but in a way I am. I need you in my life a lot more. I need for us to figure out being married while you work for John. I'm asking you to be my wife."

Lois reached out and hugged my arm. "I'd like that. As far as John is concerned, did you have something in mind?"

"I'm going to buy a house in the condo complex, and I'd like for you and me to live there, husband and wife. You can stay on with John as long as you want, but I'd like for you to consider stepping back a little from the admiral; see if you can spend less time with him. Maybe you can find somebody who can help him so you can spend time with me and the puppies. Maybe a week in DC with John and a couple of weeks with me in Florida? Or…? I'm open to suggestions."

Lois took my face in her hands. After a long kiss, she looked me in the eye. "I accept your offer of marriage. You're not stoned out of your little mind and I can see you really mean what you're asking. You know, as far as John is concerned, I think I'd like that a lot. I'm starting to get burned out. But I have a question, what would we do in Florida being together so much?"

"Lover, I have an idea. How about we go back to the bunkhouse and I'll demonstrate some of the things we can do?"

"Oh goody!"

We returned to the bunkhouse.

And I demonstrated a few of the things married folks can do...

Now, go away children...

~ ~ ~ ~ ~

The next morning Lois and I approached John with our idea.

"I wondered how long it would be before you stole her away from me," he joked. "I'd love to see you two married."

"I'm not stealing her, you just have to share her more than you do now."

John asked Lois, "Do I get to be part of this wedding thing?"

I smiled at John. "I was going to ask you to be my best man."

"I'd love that. Any idea when you two want to get married?"

Lois said, "We haven't gotten that far along with our plans. We just wanted to warn you what was coming up."

"Do you have any idea who we might get to take over some of your duties? Are we going to need two people to take your place?"

"The young lady down in personnel that's helped us a few times before, you know, the one you like so much."

"You mean the one with the…"

John held his hands in front of his chest.

"Yes, John." Lois said. "My God, you men are all alike."

"Yeah, but you love me. Do you think our young lady can handle the job? You do so much for me."

"Why thank you John for finally realizing just how much I do for you. But I think she can handle you and that's the hardest part of the job."

"Am I really that difficult?" John asked with a hurt tone.

"John, I love you and I refuse to lie to you. Yes, you really can be that difficult. Like sending Matt off to do something and then telling him not to tell me what he's doing"

"All right, all I ask is you make sure your replacement is up to speed and you're available if things turn to shit and I need you. Actually, since Matt is stealing you away, I think he should also be available should I happen to need him."

I didn't like that caveat, but I also knew I needed to keep my mouth shut if I wanted Lois free to spend time with me in Florida.

"That's fair. When we get back, we can make plans. I'll keep you in the loop." Lois told him.

~ ~ ~ ~ ~

We're still working on setting a wedding date. So far everybody we've told wants an invitation. When Heather found out I'd finally proposed, she hinted that Digger might consider doing the same. Digger is hinting about doing a two-fer. I can see this whole thing easily getting totally out of hand.

Lois is helping John train another Lois. The young woman from personnel seems to be working out.

And the best part is, John is very enamored of her. The truth be told, I think she's rather impressed with John as well.

Both are good things.

But right now, I have things to do and a wedding to plan, so I think I'll end this tale now.

I'll see you around...

The End

Well, perhaps not ... but this is a good time to leave

ACKNOWLEDGMENTS

Thank you to my editor Ellen Campbell and to Kevin G. Summers for another great cover design and for formatting this novel. What you hold in hand is a testament to their help and assistance.

This book has been a real challenge. For several months I had a problem with a detached retina in my right eye and getting it repaired prevented me from writing for several months. It seems that no sooner was my eye back to normal then the pandemic broke out which really screwed everything up. On top of that, what should have been a couple of months of editing turned into over eight months. For one reason or another, it seemed like everything that could go wrong did go wrong. But here it is, a lot later than planned, but still I got it finished.

I have been asked if there will be another Matt Preston novel. To be honest, I really don't know. I have a few ideas and I have written a little of what might be the start to seven, but after the long road to get this novel finished, I just don't know if I want to do it again. I got spoiled with the first five because they went so quickly. They were easy to write and get edited and put together. This last one was a real labor and not necessarily a labor of love. All I can say is stayed tuned.

A huge thank you to my youngest daughter, Robyn. Even more than in my previous books, her constant asking, "Is it done yet?" helped my stay motivated and is also a big reason this book was finished. If for no other reason than to get her off my back, this book is done! Here it is Robyn. I'm sorry, but I really don't know if there is another book to come.

I wish to acknowledge my two new puppies, Bijou and Boots. Without them I'd probably grow roots sitting in front of the computer. When they come and paw at my legs letting me know they want to go outside, I have to move and take them for a walk. They are very healthy to have around. This past year when we all we could do is stay home, it was nice to have them to take outside and go for walks. They are interesting and so much fun to have around. I would like to thank OrlandoCockers and Sandra Creech. Sandra has provided us with two darling little girls.

Finally, as always, I wish to express my gratitude to my wife, Sandy. All of you are aware without her Matt Preston would not exist, or at least not on paper. He has been in my head for a long time. Thank you, Sandy for your help, your support and your encouragement. Turn back the covers, I am on my way.

And so, another Matt Preston adventure is completed. I wish I could say there would be another one, but I just don't know. This one has robbed me of my desire to write more. Time will tell. For now, I'm finished. I will have to let the ideas percolate in my brain, and we will see if anything comes out.

As always, thanks for reading …
Good Night

THANK YOU

Thank you for reading *347 Million*. If you enjoyed this novel, I would appreciate it if you would help others enjoy this book, too. Some ways to share it are:

Recommend it. Please share this book by recommending it to friends, reader groups and discussion boards which help readers find books. It can also be found in Kindle Unlimited at Amazon.

Review it. Please post a review on one or more of the websites or pages listed below. Even a short review will do, tell others what you liked about this book. Also please tell your friends! (If you didn't like it let Matt Preston know… just kidding! An author lives for feedback of all kinds.)

By the way, word of mouth and reviews are an independent author's lifeblood. It helps others find our work and decide if they would like this book as well.

Amazon:
https://www.amazon.com/s?k=paul+shadinger&ref=nb_sb_noss

Or call up the purchase page for this novel and click on the book cover from there scroll down the page, and find the 'Review this Product' button to leave a review.

Goodreads:
https://www.goodreads.com/pshadingerauthor

Readers Favorite:
https://www.readersfavorite.com/book-review/347Million

To contact Paul:
pshadingerauthor@outlook.com

Follow Paul on:
https://www.facebook.com/pshadingerauthor
Twitter: @paulshadinger

And

Paul's Website
https://www.paulshadingerauthor.com